ALMOST GOT HIM

Scrambling to his feet, John ran to cut the fleeing outlaw off, hoping to get a clear shot when Boot was on horseback. To further frustrate the lawman, however, Boot pulled Lilly up behind him on his horse, and grabbing the reins of Lilly's horse, he bounded out of the clearing at a gallop, the mules following behind on the lead rope. Cutting across the clearing, John was in a position to fire, but with Lilly behind Boot, he couldn't take the chance. He was left with no choice but to let the outlaw go. . . .

DUEL AT LOW HAWK

Charles G. West

BERKLEY
New York

BERKLEY
An imprint of Penguin Random House LLC
penguinrandomhouse.com

Copyright © 2007 by Charles G. West
Penguin Random House supports copyright. Copyright fuels creativity, encourages
diverse voices, promotes free speech, and creates a vibrant culture. Thank you for buying
an authorized edition of this book and for complying with copyright laws by not
reproducing, scanning, or distributing any part of it in any form without permission.
You are supporting writers and allowing Penguin Random House to continue to
publish books for every reader.

BERKLEY and the BERKLEY & B colophon are registered trademarks of
Penguin Random House LLC.

ISBN: 9780593441466

Signet mass-market edition / July 2007
Berkley mass-market edition / August 2022

Printed in the United States of America
1   3   5   7   9   10   8   6   4   2

For Ronda

Chapter 1

It was a chilly spring morning when they opened the outer gate at Arkansas State Prison and ushered Boot Stoner outside the wall. When the gate closed behind him, one of the guards commented to another, "We sure as hell ain't doin' the world no favor by lettin' that son of a bitch outta here."

Twelve long and bitter years had passed since Boot had last been outside the high walls. He was sixteen when they sent him up to do time for cattle rustling and stealing a horse. If he heard the guard's remark, he paid it no mind. He had other things to think about. Owning nothing more than the suit of clothes the state of Arkansas issued him upon release, he was penniless and far from home. It was two hundred miles, as the crow flies, from Little Rock to the trading post his father had built eighteen miles north of Fort Gibson in the Cherokee Nation, and Boot had no way to get there other than on foot. Home was the only place he knew to go at this juncture in his life, even though his father had kicked him out long before he was arrested.

He took one last look at the place that had been his home for the past twelve years and vowed right then never to return. This promise to himself was not made because he had learned his lesson and planned to walk the straight and narrow—far from it. As he saw it, society owed him a helluva lot for locking him up for most of his young years, and he intended to collect upon that debt with interest. As for his vow never to return—the law would have to kill him next time. He had seen all of the inside of those walls he intended to see. With these thoughts in mind, he turned to face west and started walking.

Boot had been given a paper verifying his time served, and advised that he must report to the federal district office in Fort Smith within five days. There had evidently been no consideration given to the fact that he would have to walk a hundred and twenty-five miles in that time. It made little difference to Boot Stoner. He planned to ignore the directive anyway.

Although just appointed to the Western District the year before, Judge Isaac C. Parker was a name with which Boot was familiar, and he had no intention of ever seeing the man. His only plan was to head straight for Indian Territory. If the opportunity presented itself along the way, he would steal a horse to carry him. If not, he would walk every step of the way. Lean and hard, and prison-tough, Boot was capable of walking to the Pacific Ocean if necessary.

There were certain things that he intended to give

some long-awaited attention. Foremost among these was to settle with one Jacob Mashburn. Mashburn's testimony was the key piece of evidence that slammed the prison door on Boot Stoner. Boot knew there was no chance that Mashburn had seen him steal a horse from his corral. But Mashburn pointed him out and swore that Boot was the man. The fact that Boot actually did steal the red roan was beside the point. It was in the dark of night, and Mashburn could not have been certain if the thief was Boot or any of the other three rustlers who stampeded the cattle. The fact that Boot was a half-breed seemed to help the judge believe Mashburn's eyewitness report. At any rate, Boot planned to make Mashburn pay for his testimony.

He walked until dark on his first day of freedom, leaving the town of Little Rock behind him. Passing isolated farms along the dusty road, he gave no thought to food or drink until the sun began to settle upon the horizon. Approaching a modest farmhouse in the twilight of the evening, Boot decided it was time to acquire the supplies and transportation he needed.

Five-year-old Margaret Woodcock slipped out of the house and ran to the barn to say good night to the new calf. Margaret's father had told her it could be her calf, but she would have to accept the responsibility for feeding and taking care of it. A week old now, the calf still looked to its mother for nourishment in spite of Margaret's attempts to feed it from a pail. Her father said it was important to wean the calf from its mother as soon as possible, so Margaret had faithfully accompanied her father at milking time every day. And after he had drawn milk for the family, he left some in the bottom of the pail. It was Margaret's job to wet her fingers with milk and put them in the calf's mouth. When the calf began to suck the milk from her fingers, Margaret would gently lower the calf's head into the bucket where, hopefully, it would learn to drink. Since the new calf was reluctant to learn, Margaret had decided to name it Pokey.

Only mildly surprised to find the barn door slightly open, Margaret stepped inside the dark interior and paused for a moment to let her eyes adjust to the darkness. It was a small barn with only four stalls, and Pokey was in the first stall, with her mama. Margaret went directly to the stall, oblivious to the dark shadow by the rear wall, where her father's mule was kept.

"Pokey," Margaret scolded, "if you don't start drinking out of that bucket in the morning, I don't know what—" Her words were cut off by a huge hand that clamped down over her mouth so tightly that her teeth brought blood to the inside of her lips. Swept off her feet and carried roughly to the rear of the barn, Margaret tried in vain to scream.

Terrified, she tried with all her might to struggle out of the grasp of her abductor, but soon found it was impossible. In a few minutes' time, she exhausted herself. Once she stopped struggling, she felt the hot breath of her assailant close to her ear. "If you make one little squeak, I'll choke the life outta you," Boot threatened. "You understand?" She nodded fearfully, her eyes wide with terror, the stale stench of sweat filling her nostrils.

With one hand firmly in place around the child's neck, Boot slowly removed the other from her mouth. "Now," he said, "if you behave yourself and tell me what I wanna know, maybe I won't kill you." She made no response beyond an expression of total terror. "Who's in the house?" he asked. "Your mama and daddy? Anybody else?" She answered with a nod and a shake of her head. He thought it over for a moment. His initial plan had been to simply steal the mule, and maybe take a couple of the hens nesting in the barn for his supper. But now he had to do something about the little girl who had stumbled in at the wrong time. He could simply tie and gag her and be on his way, but as he thought about it, a better idea appealed to him. The little farm was isolated enough. Who would know what happened here? With a grim nod to himself, he smiled at Margaret and slowly tightened the hand around the child's throat. Unable to cry out, she flailed her arms and legs frantically until her windpipe was crushed and she became still. Boot took no particular satisfaction in the taking of a human life. It was merely a matter of convenience, the elimination of a possible minor irritation. In fact, the child was his first murder, and it meant little more to him than the killing of a sickly puppy. Dropping the limp body in the hay, Boot picked up a pitchfork and started for the house.

Constance Woodcock turned to glance at the door when she heard it open. About to remind Margaret that it was past her bedtime, she gasped instead, stunned by the appearance of the dark, ominous stranger who burst into the room. Hearing her gasp, Robert Woodcock, who was seated at the table, sprang to his feet and rushed to his wife's defense. The half-breed, in cold, unhurried response, shoved Constance aside and met her charging husband head-on. Caught by an upward thrust of the pitchfork, Robert uttered a sickening gasp as the tines pierced his abdomen. Holding the handle like a battering ram, Boot drove the hapless farmer across the room and into the opposite wall. The force of his thrust drove the tines of the pitchfork through Robert's slim body and pinned him to the wall.

Distracted for an instant, Boot turned in time to see the woman scramble up from the floor, horrified by the sight of her husband writhing in agony. She glanced at the fireplace and the double-barreled shotgun propped beside it. Boot followed the direction of her gaze and took a step toward the fireplace. Abandoning thoughts of reaching it in time, Constance bolted through the open doorway, running for her life. Boot grabbed the shotgun, broke the breech to make sure it was loaded, then charged out the door after her. In her fright, Constance could not generate rational thought. Her only reaction was to run. Had she chosen to find a place to hide instead, she might have had a chance, but in her panic she simply ran down the path toward the road. Even in the darkness, she was an easy target. Boot ran after her for a few yards before stopping to take careful aim. At that distance, the shotgun blast knocked her down, but, much to Boot's surprise, she almost immediately tried to struggle to her feet. Disgusted, it occurred to him then that Robert Woodcock's shotgun was loaded with bird shot.

Walking unhurriedly down the path then, Boot kicked Constance over on her back and set upon her with both hands around her neck. When she at last ceased to struggle, he dragged her body out of the path so that it could not be seen from the road. Returning to the house, he stood before the dying man pinned so grotesquely to the wall and coldly considered Robert's pitiful suffering. Irritated by the sniveling whining, Boot placed the muzzle of the shotgun inches from Robert's face and pulled the trigger. With all quiet now, he began to take inventory of his gains.

With the Woodcock's home and belongings completely at his disposal, Boot decided there was no need for haste. It was fairly late in the evening by then, and he figured there was little possibility of neighbors coming to call. He gave a thought toward the probability that the farmer might have a hired hand who could conceivably report for work in the morning. Even so, that gave him the entire night to satisfy his needs.

His first priority was food. He had not eaten a solid meal in ten years, having survived on the gruel prepared by the prison kitchen. In view of this, he decided he would now have a feast. Remembering the calf in the barn, he found a butcher knife in the kitchen, went out to the barn, and slaughtered Margaret's pet. He roasted it over the fire in the fireplace and stuffed himself with the tender beef, oblivious to the grotesque corpse pinned to the wall. When he was properly filled, he ransacked the house for anything useful. Taking the shotgun and some staples from the kitchen, along with a blanket, he went back to the barn to find a bridle for the mule.

With still a good two hours before daylight, Boot departed the Woodcock homestead. His new possessions bundled in the blanket and the shotgun in his hand, he gave the mule a kick. After a reluctant response, the mule stepped around the tiny body lying in the hay and started toward the open door. The stoic rider gave no thought to the innocent child.

It was a long ride on a slow-walking mule to Indian Territory. Neither verbal nor physical abuse proved effective in influencing the reluctant mule to increase its leisurely pace. It was infuriating to Boot Stoner, and though he threatened to stick his shotgun in the stubborn animal's ear, he had no choice but to put up with it. A slow ride still beat walking to Oklahoma Territory.

Crossing into Indian Territory south of Fort Smith, on the northern fringe of the Winding Stair Mountains, Boot noted that almost five full days had passed since leaving the bodies of the Woodcock family behind. He made his way past the San Bois Mountains, reaching the Canadian River, where he made camp, at nightfall. The river was fairly wide at that point, but the water was not deep. He elected to wait until daylight to cross over. Though shallow, the river had many holes, as well as some areas of quicksand. It was best to be able to see where he was going. When morning came, he crossed over without mishap and set out on a more northerly course. The next river to cross would be the Arkansas, which would offer a greater challenge to ford.

Another three days saw him finally reach the Arkansas River. After spending a good portion of the afternoon searching for a way to cross, he decided to swim the mule across. With no desire to take a swim, the mule refused to enter the water until Boot set upon it, using the shotgun as a club. After a brutal assault upon the poor critter's head that cracked the stock of the gun, the mule gave in. It proved to be an accomplished swimmer. With Boot hanging on to its tail, holding the shotgun up over his head and a half dozen matches in his teeth, the mule made the other side some fifty yards downstream from the point of embarkation.

Soaked to the bone in the chilly water, Boot staggered ashore behind the mule, cursing and shivering. Scrambling up the bank, he released the mule's tail, which proved to be a huge mistake, for the mule kept going. Having had enough of Boot's abuse, the slovenly animal decided to divorce his new master and, consequently, took off through the trees at a gallop. Enraged, Boot ran after the mule for a couple of dozen yards before stopping to level the shotgun at it. The hind end of a mule is a fair-sized target, especially with a shotgun, and Boot didn't miss. Unfortunately for him, however, the only shells he had found were loaded with bird shot, and at that distance simply peppered the mule's behind, causing it to run faster.

Frustrated to the point of exploding, Boot fired the other barrel at the departing mule. It was out of range by then, and showed no inclination to stop. On foot again, the irate half-breed retraced his steps to pick up the matches he had managed to keep dry, but lost when he opened his mouth to shout blasphemies at the departing mule. At that moment, the matches were more precious to him than the soggy blanket of stolen supplies he had managed to hang on to. Grumbling and shivering, he selected a spot to camp in the hills north of the river where there was plenty of wood for a fire. The next day, with his things dried, he set out on the last short leg of his journey. With the Boston Mountains on his right, he walked north up the valley toward Wendell Stoner's trading post on the Grand River.

Wendell Stoner had built his trading post on the bank of the Grand, or the Neosho, as some called it. The trading post consisted of a store for his trade goods and a cabin attached to it for his living quarters. With treeless prairie for hundreds of yards both north and south of his store, Wendell could see his customers approaching from a great distance. On this spring afternoon, a lone stranger on foot was sighted by Wendell's wife, Morning Light. She called to her husband. Wendell came to the door and peered out across the open grassland. He made no comment, his eyes riveted to the approaching figure. Then he turned to look at his wife for a long moment. Her eyes reflected the dread concern that he had instantly felt. Turning his gaze back toward their visitor, he knew even at that distance there was no mistaking the slight slouch in the man's walk, as if constantly stalking something or someone. *It was Boot.* He was sure of it, and a feeling of trepidation, absent for these past twelve years, now returned with renewed angst. Carrying a bundle in one hand, and with what appeared to be a shotgun propped on his shoulder, the prodigal son had returned. Looking up then, Boot discovered his mother and father watching him. Just as they had, he gave no sign of greeting as he neared the little store.

Boot dropped his bundle and propped the shotgun against it. "Well, if it ain't Mama and Papa come out to meet me," he said, a smirk displayed prominently across his surly lips. "You two don't look like you're too glad to see me."

"What the hell are you doin' back here, Boot?" Wendell Stoner demanded. "Did you break outta prison?"

Boot laughed. "Hell, no. I served my time, so they had to let me out." He shifted his gaze to his mother, who simply stood wringing her hands in despair. The sight of the quiet Cherokee woman's anxiety served to amuse him. "I knew my mama would wanna see me as soon as I got out," he chided. Back again to Wendell, he said, "I need some things."

"I told you when you started running with Billy Sore Foot and that bunch not to come round here no more. You've caused me and your mother enough grief, so you'd best just keep right on walkin'."

Boot smirked and grunted contemptuously. "Now ain't that a fine way to welcome your only son back home?" The smirk vanished from his face then, replaced by a deadly serious frown that indicated he was tired of playing around. "Like I said, I need some things. The sooner I get 'em, the sooner I'll be on my way."

Reluctant to help his belligerent offspring, but grudgingly willing to do whatever was necessary to be rid of him, Wendell replied, "There ain't much I can help you with. Some food, some clothes maybe. That's about it."

"And a horse, and a rifle, and some cartridges," Boot said. He was about to say more when a slight movement from the corner of the cabin window caught his attention. "Who the hell's inside?" he demanded.

"Nobody," Morning Light quickly replied.

"Nobody, hell," Boot snapped back. "I just saw somebody peepin' out that window."

"It ain't nobody," Wendell said. "It's just your sister. Leave her be."

"My sister?" Boot exclaimed, surprised. "Hell, I didn't know I had a sister."

"She ain't really your sister. She's a little Creek girl we took in two years ago when her parents was drowned. She ain't no concern of yours."

"Well, I'll be . . ." Boot said, stroking his unshaven face thoughtfully. "Come on out here, sister," he yelled, "so's I can take a look at'cha." When there was no response, he lost interest and quickly changed the subject. "You know, I've been walkin' a long way. I'm tired and hungry. Looks like when a man comes home after twelve years, he oughta be offered somethin' besides rude talk."

"I reckon we can give you somethin' to eat," Wendell said, "but don't go gettin' no ideas about stayin'." He nodded to his wife. She went inside immediately.

"What's my sister's name?" Boot asked.

Wendell hesitated, then said, "Lilly, if it's any of your business."

Boot snorted, amused. "Yessir, this is one fine homecoming," he said sarcastically.

In a few moments, Morning Light returned with a plate of food and handed it to Boot. He immediately set upon it with a ravenous appetite, gobbling down half of it before coming up for air. "Cold beans and biscuits," he said. "Some banquet for my homecomin'."

"That's all there is right now," Morning Light said.

"Ain'tcha got no coffee?"

Morning Light fixed an impatient frown upon him before calling to her adopted daughter. "Lilly, pour a cup of coffee and fetch it here."

A few moments later, a slight Creek girl appeared in the cabin doorway holding a cup of coffee. Boot looked up, obviously surprised. "Well, Lilly," he said with a broad grin, looking her over with an unabashed scrutiny, "no wonder they was hidin' you. You ain't no little girl a'tall. How old are you?"

Instinctively protective, Morning Light took the

cup from her daughter, and stepped between the girl and the unwelcome guest. "She ain't but fourteen, near as we know. Never you mind about her."

Boot merely smiled in reply, but continued to ogle the young Indian girl. When Lilly had returned to the cabin, Boot cleaned up the last of the beans and tossed the plate on the ground. "All right," he announced, "let's go in the store and see what I need." Without waiting for Wendell's reaction, he pushed by his father and walked into the store.

Following immediately behind him, Wendell informed the unruly half-breed, "I worked hard for this merchandise. I ain't plannin' to give it all away to the likes of you."

"Hell, I don't want all of it," Boot replied as he took inventory of the shelves. "I just want what I need."

"I don't owe you a damn thing," Wendell stated.

"Well, somebody does," Boot snapped back, "and it looks like you're the only one standin' here." He began picking items off the shelves—a pair of trousers, a shirt, some tobacco, a coat—and laid them on the counter. "I need a rifle," he said. "I see cartridges, but I don't see no rifles."

"You know I don't sell guns."

"But I bet, by God, you've got a couple in the cabin," Boot shot back. "I expect I'll be needin' one, and a pistol, too."

"You can take them clothes there," Wendell stated forcefully, "and that's all I'm givin' you. Take 'em and leave us be."

Boot paused to give his father an impatient glare. "Old man, you don't understand, do you? I'll decide what I'll take. When I get through here, we'll take a look at them two horses you got in the corral back there. I'm damned tired of walkin'."

"I'll be Gawdamned," Wendell exclaimed, drawing the line. "You ain't takin' no horse!"

"We'll see about that," Boot said, and pushed through the door to the cabin with Wendell right behind him. He knew exactly where he was heading. Striding past the startled Creek girl, he made straight through the curtain that closed off his parents' bedroom. "I see you keep 'em in the same place," he said as he picked up one of the two rifles propped in the corner by the bed.

"Put it back, Boot."

Ignoring his father's command, Boot held the rifle up to examine it closely. Turning it one way and then another, he marveled, "This is one of them new Winchesters, ain't it?" He glanced briefly at the other rifle propped in the corner. "I remember that old Remington, but this here Winchester, that's a helluva rifle. An old man like you ain't got no use for a rifle like this."

"I'm warnin' you, Boot," Wendell threatened, determined to stand up to his renegade son. Boot continued to ignore him, still admiring the new rifle. Realizing that his threats were toothless, Wendell compromised. "You can take the Remington, and I'll give you cartridges to go with it. But I need the Winchester."

Boot laughed. "That old Remington is good enough for you, old man. You ain't got nothin' to shoot at but jackrabbits and groundhogs. I've got better use for this one. Hell, I'll even leave you my shotgun." He started to walk out. "Now, I'll need your saddle."

"I ain't got no saddle to spare, and I'll be damned if I'm gonna let you take mine or Morning Light's." Wendell reached out and grabbed Boot by his sleeve as he started toward the door, determined to fight for his property. "No horse and no saddle!" he screeched. "Now get the hell off my land."

His anger flaring, Boot jerked his arm free. "I'm warnin' you, old man."

Wendell lunged for the rifle in Boot's other hand, but his son was quicker than he. He stepped back quickly and struck Wendell with the butt of the rifle. Lilly, too terrified to make a sound up to that point, screamed when she saw her father crumple to the floor. At the sound of the scream, Boot whirled around just in time to confront his mother with a pistol in her hand. His lightning-quick reaction was to level the Winchester and pull the trigger, though he wasn't even sure it was loaded. The crack of the rifle split the room, the bullet slamming into Morning Light's breast. The pistol dropped from her hand, clattering on the plank floor. Morning Light stood staring wide-eyed for a brief moment before sliding down the wall to collapse on the floor. Wendell, on hands and knees, staggered to his feet and lurched toward Boot in an attempt to avenge his wife. Boot easily avoided the attack, cocked the rifle again, and put a bullet in his father's forehead.

Rendered paralyzed by the horrible scene playing out before her young eyes, Lilly was unable to move for several long moments. Standing over his murdered parents, Boot stared dispassionately at the bodies that had given him birth. "It's their own damn fault," he stated coldly. "They shouldn'ta come at me like that." Suddenly realizing that she might be next, Lilly brought herself out of her paralysis and bolted for the door. Boot charged out after her.

The young Creek girl was lithe and swift, but she was no match for Boot in an all-out sprint. The half-breed overtook her before she had run fifty yards, taking her down as he dived for her legs. The two of them rolled over and over in the meadow grass with Boot winding up on top. "Ain't no use in you runnin'," he panted. "I ain't fixin' to kill you—little sister," he added with a malevolent grin. "I got better use for you." Keeping a firm grip on the girl's arm, he got to his feet and pulled her up. "Now I expect we'd best get ready to travel."

Boot tied Lilly hand and foot and left her lying on the floor next to her adoptive parents while he ransacked the store and cabin for anything useful. Satisfied that he was now armed and supplied, he went out to the corral to saddle the two horses. Just as he was about to lead the horses out of the corral, he saw two riders approaching the trading post. He paused to study them for a few moments before deciding they were harmless visitors.

With rifle in hand, he walked out to the front of the store and awaited them. When they were a little closer, he identified them as Cherokees, probably regular customers of his father's. "Howdy," the older man greeted Boot, speaking in English and obviously curious about being greeted by a young man with a rifle. "Need flour and salt," he said. "Where's Wendell?"

Boot did not reply at once, still studying Wendell's customers, a cynical smile on his face. When the old man started to repeat his question, Boot spoke. "Wendell ain't here. Him and Mornin' Light's gone on a trip." The two Cherokees exchanged confused glances, not sure what to think. To the older man there was something familiar about the stranger. He felt sure he had seen him before, but he would have to give it some thought before it came to him.

"The store's closed," Boot said.

The Cherokees considered the surly young half-breed standing before them, casually cradling Wendell's rifle, and decided it best to take their leave. Without further questions, they wheeled their ponies and departed.

Boot went inside the cabin and announced, "Come on, girl, it's time to go."

Chapter 2

Wendell Stoner's saddle was nothing a man could brag about. Old and worn, the girth was frayed on both edges, causing Boot to wonder how much longer it would be before the strap separated and dumped his behind on the ground. It would have to do for a while, he decided—at least until he had an opportunity to find a better one. Morning Light's saddle was in much the same condition, bearing evidence that neither saddle had been used very often. It was a light Indian saddle, made of wood, with carved cantle and horn. When he placed the saddle on the little gray mare's back and drew up on the girth, it caused the weathered wood to split. Disgusted, Boot pulled the saddle off and threw it aside. Glaring at the girl cowering in the corner of the corral, her hands tied to the rail, he snarled, "You an Injun, ain'tcha? You can ride bareback."

Boot assumed from the condition of the saddles that the horses had not been ridden recently, so after he threw the saddle on Wendell's bay pony, he stepped aboard to test the spirit of the animal. As he had suspected, the horse had been allowed to get a little rank in attitude and was not at all inclined to carry a rider on its back. Lilly watched wide-eyed and terrified as the horse bucked around the corral, but Boot proved to be more than the bay could handle. Unable to buck its burden out of the saddle, the horse then attempted to scrape Boot off against the rails. As before, Boot avoided catastrophe and remained in the saddle. When the bay exhausted its efforts and submitted to its new master, Boot dismounted. Then he tied the reins to a post and fetched a pitchfork from the lean-to that served as a barn. Approaching the weary horse again, he whacked it repeatedly across the face with the handle of the pitchfork until the handle broke in two. With the animal screaming in pain and jerking at the reins, Boot then grabbed the bridle and pulled the bay's head down. Looking the horse in the eye, he snarled, "I reckon you know who's the boss now, you son of a bitch. The next time you try to buck me off, I'm gonna put a bullet in your pea brain." The horse must have understood. When Boot stepped up in the saddle again, the bay was as polite as could be, having learned a little about its new master.

Untying Lilly then, Boot pulled the cringing Creek girl over to the mare. Holding her wrist in one hand, he grabbed a handful of her hair with the other, jerked her head back, and glared down into her face. "These horses, these rifles, this pistol, these packs—they all belong to me, because I was strong enough to take 'em. You understand?" When she was too terrified to respond, he yanked her head back harder. "You understand?" he demanded.

Fearing for her life, she replied in a barely audible voice, "Yes."

"This horse tries to run away, I shoot him," he said. "You understand that?" She nodded. "You belong to me, just like that horse and those rifles. You understand *that*?" Again she nodded, her eyes filling with tears. He gave her hair another jerk. "You ever try to run away, you get the same as the horse." He did not have to ask if she understood again. Her eyes answered without being asked. He put her on the mare's back then and, holding the reins in one hand, climbed up on the bay. Crossing over to the west bank, he headed north, following the river.

Dusk found them only two hours away from the grim scene Boot had left behind. He continued on until he found a place to camp that suited him. Leading her pony down near the water's edge, he instructed Lilly to gather wood for a fire while he unsaddled his horse. Aware of his eyes constantly watching her, she did as she was told. Longing to escape, but afraid to try, she moved among the cottonwoods, picking up dead branches until she had gathered an armload. With fingers trembling almost uncontrollably, she built the fire, using flint and steel that Boot had found in the cabin. While she bent over the flame, blowing it into life, he sat down with his back against a log, watching her. When the fire showed signs of permanent life, he pointed toward the packs and said, "Cook me somethin' to eat."

After he had his fill of bacon and beans, he told her to eat. Still too terrified to be hungry, she nevertheless attempted to stuff some of the food down. When she finished, she started to take the pan down to wash it, but he stopped her. "Leave it for now," he ordered. "You can wash it later. C'mere." The moment she feared had come. There was no mistaking the look in his eye. "I said come here, dammit!" he demanded when she hesitated to obey. The stark expression of fright in her eyes brought a malicious smile to his face. "I ain't gonna hurt'cha. Hell, we're gonna have some fun." He got up and went to her.

"Please don't," she whimpered, taking a step backward, but too terrified to run. "Please don't hurt me," she begged as he grabbed her wrist and pulled her close to him. "I'm your sister," she pleaded in desperation.

He laughed. "Hell, you ain't my sister. Even if you was, it wouldn't make no difference. I been locked up for twelve years and I'm damn sure overdue." Twisting her arm, he forced her down on the riverbank and immediately started pulling at her clothes. She fought against him at first, until he tired of the struggle and slapped her hard several times. Hurt and afraid, she submitted, crying uncontrollably while he savagely attacked her body. Though seeming an eternity, it finally ended when his lust had been sated and he rolled away from her. The sweet mystery she had anticipated for several years was now revealed as a horrible nightmare of pain and bleeding, and a sickening stench of sweat and tobacco. Her precious virginity had been ripped from her body like a man would gut an animal. It was a nightmare that would reoccur daily for the next few days.

Feeling as if she were treading between the light and darkness, Lilly forced her body to respond to her captor's demands the following morning when they broke camp and continued north along the river. With no certainty that this day would not be her last, she trailed along behind the stoic half-breed in silent despair, the image of Wendell Stoner and Morning Light's corpses constantly returning to haunt her mind. A little before noon, they neared a small cluster of buildings.

Jacob Mashburn hauled back on the traces, pulling his mule to a stop when he spotted two riders approaching down near the river. He leaned on the plow for a few moments while squinting against the sun in an effort to identify them. It appeared to be a man and a woman, and they were evidently coming to his place since they had veered away from the river.

Jacob didn't get many visitors, something that satisfied him, but his wife lamented. He and Lucille had carved out a respectable little ranch in the Cherokee Nation, raising a few head of cattle and growing what vegetables they needed on a small patch by the river. His only regret was that they had no children. He didn't know who was to blame, he or Lucille, but it was evidently God's will, so he didn't question it.

Within fifty yards of his garden now, the two riders were still unrecognizable to Jacob. He pulled a bandanna from his pocket and wiped the sweat from his eyes. As near as he could tell, the two were strangers to him.

"Mr. Jacob Mashburn," Boot announced as he pulled the bay to a stop before him.

"Yessir," Jacob replied, puzzled to find that the stranger knew his name.

Boot chuckled, obviously amused. "It's been a while, but you look pretty much the same as the last time I saw you."

Jacob smiled and scratched his head, trying to place the stranger. "I swear, mister, you've got the advantage on me. I can't remember you. Musta been a while back."

"Twelve years and some," Boot replied. "I expect I have changed a little. Prison'll do that to a man." His smile widened a bit when he saw the sudden look of concern in Mashburn's eyes. "You was pretty damn sure you knew me when you pointed your finger at me in that courtroom."

Totally alarmed at this point, his blood freezing in his veins, Jacob recognized the cruel face of the half-breed bandit he had testified against in court. With no other recourse available to him, he turned and ran toward the house. Boot, still grinning, took his time to raise his Winchester. Sighting it on a spot between

Mashburn's shoulder blades, he squeezed the trigger. Jacob fell facedown in the row he had just plowed.

With no knowledge beforehand of Boot's intentions upon approaching the homestead, Lilly was almost thrown from her horse when the mare was startled by the rifle shot. Horrified by the wanton taking of life, she cried out uncontrollably, only to receive a menacing scowl from Boot. When the frightened girl was sufficiently cowed, he walked his horse up to the body lying in the garden. To be sure Mashburn was dead, he put another bullet in the body. Hearing a cry of alarm from the house then, he looked up to see Lucille Mashburn running toward them. In a move that was almost casual, he raised the rifle and shot her. After taking a half dozen steps more, she fell dead.

Boot watched the house carefully, unsure if the man and wife were the only people there. When there was no response of any kind from the house or outbuildings, he returned the rifle to its saddle sling and nudged the bay forward. "Come on," he said to Lilly. "Let's go see what we can find in the house."

Just as he had done in his parents' house, Boot ransacked the place, taking what was useful and destroying the rest. Finding a silver chain with a cross, he tossed it to Lilly and told her to put it on. "It's a good luck charm," he said, laughing. For himself, he took a gold watch and a handful of gold coins he found in a box under the bed. Rummaging through a trunk at the foot of the bed, he found a silk vest that delighted him so much he had to put it on immediately. "How you

like your man now?" he asked Lilly as he strutted before her, preening like a peacock and laughing when
she didn't know how to reply.

They spent the night at Jacob Mashburn's place,
sleeping in his bed. Lilly was subjected to another
brutal attack upon her body. Knowing it was useless to
resist, she made no attempt to fight him, suffering
with silent tears while he satisfied his savage needs.
When he was finished with her, he tied her wrists to
the bedpost, leaving her to sleep as best she could.
The following morning, Boot rigged packs for two of
Mashburn's mules and loaded them down with supplies and loot from the house. Deciding he favored
Jacob's saddle over the one taken from his father, he
relegated Wendell Stoner's saddle to Lilly. Making it
a point to leave nothing of Mashburn's unharmed, he
methodically shot all the livestock that were not fortunate enough to escape his wrath. He spared one cow,
which he tied to a lead rope and hooked onto the pack
mules. "We'll butcher this'un when we get up in the
hills and make us a camp."

With a full belly and two pack mules loaded with
food, cooking utensils, and ammunition, Boot was
well supplied to hole up for a spell. In a final act of
contempt, he set fire to Mashburn's house and
watched it burn for a few minutes while he thought of
the twelve long years he had waited to extract his
vengeance. There had been few nights when he had
not lain awake thinking about the man who had testified against him. He had vowed that he would destroy
the man completely, wipe him off the face of the

earth, along with his family and livestock. That promise had been fulfilled now, but he felt no satisfaction that the debt had been paid for his years of incarceration. In a sudden burst of anger, he pumped three more slugs into Mashburn's body before crossing back over the river and striking out east, toward the Boston Mountains near the Missouri border.

Chapter 3

Nothing about the man would cause a person to stare openly. On a public street, one might pass him by without so much as a casual glance. That is to say, unless you happened to notice him standing next to another man. Then you might possibly notice the width of his shoulders, or the discerning eye that quietly evaluated his surroundings. John Ward would hardly be regarded as a handsome man, but there was an honesty in his face that reflected a solid core deep inside him, evidence of an inner strength and patience. Patience—some on the wrong side of the law might call it relentlessness, for John Ward was well known among the rabble of fugitives who sought refuge in Oklahoma Territory.

It had been a long hunt, almost two weeks since he had struck Rafe Wilson's trail just north of the Winding Stair Mountains. Doggedly, John had followed Rafe through the Winding Stairs, across the Kiamichi River, and into the mountains of the same name. From

camp to camp, he had tracked the fugitive from Judge
Parker's jail in Fort Smith all the way to where he now
sat in the saddle, looking down at a shanty that served
as a saloon on the banks of the Red River.

In no particular hurry, now that his quarry was in
sight, he studied the horse tied out front of the dilapi-
dated cabin. It was without question the red roan Rafe
had stolen when he escaped from jail. A wild young
fellow, Rafe had only six months left to serve on an attempted bank robbery conviction. Now he could look
forward to an extended stay in the jail below the
courtroom in Fort Smith, with jailbreak and horse
thievery added on. John grunted and shook his head in
bored amazement at the antics of such hotheaded
young men. He nudged his horse gently, and the big
buckskin gelding took him down to the river.

Pulling up beside the roan, he eased his Winchester
out of the saddle sling and dismounted. He paused for
a few moments, listening to the tormented sounds of a
banjo inside, punctuated at odd intervals by some
drunken whooping and hollering. The heavy frailing
of the banjo would be the work of Skully Adkins, the
proprietor of the seedy saloon. John was already familiar with Skully and his rotgut whiskey trade with
the Choctaws. He assumed the whooping and hollering was the alcoholic release of the man he had come
for, Rafe Wilson. He pushed the door open and
stepped up into the room.

Though still early in the evening, the inside of the
cabin was bathed in darkness, relieved only slightly
by a lantern on the end of the crude bar. John stood in

the doorway for a few moments, unnoticed by the bartender and his inebriated customer. At the single table in the bar, Skully was entertaining with a few of his homemade licks on the banjo, while Rafe proceeded to empty a bottle of Skully's worst. The deputy marshal walked up to Rafe, whose back was turned. "Rafe Wilson," John said.

Startled, Skully almost fell off the chair back he had been perched upon. Rafe, on the other hand, was too far into the bottle to react instantly. He turned around to scowl at the lawman. "Who the hell wants to know?" he slurred.

"John Ward," Skully answered for him.

"Finish your drink, Rafe," John answered calmly. "It's the last one you'll have for a while."

"Who the hell are you?" Rafe insisted.

"I'm a deputy marshal," John replied. "And I expect you know why I'm here. Now get on your feet."

"The hell I will," Rafe shot back. "You can't arrest me. I'm in Texas."

"You're still in Indian Territory. Texas is across the river." Without turning his head to look at him, he cautioned the bartender, "You just set yourself down in that chair, Skully." Back to Rafe, he said, "I'm not gonna tell you again, Rafe. Get on your feet."

Rafe didn't move right away, but said, "All right, I'll go peaceable." He shuffled his feet under him and started to get up. Halfway up, he made a sudden lunge and turned with his pistol in his hand. Expecting something of the sort, the deputy was ready with his rifle. He cracked Rafe across the head with the barrel of the Winchester, knocking him to the floor. When the barrel struck him, Rafe pulled the trigger of his pistol in reflex, the bullet whistling beside Skully's left ear. Thinking he was shot, Skully fell out of the chair and rolled up under the table. Rafe tried to struggle up on all fours, but the effect of the blow to the head, on top of two-thirds of a bottle of whiskey, was more than his addled brain could handle. John reached down and took the pistol from his hand.

"I expect we can get started back to Fort Smith now," John said, his words dry and without emotion, "unless there's some more tricks you'd like to try." He reached down, grabbed Rafe by the back of his collar with one hand, and dragged him across the floor. "Get on your feet," he ordered when he got to the door.

"I'm tryin' to, dammit," Rafe pleaded as he grasped the doorjamb in an effort to help himself up. "You cracked my skull," he slurred.

"Hey, wait a minute, John Ward." Skully, realizing now that he hadn't been shot, scrambled out from under the table. "He owes me some money for all the whiskey he drank."

With little interest in the bartender's plight, John replied, "I expect you just poured that rotgut into him outta the kindness of your heart. I doubt if Rafe, here, has two bits to his name."

"I ain't got no money," Rafe confirmed in a low grumble, his head obviously causing him pain.

"Why, you low-down son of a bitch," Skully spat. "And I even played the banjo for you. That whiskey cost me a lot of money."

"I doubt that," John said as he helped a still-staggering Rafe Wilson up in the saddle.

"How 'bout you, Marshal?" Skully inquired, searching for some way to cut his losses. "You could stand a little drink before you start back, couldn't you?"

"I reckon not," John said as he tied Rafe's hands together and secured them to his saddle. He tied the reins of Rafe's horse behind his own saddle. Without another glance at the distraught bartender, he climbed up on the buckskin and headed back the way he had come.

There were no more than a couple of hours left before dark, but John rode the horses hard until stopping to make camp. Glancing back at his prisoner frequently, he could see that Rafe was in no condition to give him much trouble for a while yet. Obviously sick as a dog, a result of Skully's poison, the miserable young man lay on his horse's neck for most of the two hours. When they finally stopped for the night, John noticed a sizable streak of vomit down the roan's withers. Feeling more compassion for the horse than he did for the man, he dipped some water from the river and doused the horse's side. "I'll make us some coffee," he said when he pulled Rafe from the horse. "Maybe that'll cut some of that whiskey in your gut." With another glance at the roan's wet withers, he added, "If there's any whiskey left in you." Rafe responded with a tortured look and no reply.

After a while, and some of John's coffee, the prisoner regained a measure of stability, even to the point of trying to eat a little of the hardtack John offered.

"I'd just as soon you shoot me instead of takin' me back to that stinkin' jail in Fort Smith," Rafe finally uttered.

"I expect I could do that," John replied. "Make it easier to carry you." He took a couple of sips from his coffee cup. "But Judge Parker frowns on havin' to try dead men." He could sympathize somewhat with Rafe's objection. The jail at Fort Smith was in the basement of the court building, and there wasn't much in the way of ventilation for the prisoners. With summer not far off, it would only get worse. The stench from the prisoners' urine had gotten so bad during the past summer that the tubs they used for that purpose were placed in the big fireplaces at each end of the building in hopes the fumes would go up the chimneys. It didn't help a great deal. John could remember smelling the stench in the courtroom above the jail.

"I've heard 'em talk about you in Fort Smith," Rafe said. "They said you was a reasonable man. You ought not send a man back to that *hell on the border.*" He paused, trying to determine if his words were having any effect on the imperturbable lawman. "You know, you was right. I ain't got no money on me, but I know where I can get my hands on a bunch of it. I'd be willing to split it with you, fifty-fifty, if you was to just let me get on my way to Texas."

"Well, now that's hard to pass up," John replied facetiously. "I'll think it over while we ride back to Fort Smith. Meanwhile, let's get a little sleep. We'll be ridin' hard tomorrow." With that, he tied Rafe to a tree for the night.

*   *   *

Five days of hard riding found John Ward leading a sullen and subdued Rafe Wilson through the streets of Fort Smith. He made straight for the jail, where he turned his prisoner over to Seth Thompkins, the jailer. "I'll tell the judge you didn't try to cause any trouble on the way back," he said as a parting gesture to Rafe. "Maybe he'll go a little easier on you." A few minutes later, John was sitting, hat in hand, patiently waiting outside Judge Isaac Parker's office.

After a considerable wait, the office door finally opened, and Judge Parker escorted two well-dressed citizens of Fort Smith out into the hall. The two gentlemen barely cast an eye in the direction of the weather-bronzed, trail-worn individual waiting to see the judge. After bidding his visitors good day, the judge held the door open and said, "Come on in, John. Glad to see you made it back all right. I assume you brought Wilson back with you."

"Yes, sir," John replied respectfully. "He's back in the jail."

"Any trouble?"

"No, sir, no trouble. He came back real peacefully."

"Good job, John. I expect you're probably ready to take a little time off. You've been going at it pretty steady for the past few months."

"Well, I have been thinkin' about doin' a little huntin' and fishin'—maybe take a couple of weeks off if there's nothin' you've got for me right away."

"No," Judge Parker said, signaling an end to the

conversation. "You go on and enjoy yourself. I wish I could go fishing with you."

"Thank you, sir." John grasped the hand extended toward him, shook it, and was on his way.

The judge stood behind his desk and watched the quiet lawman until John carefully closed the door behind him. Then he sat down and started to look through the court docket for the following week, only to become bored with it after a few seconds. It had been a long and busy morning. He stood up and walked to the window.

Looking down on the street below, he saw John Ward as the broad-shouldered deputy marshal descended the steps of the courthouse and walked toward his horse. *A good man,* he thought as he admired the bearing of the deputy. A big man, yet he moved with a certain animal grace that suggested the reflexes of a cat. *Relentless* was the word that always came to mind when Parker thought of John Ward, and John was always his first choice to handle the most dangerous assignments. Possibly he was being unfair when he singled out the quiet lawman for the most difficult and dangerous jobs. In his defense, however, he would cite the fact that John Ward was a loner. He had no family to worry about, no wife waiting at home to cause him to hesitate in a life-threatening situation, no children who might become fatherless if his reactions ever proved to be a bit too slow. John Ward was not burdened with a complicated mind. He saw the right of things, and acted accordingly—uncomplicated, but by no means simpleminded. Parker shook his head in admiration, thankful that the sometimes dispassionate lawman worked for him.

John Ward laid the bridle he had been mending in his lap and glanced up toward the tiny trail that led to his cabin on the Poteau River, waiting to see who his visitor might be. He wasn't accustomed to many visitors. Usually it turned out to be someone who had gotten lost and wandered off the road to Fort Smith. John spent very little time at the cabin himself. He only used it when taking a little time off from his regular duties as a deputy marshal.

After a few seconds passed, a horse's head appeared, pushing through the juniper bushes that lined the narrow path. John recognized the rider as Nate Simmons, and knew his little vacation was most likely about to end. He set the bridle aside and got up to greet Nate.

"John Ward," Nate called out, not seeing John at first.

"Nate," John greeted him and stepped out into the tiny clearing so Nate could see him.

"Howdy, John," Nate replied. "Didn't see you there." He reached up and wiped away a little blood from a scratch on his face. "Why the hell don't you cut a decent road into this place?" John didn't bother to answer, so Nate proceeded to state the purpose of his visit. "Judge Parker sent me after you. He said to tell you it was important, and he needs to see you right away."

The message didn't surprise John, in spite of the

fact that he had just left the judge no more than three days before. Whenever he was summoned personally by Judge Isaac C. Parker, it was always important, and it usually meant someone had to be tracked down. The judge had any number of deputy marshals he could assign to arrest somebody, but if the job was likely to be long and dangerous, John Ward was his preferred agent. This fact never impressed John. He accepted it as simple evidence that he was long on experience and diligent in doing his job. Nodding thoughtfully in response to Nate's comment, John asked, "Know what the judge has got on his mind?"

"I don't for a fact, John," Nate replied as he dismounted. "Have you got anythin' to cut the dust in my throat? I swear that's a dusty ride out from Fort Smith."

John smiled. "Yeah, I reckon it is, especially since we've had rain for the last two days." He turned and walked toward the cabin. "Come on inside. I think I've got a bottle around here somewhere." He went to a tiny cupboard and took a bottle from the top shelf. From the lower shelf, he took a cup, then handed them both to Nate. "Help yourself. The judge didn't say anything more about it?"

Nate poured the cup half full. "Nope. But if I had to guess, I'd suspect it might have somethin' to do with some trouble over in the Nations. Somebody sent word last week about some killin's over on the Neosho."

Again, John nodded thoughtfully. "All right, I'll get a few things together and ride back with you." He cocked an eye at Nate. "I reckon Judge Parker gave you instructions to fetch me back with you."

"Well, yeah, I reckon," Nate replied. Parker's orders had specifically been to bring John Ward back right away, but Nate had been hesitant to suggest that to the deputy marshal. John Ward was not the kind of man you ordered to do anything.

It didn't take John long to get ready. He traveled light. Long accustomed to living off the land, he needed few supplies: flint and steel, some salt, some coffee, a frying pan, and a coffeepot. Usually he carried a supply of jerky and hardtack for times when game was scarce. His bedroll, being too bulky to carry behind his saddle, was left in the cabin in favor of one blanket. With his gear ready to pack, he whistled for his horse. Almost immediately, the buckskin gelding loped up from the river and appeared at the corner of the cabin. The two horses greeted each other with a series of low whinnies; then the buckskin John had named Cousin plodded obediently over to his master. John saddled the horse, walked over to pull the cabin door to, then stepped up on the buckskin.

"Ain'tcha got no lock on that door?" Nate asked.

John shrugged. "If somebody wants to get in that cabin while I'm gone, I'd prefer they didn't break the door down." He turned the buckskin's head toward the trail and led them out to strike the road to Fort Smith.

"Well, it appears Nate Simmons didn't have any trouble finding you." Judge Parker looked up from his desk when the open doorway was suddenly filled with the formidable figure of Deputy Marshal John Ward.

"No, sir," Ward replied. "I was at the cabin."

Parker motioned toward a chair. "John, I know you were planning to take a little time to do some hunting and fishing, but something's come up and I need you to take care of it."

"Yes, sir," was John's simple reply, his face expressionless.

Parker could not help but marvel at the man's attitude. He had just recently returned after a month tracking down a gang of horse thieves over near the Cimarron River, in cooperation with the Osage native police. No sooner was he back than the judge had called upon him to bring in Rafe Wilson. The man deserved some time off, but Parker felt none of his other deputies were as qualified as John Ward for the job required. If John felt he was being taken advantage of, he gave no indication. But then, Parker reminded himself, the solemn deputy never showed any emotion to amount to anything.

After John settled his imposing frame into one of the judge's side chairs, Parker continued. "We've got a real wild one raising hell in the Nations, a killer, and I'm afraid he's going to do a lot more if we don't stop him. We know who he is, a half-breed Cherokee named Boot Stoner. He's the son of Wendell Stoner and an Indian woman. Stoner ran a trading post on the Grand River in the Cherokee Nation. You most likely knew him."

"I did," John answered, aware that the judge spoke

of Wendell in past tense. He knew Wendell very well, and his wife, Morning Light. He had often stopped there when passing through that valley. They were good folks. He knew about their son Boot, but he had not been involved in the boy's arrest. "Has somethin' happened to Wendell?"

"He and his Indian wife were murdered by their son." He paused a moment to let John react to his words before continuing. "Boot Stoner was released from the penitentiary in Little Rock two weeks ago. He was supposed to report in here, but he failed to do so. He was identified by two Indians at his father's store. They were certain it was the same boy who was sent away twelve years ago. The next day, another Indian went to the store and found Wendell and his wife dead."

"There was a daughter," John said, "a young girl about fourteen or fifteen."

"She's missing," Parker replied. "At least, if he killed her, the body wasn't found. I expect Boot must have taken her with him." He paused again while John shook his head solemnly. "We found out also that a man and his wife and a little girl were murdered just outside of Little Rock on the same day Boot was released. Their home was on the road he most likely would have taken. I wouldn't be surprised if that was not more of Boot's work." He gestured toward a map of Indian Territory behind him on the wall. "John, this savage has to be stopped. He's leaving a bloody trail across the whole territory. He's been out of prison for only two weeks, and already five people have been murdered and one young girl abducted. How soon can you ride?"

"I reckon I can start out for Stoner's trading post as soon as I leave here. I'll need to pick up some extra cartridges for my rifle."

"Fine," Parker said. "I knew I could count on you. I'll give you a voucher for your ammunition." He got to his feet and extended his hand. "And, John, you be damn careful."

"Yes, sir," John replied softly.

After riding a ferry across the Arkansas River, John Ward turned the buckskin west, making his way through the hill country known locally as Cookson Hills. Skirting Fort Gibson and the town of Tahlequah, he rode north up the Grand River valley, west of the Boston Mountains. It was better than sixty miles to Wendell Stoner's trading post. John sighted the store late in the afternoon of the third day out.

There was enough daylight left to take a look around Stoner's house and store. He found a couple of fresh graves in a grove of cottonwood trees. *Probably dug by the native police or friends of Wendell's,* he thought. Stoner's store was about twelve miles from Tahlequah—the little town that had become the capital of the Cherokee Nation—and that was most likely where the Cherokee police had ridden from, since it was closer than Fort Gibson. The trading post was probably a little over eighteen miles from the army post. Fort Gibson was located on the same river as Stoner's in an area the Cherokee called Muskogee, about three miles from the convergence of that river with the Arkansas and the Verdigris.

John studied a set of tracks that led north along the river. They were fresher than the other tracks around the store: two horses, both carrying riders, or one rider and a packhorse. He felt fairly certain that this was the trail he was looking for. Glancing over his shoulder at the sun, which was almost resting on the distant hills, he knew his search would have to continue the next day.

A hunter accustomed to riding alone, he methodically went about the routine of making his camp. Like any man who lived in the wild, he took care of his horse first, leading the buckskin down to the water to drink. Afterward, knowing that Wendell Stoner would not mind, especially now, he found some oats in the lean-to back of the corral and gave Cousin a generous measure. The horse was accustomed to surviving on prairie grass, so it was appreciative of the occasional treat. After Cousin was taken care of, John hobbled the horse and left it to graze while he gathered some wood for a fire. It wasn't absolutely necessary to hobble the buckskin—the horse wouldn't wander far— but John wanted it close in case he needed it in a hurry.

He took a look around in the store in case there was anything useful left, but the shelves were stripped bare. No doubt the folks who buried Wendell and Morning Light had seen no reason to leave useful items on the shelves. "Ain't nothin' I really need, anyway," he muttered and went down near the water to tend his fire. Instead of using Wendell's cabin, he chose to camp outside in the open. After a meal of coffee and bacon, he rolled up in his blanket, using his saddle as a pillow, and was soon asleep.

His eyes blinked open, awakened by something. He wasn't sure what. Feeling not fully awake, he nevertheless reacted automatically. Rolling over on his stomach, he pulled his rifle up close to him and waited, listening. He could see nothing moving in the darkness of the moonless night, but he knew something had jarred him from sleep. Then he heard his horse snort inquisitively, and he knew that was what had awakened him. The buckskin was aware of another horse nearby.

After carefully freeing himself from his blanket, he rolled away from his saddle and the firelight. Once in the deeper darkness, he crawled up to the edge of the cottonwoods where Wendell and his wife were buried, and positioned himself where he could watch his camp. Long moments passed with no sign of anything moving. Then he caught sight of a shadow darting from one tree to another along the riverbank, making its way down to his fire.

Waiting a few moments longer to make sure there was only one shadow in the trees, John rose silently and worked his way around behind his unannounced visitor. Following along in the intruder's footsteps, he could now determine that it was a man, and appeared to be an Indian. He caught up to him just as the Indian pulled a knife from his belt and charged out into the firelight, heading for John's saddle. Acting quickly, John kicked the Indian's heel, causing him to stumble and fall face-first across the saddle. He rolled over at once, only to find himself staring into the muzzle of John's Winchester.

"Two Buck!" John exclaimed when he recognized the young Cherokee who sometimes worked for Wendell Stoner.

"John Ward, don't shoot!" the Cherokee pleaded. "I didn't know it was you."

John lowered the rifle. "Hell, Two Buck, I'm not gonna shoot you. What the hell are you doin' here?"

Two Buck got to his feet and put the knife back in its sheath. "I saw your fire. I thought you were Boot maybe, come back. How you hear me, anyway?"

"My horse," John said, and tilted his head toward the buckskin. "He musta smelled yours back in the trees there." He stepped past Two Buck and picked up a stick to poke up the fire. "What made you think Boot Stoner would be here in the middle of the night?"

"I don't know." Two Buck shrugged. "I just thought I'd come back. I didn't think anybody'd be here. Then I saw your fire. I'd like to kill that son of a bitch."

John studied the young man's face for a moment. "You were the one that buried Wendell and Morning Light, weren't you?" Two Buck nodded. John knew that Two Buck was quite fond of Wendell and his wife. Wendell had let him take care of the horses and do odd jobs around the store. Over the years since Boot had been in prison, Two Buck had become more of a son to Wendell than Boot had ever been. So it was little wonder the young man wanted to extract vengeance from the half-breed.

After a long silence, during which Two Buck stared thoughtfully into the fire, he asked, "The soldiers send you to look for Boot?"

John nodded, then said, "Well, no, not the soldiers. Judge Parker sent me to get him."

Two Buck looked up anxiously into John's face. "Let me go with you. I can help you track."

"I don't know." John hesitated. He usually worked alone, but the earnest pleading in the young man's eyes was hard to reject. "I ain't used to workin' with anybody, and there ain't no tellin' how long this is gonna take."

"I don't care how long it takes," Two Buck insisted. "We gotta find him."

"Well, all right," John relented. "You can go till you start gettin' in my way, I reckon."

"I won't get in your way, John Ward. I'll help you."

"Yeah, I reckon," John replied, already wondering if he had made a poor decision. He suspected that Two Buck was more concerned with rescuing Lilly than he was over punishing Wendell's murderer. "We'll start at first light. Now, dammit, I need to get some sleep."

"They're headed for Mr. Mashburn's place," Two Buck remarked after he and John had followed the obvious trail left by Boot and his captive for half a day.

"Looks that way," John agreed. He had met Jacob Mashburn once when riding through the Nations, but he really didn't know the man.

They continued on for the better part of two hours, following the tracks of two horses before first sighting the flock of buzzards in the distance. *That doesn't look good,* John thought. There must have been twenty or more of the grisly birds forming a macabre cloud just beyond a line of trees by the river. Once they passed the trees, they saw the burned-out ruins of Mashburn's house and the cause for the great gathering of scavenger birds. It was a feast on a grand scale and, by this time, almost finished. There were carcasses strewn about the corral and outbuildings, most of them cattle, some mules, all of them almost totally devoid of flesh. Closer to the house, John spotted the remains of Jacob and his wife, already little more than skeletons, their clothes ripped and shredded by the sharp beaks and claws of the screeching diners.

John and Two Buck were stopped cold for a few long seconds, repulsed by the grisly scene before them. Too late to rescue the Mashburns' bodies from the indignity of their fate, there was little point in attempting to end the ghastly feast. In fact, the banquet had gone on for so long and grown so in intensity that the two riders were the intruders, and the brazen birds were not inclined to retreat. The most the two trackers could do was to rescue the remains of Jacob and his wife and carry them down behind the ruins of their house for burial. It was a grim and pitiful funeral for the man and wife, amid a chorus of screeching and screaming buzzards in place of hymns by a choir.

"That's about all we can do for them," a somber John Ward said when the grave was finished. He didn't comment on it, but he was thinking that Boot Stoner had a bloodlust that went beyond burning and looting. He suspected the half-breed had begun killing for the sheer satisfaction it brought him. If that was the case, John feared that anyone in Boot's path had just been served a death warrant. He was afraid there was a mad dog loose who was going to leave a bloody trail across the territory. "We're done here," he said to Two Buck. "Look for a trail outta here."

As before, there was no effort on Boot Stoner's part to cover his trail. It would have been difficult to hide at any rate, even as old as it was. Two horses, two mules, and what appeared to be a cow left a clear path away from the Mashburn ranch, leading toward the mountains east of the river. Feeling a renewed urgency, John started out at an easy lope with Two Buck close behind.

The half-breed's trail led them up into the mountains, following a stream that led to a small meadow. Here Boot had made camp and butchered the cow. From the evidence left behind, he had remained there for two or three days before leaving the mountains again and striking out to the northwest.

John paused to watch Two Buck as the young Cherokee studied the sign left in the campsite. Meticulously examining every scrap of evidence—footprints, bent twigs, disturbed brush and grass—the young man was trying anxiously to create a picture in his mind. After watching for a while, John expressed the thought that Two Buck was wrestling with. " 'Pears she's still alive," he said softly.

Two Buck flushed, embarrassed that his thoughts were so obvious. "Looks that way," he replied, reluctant to say more even though it was apparent that John Ward saw through his attempt to feign indifference. "That son of a bitch needs killin' bad. The Stoners were decent people."

"That's a fact," John said. He hesitated for a moment, deciding whether or not to say more. Then he advised, "I know it ain't good to think about, but there's no tellin' what kind of condition we're likely to find Lilly in, even if she's still alive. You'd best not get your hopes up too high."

In the saddle again, they followed Boot's trail out of the hills. After reaching the valley once more, John pulled up and searched the land before him. "The way he's heading, he'll strike the Neosho again." It was anybody's guess where Boot was going. Maybe Boot didn't know himself, but if he continued in the same direction, he'd soon end up in Kansas. The fact that Kansas was out of John's jurisdiction bothered the lawman not in the least. When it came to hunting down a mad dog, John did not concern himself with legal boundaries. If he had to go to Canada to get Boot, that was where he would go.

Chapter 4

Boot Stoner pulled his horse to a stop and paused to look at the railroad tracks before him. They had not been there the last time he had ridden through this part of the territory with Billy Sore Foot and Henry Dodge. He took a few moments to speculate upon the tracks, wondering where they went. Finally, he turned to Lilly, sitting patiently on her pony behind him. "You know about this railroad?"

Rolling baleful eyes in his direction, she answered. "It's the MKT," she replied dutifully. Much as a mustang horse is broken, Lilly had been brutally broken over the past two weeks. Resigned to the cruel use of her body, and learning well the lesson that resistance brought savage punishment, she had reconciled herself to her new existence as Boot Stoner's property.

"MKT?" Boot questioned.

"Missouri, Kansas, and Texas Railroad," she explained.

Boot thought about that for a few moments. "Well,

I'll be . . ." he mused. "So if we go that way," he said, pointing down the tracks to the south, "we'd end up in Texas." Then he gazed in the other direction. "If we go that way, we'd end up in Missouri." He scratched his head then as if amazed. "Well, I'll be . . ." he said again, and kicked his horse into motion, crossing over the tracks and continuing in a westerly direction. She followed without a word from him, the pack mules on a line behind her.

Boot had a notion to go to Kansas, but he was not figuring on following the railroad. Railroads spawned towns and telegraphs, and he deemed it healthier for him to stay away from telegraphs. He had no doubt that the law was already on to him, so he planned to stay away from the big towns and ride the wild country. Kansas remained in his mind, but first he was going to Jackrabbit Creek to see if he could hook up with Billy Sore Foot. While in prison at Little Rock, he had talked to a man who knew Billy. The man had said that Billy had managed to evade the law and gone back to Jackrabbit. Billy was a couple of years older than Boot. He wondered if Billy had changed as much as he had. It would be real interesting to see his old partner again.

There might have been new railroad tracks splitting the Cherokee Nation, but Jackrabbit Creek had not changed since Boot had seen it over twelve years ago. It was still a cluster of four shacks, two on either side of the creek at a point where it took a sharp turn back on itself, reminding one of a jackrabbit's hind leg. A half dozen dogs started barking when Boot and Lilly were still a hundred yards away, and a few children who were playing on the creek bank stopped to look their way.

Boot continued toward the first of the four shacks, walking his horse slowly up to a rickety porch that had separated from the front of the house at one end. The barrel of a rifle was just barely showing in the dark interior of the doorway. "That you, Billy?" Boot sang out as he pulled up to the porch.

"Who wants to know?" The reply came back from the dark.

"You sure as hell got cranky since I saw you last," Boot responded with a wide grin.

A stocky man with a large head stepped out onto the porch, still holding the rifle before him. Dark, brooding eyes searched the face of his visitor from under heavy woolly eyebrows. There were a few moments when nothing was said, then, "Boot? Is that you?"

"Ain't nobody else."

"Well, I'll be go to hell!" He propped the rifle inside the door and walked out to shake Boot's hand. "I swear, if you ain't a sight for sore eyes. Hell, I figured you'd rot inside that damn prison. Step down and come on in. I reckon I might be able to find a little somethin' to cut the dust." He stepped back as if to take a broader look, staring first at Lilly, then at the two pack mules loaded with supplies taken from Jacob Mashburn's ranch. "Yessir," he allowed, "you're a welcome sight, all right. I see you got yourself a little gal, too. Looks like you ain't wasted no time. When did you get out?"

"A couple of weeks ago," Boot answered as he threw a leg over and slid down from the saddle. "This place looks like it's seen some hard times," he said. As he dismounted, other faces appeared in the doorways of the other three shacks, but no one came outside. Turning to look at Lilly, Boot said, "Get down, girl."

Billy's eyes never left the young girl as she obeyed Boot's order. "Damn," Billy said, "she's a pretty little thing."

"Creek," Boot stated, "and she belongs to me."

"Creek don't make no difference to me. She's a pretty little thing." A malicious smile spread across his leering face when Boot cocked his head back and frowned. "Don't go gettin' your back up," Billy said. "I'm just lookin', that's all." He stepped up on the porch and waited. "Come on in the house. This sure as hell calls for a drink."

Boot tied the horses to the porch post, leaving the mules to stand on the lead rope tied to Lilly's saddle. While the horses were being tied, Billy walked over to the edge of the porch and called to the shack next door. "Henry! It's Boot Stoner."

Almost immediately, a thin, gaunt man with a full beard stepped out, holding a shotgun. "Well, damn me, Boot Stoner," Henry Dodge exclaimed, as surprised to see the half-breed as Billy Sore Foot had been. He stepped off the low stoop and walked across the dirt yard between the two shacks. "Howdy, Boot." Boot took his hand and they shook. Henry turned to

Billy then and said, "The last time I seen you, you was hightailin' it across that ridge after we split up with them cattle."

"That's a fact," Boot allowed, thinking to himself that if he had not chosen to split with the rest of the gang, he might not have been the only one who got caught.

The same thought must have occurred to Henry because he remarked, "It's a damn shame you was the only one they could pin that job on. But them's the breaks."

"Yeah, them's the breaks, all right," Boot replied sullenly. "Twelve years' worth of breaks."

Seeing the tone of conversation going sour, Billy spoke up. "Yeah, it's a damn shame, but there weren't nothin' nobody could do about it. And you're out now, and don't look no worse for wear, so come on in and let's have a drink." He flashed Boot a wide grin. "Yessir, ol' Boot's back." He nudged Henry playfully. "And got him a woman."

"I see he has," Henry said, having already looked Lilly over thoroughly. Older than Billy, the sap no longer rose as high in Henry, nor as often, as it had in years past. Still, he liked to look at fair young women. And Lilly was the fairest and youngest female seen around Jackrabbit Creek for quite some time.

Inside the house, Lilly was subjected to additional scrutiny, although this time it was devoid of admiration. Next to a small stove in the kitchen, Rena Big Dog stood, stoically watching her husband's guests. A Cherokee, Rena did not like Creeks, and she had heard through the open door when Boot remarked that Lilly was Creek. Being fat and past thirty, Rena was also unfriendly toward slim young women, white or Indian, especially when they caused a certain gleam in her husband's eye.

"Fetch me the bottle," Billy ordered. Her sullen expression unchanging, Rena did as she was told. She reached in a cupboard and produced a half-empty bottle. Placing it on the table, she then got three cups from the same cupboard, all the while keeping an accusing eye upon Lilly. "Set yourselves down, gents," Billy said cheerfully. "We'll drink to havin' ol' Boot back."

The half bottle of whiskey was soon emptied while they sat around the table. The talk was mostly about the state of things in the territory since Boot had been away. "Things has been pretty hard around here lately," Henry summed up. "We ain't been doin' as many jobs as we used to—gettin' old, I reckon. We hit a few farmers in Kansas, and two banks that kept us in high cotton for a while, but not much lately. Mostly, we've been holed up back here in the Nations."

Boot tossed back the remaining whiskey in his cup and set it on the table. He was not particularly pleased with the conversation. He had come seeking out his old partners, expecting to pick up where they had left off before he was caught by the law. Now, sitting around this table, all he seemed to hear from Billy and Henry was talk of lying low, afraid of the army at Fort Gibson and afraid of the new judge at Fort Smith.

Growing more and more disgusted, he finally asked, "When was the last time you went out on a job?"

Billy shrugged and looked at Henry. "Hell, I don't know. I reckon three, maybe four weeks ago. When did we steal them cows over in Oswego, Henry?"

"I expect it was a month ago," Henry replied.

Boot frowned. His old partners had obviously lost the nerve or the inclination. He quickly decided he had wasted his time in coming here. "Anybody else ride with you?"

"Virgil and Lem," Billy answered. When Boot raised a questioning eyebrow, Billy explained. "They live in them two houses across the creek, Virgil Potts and his half-wit cousin, Lem Stokes. They joined up with me and Henry not long after you left—set up in them two old shacks across the creek."

While the three men sat around the table talking, Lilly sat down on a stool in the corner of the shack, trying to attract as little attention to herself as possible. As cruel as Boot was, she feared more for her safety in the presence of these two vile-looking fugitives. When Billy Sore Foot commanded Rena to prepare some food, Lilly was afraid not to offer to help. However, the scowl she received from the Cherokee woman was enough to make her withdraw to her stool again. "Don't let her scare you, honey," Billy said, chuckling. "She don't like seein' no sweet young thing traipsin' around her kitchen." When Boot cocked an eye in response to Billy's comment, Billy laughed again. "I swear, Boot, you get your back up ever' time I look at that gal. I don't mean no harm. Hell, me and Henry's got a little job planned that you might wanna come along on."

"What kinda job?" Boot asked, only partially interested.

"We've been keepin' an eye on a little settlement over in Kansas—Oswego. Last time we was over that way, lookin' for livestock, we couldn't help noticin' how much that little town has growed. And there's a feller built a general store on the south end that sure looks mighty prosperous. Right, Henry?" Henry nodded emphatically. Billy continued. "Me and Henry is of a mind to pay that store a little visit. Hell, that man's bound to be packin' money away. There ain't no other place around for folks to buy their goods."

"They got a bank over there?" Boot asked.

"Nah. Town ain't big enough to have a bank yet," Henry answered. "That's why we're pretty sure the owner of that store must have all the money in town."

"Them other two fellers you mentioned—are they figurin' in on this deal?"

"Well, sure," Henry replied. "Lem and Virgil is part of the gang."

Boot considered it for only a few moments. It seemed like a mighty small job to be split five ways. "I expect not," he decided. "I'll be better off by myself."

Billy threw the empty whiskey bottle out the door. "Hell, you can at least think it over for a minute or two before you say no." He turned then to his partner. "We need some more whiskey. We got a lotta talkin' to do. Henry, why don't you go see if Virgil's got some?"

When Henry started to get up, Billy stopped him with a wink of his eye. "Never mind. Hell, I'll go myself."

Using a felled tree as a footbridge, Billy Sore Foot crossed over the creek and, without knocking, walked into one of the cabins. "What the hell . . . ?" Virgil Potts exclaimed, his bare backside shining as he labored between the ample thighs of an Indian woman.

"Get up from there, Virgil," Billy said. "We got bigger fish to fry." He went straight to the cupboard while Virgil extricated himself from the massive embrace of his woman.

Not without a sense of humor, Virgil replied, "There ain't many fish bigger'n Sally Red Beads. I was about finished, anyway."

"Where's your likker?" Billy asked, then found it on the top shelf. Grabbing the bottle, he asked, "You know who's settin' over at my table right now?"

"Who?" Potts asked.

"Boot Stoner."

"Who?" Potts repeated.

"Boot Stoner. I told you about Boot—used to ride with us till the law caught him. He just got outta prison over in Arkansas."

"Well, what the hell do I care?" Virgil asked. "What's he want, anyway? You ain't askin' him to throw in with us, are you?" He rolled over and sat on the edge of the cot. "We ain't hardly got enough to share as it is."

"See, that's the thing," Billy said with a grin. "Boot don't wanna join up with us. But he come ridin' up with two pack mules loaded down and a young gal.

I'm thinkin' we could use all that stuff. Includin' the gal," he added with a wink. "I say to hell with him if he don't wanna join up with us."

Virgil was immediately intrigued by the suggestion. "What if he don't wanna share his stuff with us?"

"Share it?" Billy replied. "Hell, I ain't talkin' about sharin' nothin'. Boot Stoner ain't likely to share nothin', anyway. We're gonna have to kill him."

Virgil considered that possibility for a moment, then said, "Oh . . . well that makes sense then."

"We'll most likely be doin' the law's work for 'em, anyway," Billy said, the grin returning to his swarthy face. "From the trail he's left between here and Arkansas, I'd be surprised if there ain't a lawman on his tail already, and leading right to us." With the whiskey bottle in his hand, he started for the door. "Get Lem and come on over to my place."

Back inside Billy's cabin, Henry Dodge had been trying to convince Boot to reconsider his decision to move on. He had caught the significance of Billy's wink when he left to get more whiskey, and his mind was running in the same groove as Billy's. Two pack mules of goods was a helluva lot for a man just out of the hoosegow. Like Billy, Henry was itching to see what was in those packs. Boot was adamant in his decision, however, and there was no amount of talking on Henry's part that could make him change his mind. He was preparing to take his leave when Billy returned with the whiskey.

"Here we go!" Billy sang out cheerfully as he walked in the door, waving the whiskey bottle. He set the bottle down hard in the middle of the table. "Let's have a drink to the good ol' days before Judge Parker came to Fort Smith." He filled the glasses. "Virgil and Lem will be here in a minute or two. They're good boys. Lem Stokes is a little tetched in the head, but he's handy to have around when you need an extra gun. He don't shit without Virgil tellin' him to. Virgil's right as rain, though."

Seeing no need in turning down one more drink, Boot sat down again.

One drink led to another, with most of the talking done by Billy Sore Foot, and mostly about the good ol' days when Boot was just a wild kid, and the three of them were the principal hell-raisers in the Cherokee Nation. The reunion was joined by Virgil Potts and Lem Stokes after the second round. They both nodded to Boot and favored him with wide smiles. Boot paid little attention to the pair, responding with a brief nod before returning his attention to the bottle.

On her stool in the corner, Lilly became more and more worried, especially with the arrival of the last two. Both men leered at her as they seated themselves on a rough bench at the table. Of the same cut as Billy and Henry, Potts had a particularly lecherous gleam in his eye. His friend, the man identified as Lem Stokes, openly gaped at her with the primitive expression of a hound dog. Averting her eyes to avoid contact, she returned her gaze to Boot. He seemed unaware of the potential danger building as the level in the bottle went down. As miserable as her life had become with Boot Stoner, she shivered when she considered her fate if she were to somehow fall into the hands of the other four.

It was bound to come to a head. When Billy figured the group had mellowed sufficiently from the alcohol, he broached the subject that Lilly feared might come. "It's been a mighty long time since I've had a roll in the hay with a young gal like her," he announced with a confident grin that exposed all but his back teeth. "Since we're partners, I know I'd be proud to share with you, if things were the other way around."

"That's what I was thinkin'," Virgil Potts spoke up. "It's got to where ridin' Sally Red Beads ain't much better'n plowin' a field." His comment brought a brainless grin to the face of Lem Stokes.

Boot Stoner's face clouded up immediately. His eyes narrowed to little more than two slits aimed directly at Billy Sore Foot. "I ain't your partner, and I damn sure ain't plannin' to share my woman with you polecats."

His statement was welcome news to Lilly, but it provided no confidence when she witnessed the grim expressions of the other four men. Billy's wide grin faded to form a malicious smirk. He glanced briefly at Henry Dodge before commenting. "Well now, see, Boot, maybe me and the boys here feel like you ain't rememberin' we was partners. And we're real disappointed in your attitude. The truth is, we figure we oughta have a share in whatever you're carryin' in them packs out there, too."

A deadly silence filled the tiny shack for a brief moment as everyone seemed suspended in a state of frozen apprehension. In the next instant, the silence was shattered. Virgil Potts, unable to wait a moment longer, made the fatal mistake of reaching for his pistol. Unnoticed by anyone, Boot had taken the precaution of slipping his revolver from the holster and laying it in his lap when Virgil and Lem first came in the house. The sharp crack of Boot's shot split the room as Virgil doubled over before his hand had touched the handle of his pistol.

Stunned by the sudden explosion, no one moved for an instant, then chairs went tumbling as everyone scrambled to find safety. Boot caught Lem Stokes with the next shot before he could get untangled from his overturned chair. Henry Dodge managed to get his gun out, but Boot shoved the table over on him and pumped two shots into him as he lay helpless on the floor. That left Billy Sore Foot as the only survivor, and Boot brought his pistol to bear on him while Billy, now seated on the floor, had his gun only halfway out of the holster.

Seeing that he had no chance, Billy let his pistol ease back in the holster. "You always was quicker'n anybody I'd ever seen," he said. "I don't blame you for killin' them two, but I never thought you'd turn on me and Henry. Hell, we go way back. We can start over, you and me. Why, hell, we can ride up in Kansas and Missouri, partners, like we used to, and no hard feelin's."

Boot hesitated, amused by Billy's about-face, his pistol still aimed at Billy's head. "Well, now that's somethin' to think about. I tell you what. Why don't you think about it on your way to hell?" He pulled the trigger, sending Billy Sore Foot on his way.

With her back pressed as tightly against the corner as she could manage, Lilly sat next to her overturned stool, her hands clamped tightly over her ears, her eyes wide open in terrified shock. Ignoring her, Boot turned his gun to seek out Rena Big Dog, in case she had notions of avenging her husband, but Rena had fled through the open door with the first shot fired. Boot walked outside, where he spotted Rena and Sally Red Beads running for their lives. With the two Indian women already out of pistol range, he holstered it and pulled his rifle up. He paused then, hesitant to waste the ammunition. The decision was made for him, however, when the two fleeing women disappeared over the edge of the riverbank. He shrugged and lowered the rifle. Turning on his heel, he went back in the shack to find Lilly still cowering, terrified, in the corner.

"Get up from there," he commanded. "We need to look in them other houses to see if there's anythin' worth takin'."

Finding it difficult to move, she nevertheless did as she was told and collected her shattered emotions as best she could, afraid that if she didn't, she'd be his next victim. Boot went directly to Henry Dodge's cabin while pointing Lilly toward the footbridge to the other two.

Boot conducted a none too gentle search of Henry's house, throwing useless articles on the floor and up-turning tables and chairs, all the while witnessed by the terrified eyes of a half dozen small children. Interested only in guns and ammunition, he came outside again with nothing much to show for his efforts. Glancing up, he encountered Lilly coming back across the creek. She cradled a rifle in her arms. Boot stopped to watch her, his hand casually resting on the handle of his revolver. A thin smile creased his lips as he waited to see what the young Creek girl would do with a rifle in her hands. With his gaze riveted upon her, she dutifully walked up to him and handed him the rifle. He knew then that he had succeeded in breaking her spirit. When he took the rifle from her, he reached out and grabbed a handful of her hair. Jerking her head back until she cried out, he leered down in her face for a moment before releasing her. "Get ready to ride," he ordered. "There ain't nothin' to stay here for."

Chapter 5

Approaching the MKT tracks, after crossing the Grand, John pulled Cousin to a halt when he spotted two figures on foot, approaching from the opposite direction. "Women," Two Buck said as he pulled up beside John. John nodded, then urged Cousin forward to intercept the two women.

Upon sighting the two men on horseback veering toward them, Rena Big Dog and Sally Red Beads turned at once and ran for safety, even though it was obviously futile. The horses overtook them in a matter of minutes. When Two Buck called out to them in Cherokee, they stopped and waited.

Puzzled to find the two Cherokee women alone and afoot in the middle of the prairie, Two Buck questioned them. They were reluctant to speak at first, both women eyeing Two Buck's white companion suspiciously. After looking the white man over carefully, Rena Big Dog whispered to Two Buck, "John Ward?" The Indian woman had never before seen the white lawman, but she had heard plenty about the big, broad-shouldered man who rode a buckskin horse. The name John Ward was known by every outlaw in the Nations.

Hearing his name, John interrupted the questioning. "You talk white man?" he asked. Rena nodded nervously. She then answered his questions, explaining how they happened to be there and that they were on their way to Muskogee where Sally had family. Knowing John was a marshal, she was hesitant at first to tell him that she had been living with Billy Sore Foot, thinking he might arrest her. Two Buck explained to her that John was looking for Boot Stoner. The eyes of both women lit up at that.

"Dead!" Sally Red Beads said. "All dead. He kill everybody!"

"When?" John asked.

"Yesterday," Rena answered.

"How come you're on foot?" John asked.

"No time to catch horses. Afraid he gonna shoot us."

If what Sally said was true, John thought, then it would mean that he was not that far behind. They left the two women to resume their walk from Jackrabbit Creek to Muskogee after sharing a portion of their food supply with them.

The buzzards had not yet discovered the second banquet left for them by Boot Stoner, since the entrée was inside the shack. It was a grim scene, with only flies as the early guests. The bodies had not yet begun to bloat and were still recognizable. "Billy Sore Foot," Two Buck said as he stood over the body. He then pointed toward a body lying flat on its back with a table on top of it. "Henry Dodge."

John grunted in reply. He was familiar with the names, but had never had the occasion to come face-to-face with the two outlaws. "How 'bout the other two? You know 'em?"

"Don't know," Two Buck said. "Never seen 'em."

John stood there for a few moments more, looking over the grisly leavings of the half-breed Boot Stoner. Then, with a slight nod that signaled he had finished there, he turned to leave the shack. "Well, I guess it don't matter who they are. I doubt anybody's gonna miss 'em, anyway." He was already thinking about finding Boot's trail away from Jackrabbit Creek.

"It sure ain't hard to follow his trail," Two Buck commented, taking a last look at Billy Sore Foot's body. Stepping rapidly to catch up with John, he asked, "We gonna bury 'em?"

"Not hardly," John replied without stopping to look at Two Buck. He felt no more obligation to spend sweat digging graves for the four outlaws than he would have for a rotting coyote. "Cremate 'em."

"Do what?" Two Buck asked, not understanding.

"Burn the shack," John said.

"Oh."

While Two Buck set fire to Billy Sore Foot's house, John scouted the clearing, looking for tracks that would tell him in which direction Boot had set out after his little party. It didn't take him long to spot the trail left by two horses and two mules, leading north-east. Satisfied that it was the trail he looked for, he stood up and took a long look at the sun, already heavy in the western sky. He figured one hour of daylight at best. *Might as well make camp,* he thought. *But not here in this stinking place.* The four outlaws had not been especially tidy in their living conditions. There was a filthy squalor about the little cluster of shacks that might offend a buzzard. So as not to lose the entire hour of daylight that was left, he decided to follow Boot's trail until he came across a spot that suited him. The decision made, he stepped up in the saddle and pointed Cousin northeast.

Seeing John Ward mounted and riding out, Two Buck threw part of a broken chair he was holding onto the fire he had built in the middle of the shack. The fire, barely started, was showing signs of reluctance, and Two Buck hesitated, wanting to see the cabin burn, but he was irritated at being left behind. "Damn," he finally uttered and ran for his pony. Jumping on the horse's back, he galloped after the departing lawman. "Damn, John Ward," he complained upon pulling up beside him, "why didn't you say you was leavin'?"

"Seemed obvious," was John's simple reply.

Starting out early the next morning, they picked up Boot's trail where it left the east fork of Jackrabbit Creek. Judging by the freshness of the droppings they found, John was confident that he was rapidly over-taking the cold-blooded killer. Two Buck's eagerness upon finding fresher and fresher sign was almost more than he could restrain. John was prompted to rein the Indian's excitement in, lest Two Buck should break into a gallop. "Just hold your damn horses," John cautioned. "We're catchin' up fast, and I'd rather Boot didn't know we're comin'."

They had been riding through hill country ever since early morning, and it was now growing late in the afternoon. Boot seemed to be traveling at a leisurely pace, and John figured the outlaw might set up camp before much longer. Consequently, it made sense to him to hold back a little and catch Boot in his camp. If everything went the way he figured, and the cards fell just right, he might be heading back to Fort Smith with his prisoner in the morning.

Crossing a wayward stream that curved around a long ridge, John pulled Cousin to a stop while he looked at the hoofprints on either side of the stream. "He stopped here and thought about makin' camp, judgin' by the prints. Decided to look for a better place," he added, and nodded toward the tracks leading farther along the stream. "I reckon we'd best take it a little slower from here on," he said, and proceeded to dismount. Following his lead, Two Buck slid off his pony. "We'll leave the horses here," John said, "and crawl up to the top of this ridge. Maybe we can see what's ahead before we ride into it."

Tying the horses in the brush, they made their way up the slope to the rim of the ridge, where they lay flat on their bellies and scanned the valley beyond. For a few moments, there was nothing. Then Two Buck pointed to a long clump of bushes between the cottonwood trees. John stared at the spot for a brief second before seeing a thin wisp of smoke rising beyond the leafy vines. He acknowledged Two Buck's signal with a nod, then said, "We'll wait till dark—give him a chance to crawl in his blanket."

After studying the lay of the land, John decided it best to split up as soon as the little stream was cloaked in darkness. Pointing to a shallow ravine that appeared to run down to the stream from the east, he instructed Two Buck to approach the camp from that side. "When you get to the head of that ravine, I'll move in from along the stream. If we do this thing right, we oughta be able to catch him before he even knows we're here." He paused to study the anxious young Cherokee's eyes, then added, "Keep your wits about you. Don't be surprised if the girl ain't with him." Two Buck nodded vigorously, impatient to go. "And don't go chargin' in there before I work my way down to that stream. All right?" Two Buck nodded again. "Let's go then," John said as he pushed back from the edge of the ridge.

Descending the slope at a trot, John couldn't help feeling compassion for Two Buck. The young man obviously had strong feelings for the Creek girl. John was afraid Two Buck might be devastated to find she was no longer with Boot, for that would almost certainly mean she was dead. *Maybe I shouldn't have let him come with me,* he thought.

Once he reached the bank of the stream, he looked across the expanse of scrub bushes to locate Two Buck. After a few moments, he was able to make out

the Indian's form in the deepening darkness. Waving
his rifle slowly back and forth over his head, he
waited until Two Buck acknowledged. Then he started
working his way along the stream bank toward the
fire's glow, now evident through the screen of bushes
and vines. After moving approximately twenty yards
closer to the camp, he came to a clearing. Dropping at
once to one knee to look the situation over, he at first
saw no sign of anyone near the fire. Scanning across
the clearing, he saw two horses and two mules, still
standing with saddles and packs on. It didn't surprise
him, knowing the nature of the man he was tracking.
Still, there was no sign of anyone about. Instinctively,
he quickly turned to look behind him, thinking that
maybe Boot had somehow sensed danger. However,
he could see no one.

Turning back again to watch the camp, his eye
caught some movement just beyond the circle of firelight. He concentrated his gaze upon it. After a few
moments, he realized that what he was staring at was
a prone figure seeming to bob about in the darkness.
It struck him then exactly what he was witnessing.

From the opposite side of the camp, the stark realization struck Two Buck at almost the same instant. It
was too much for the anxiety-ridden young man to
contain, for from his position, the fire provided just
enough light to give him a glimpse of the young girl's
face, staring stoically up from beneath the half-
breed's body. "Lilly!" In heartsick rage, he cried out
her name and charged into the clearing.

Although totally absorbed in the fulfillment of his

animal lust a brief instant before, Boot Stoner's reactions were lightninglike in response. His pistol always handy, he rolled off the girl, grabbing the weapon as he did. Two Buck, charging like a crazed bull, was an easy target. Boot quickly pumped two shots into the Cherokee's chest, dropping him before he could advance beyond the campfire.

"Dammit!" John Ward grunted under his breath. Raising his rifle, he tried to get a clear shot, but he only got a brief glimpse of the half-breed's body as Boot scrambled into the brush. He fired two shots in that direction anyway, knowing that it would be luck if he hit the outlaw. His miss was confirmed when a barrage of lead came back from the darkness of the brush, causing him to flatten himself on the ground. When he looked up again, it was to see Boot running for his horses. John raised his rifle again to take aim, but the half-breed was pulling the girl along behind him, shielding himself from John's rifle.

Scrambling to his feet, John ran to cut the fleeing outlaw off, hoping to get a clear shot when Boot was on horseback. To further frustrate the lawman, however, Boot pulled Lilly up behind him on his horse, and grabbing the reins of Lilly's horse, he bounded out of the clearing at a gallop, the mules following behind on the lead rope. Cutting across the clearing, John was in a position to fire, but with Lilly behind Boot, he couldn't take the chance. He was left with no choice but to let the outlaw go.

Well, he thought, *I won't likely get another chance like that. He knows I'm after him now.* There was little he could do about it at this point. Thoughts of pursuit first filled his mind, but he discarded them, knowing that he must first check on Two Buck. Turning to look back at the camp, he could see the body lying right where it had fallen, just short of the fire.

"I reckon I'll have to take time to bury him," he mumbled. He could well have been irritated with the brash young man for his premature blunder, but a genuine feeling of sorrow prevented it. In the short time he had ridden with Two Buck, he had come to like the boy, and he was truly sorry for him.

Bending over the body, John started to take Two Buck's hands to pull him up when the Indian's eyelids opened slowly. "I messed up," Two Buck whispered weakly. "I'm sorry, John Ward."

Taken totally by surprise, John let him sink slowly back to rest on the ground again. "Damn, I thought you were dead," he said.

"I think I'm dyin'. I can't feel nothin' in my chest."

"No, you ain't. Now lay still while I make sure Boot ain't circlin' back on us." Leaving Two Buck where he lay, John jumped across the stream and ran up to the top of a low rise just beyond. Boot was already out of sight. Figuring that Boot wasn't sure how many he was up against, John was pretty sure the half-breed was likely to keep moving, and as fast as he could. Disappointed, but far from discouraged, the deputy marshal turned when he heard a weak chant from the camp. Two Buck was singing his death song. Returning immediately to the young man's side, John abruptly interrupted the singing.

"Shut up that noise," he ordered. "You can't die just yet. I'm gonna be needin' your help." He unbuttoned Two Buck's shirt and pulled it open to reveal two dark bullet holes. "Hmm," he grunted, and rolled the wounded man halfway over on his side. Laying him back flat, he gave his prognosis. "Both slugs are still in you. Nothin' came all the way through. Guess you were lucky he got you with a pistol instead of a rifle." Always frank and an honest man, John told it like he saw it. "Like I said, you ain't dead, but I need to get you to a doctor or I'm afraid you will be. At least you ain't spittin' up blood, so I reckon he missed your lung." Getting to his feet, he said, "You lie still. I'll go get the horses. I've got some cloth in my saddlebags we can use to stuff those bullet holes to stop the bleedin'."

With Two Buck unable to sit a saddle, John set about fashioning a travois to carry him to a doctor. If they were closer to Fort Gibson, that would have been his choice of doctors, but he was afraid Two Buck might not make it that far before bleeding out. There was an alternative, albeit one that some might think risky. Dr. Walter Summerlin had established a small clinic, with the help of his daughter, Lucinda, in the Cherokee settlement of Red Bow. There was some question concerning the reasons for the elderly physician's presence in a remote settlement in Indian Territory. Some said it was his Christian compassion for the plight of the red man. Others, whom John Ward figured were closer to the truth, were certain Dr. Summerlin had left a practice back east in shame, mortified by the unnecessary death of a patient during a drunken attempt at surgery. It was rumored the inebriated surgeon's hand was so unsteady that he accidentally severed an artery, causing the patient to bleed out on the table.

John knew the doctor. He had stopped to visit him and his daughter on more than one occasion when his business caused him to be in the vicinity of the Indian village on the east fork of the Verdigris. The doctor had a fondness for alcohol, but in his waning years, the drink had become a demon in his system. He no longer had the tolerance for whiskey that he enjoyed in his younger years. Consequently, there were now scant degrees of intoxication: one drink and he was steady as a rock, two or more and he was a useless drunk. John Ward did not set himself up to judge the doctor's weaknesses. He knew Summerlin to be a good man morally. Sober, he was a competent surgeon. One drink and he was even better. It mattered little in Two Buck's case, however, for John was convinced that it was either Dr. Summerlin or die on the trip back to Fort Gibson for the young Cherokee. As soon as daylight permitted, he would settle Two Buck on the travois and head west for Red Bow.

Some four miles north, still pushing his horse hard across the darkened prairie, Boot Stoner finally decided there was no one following him. He reined back and dismounted to let the exhausted animals rest. They had had only one brief stop, when Boot halted long enough to put Lilly on her own horse. Now he waited for the girl to catch up to him.

"What was that you yelled out back there when them bastards jumped us?" he demanded. "I heard you yell somethin' like you knew 'em."

Lilly, fearfully obedient, answered. "Two Buck," she said softly. "It was Two Buck you killed."

"Two Buck?" Boot snorted. "Who the hell's Two Buck?"

"He worked for my father while you were in prison."

"You mean *my* father," Boot emphasized. "Wendell Stoner weren't your daddy. You ain't no kin of mine." He glared at her in the darkness to make sure she had no doubt about it. "How 'bout the other feller—the one that took a shot at us. Did you get a look at him?"

Lilly nodded, then answered, "It was John Ward."

"John Ward," Boot repeated. He had heard the name somewhere before, but he couldn't recall where. He repeated the name several times, searching his memory. Then it came to him. He was a deputy marshal. Boot had talked to a couple of fellow inmates at Little Rock who were there courtesy of John Ward. They had both said that once John Ward was on your trail, you might as well throw up your hands and surrender because he was harder to shake than the devil.

"Damn lawman," Boot murmured. "I heard of him. I bet there was only the two of 'em back there. I oughta go back there and shoot his ass." It was no more than boastful talk, for his instincts were telling him it was best to avoid this particular lawman. "But

I reckon it's his luck I ain't got the time right now. I wanna pay a little visit to that store in Oswego to see if Billy and Henry were really on to somethin' worth lookin' into." There was one additional reason to keep riding to Oswego. It was in Kansas Territory and out of John Ward's jurisdiction.

"John Ward will come after you," Lilly said. It was not meant to be a warning. She simply stated a fact that she knew was as inevitable as the morning sun.

"Is that right?" Boot snorted. "Well it'll be hell to pay for him if he does."

Chapter 6

Lucinda Summerlin stepped off the short back stoop of her father's modest frame house, carrying a basin of bloody water. Waiting until she was well away from the house, she scattered the contents of the basin across the bare ground and stood, idly watching the dusty soil soak up the water. The boy she had just stitched up had been brought to see her father after he fell from a horse and landed upon his hunting knife. The wound was not as serious as it first appeared, but it did require four stitches. Lucinda, or Lucy as her father called her, was very adept at minor first aid, having helped her father since she was a young girl. That was quite a few years back, more than she liked to think about.

Sometimes she would permit herself to wonder what her life might have been had her mother not died when Lucy was only thirteen. It was a long, painful illness that reduced her mother to little more than a skeleton before she was finally taken by God. The loss of his beloved wife was more than Walter Summerlin could reconcile. Devastated by what he perceived as an uncalled-for cruelty to one so innocent, his desperate recourse was to turn to the bottle in an attempt to drown his grief. After an extended absence, he finally resolved to deal with the loss of his wife and return to his practice. Unfortunately for him, however, alcohol had taken a firm grip upon him, and he found it impossible to function without it.

Her father's battle with grief and alcohol was a heartrending experience as seen through the eyes of a thirteen-year-old. As much as she grieved her mother's passing, she felt more compassion for her father. She had felt it was her responsibility to take care of him, so she stood by him in his darkest moments, forsaking a life of her own in order to help him carry on. Still, she found herself wondering how different her life might have been if she and her father had been able to remain in the east.

"Little use in spending wasteful thoughts on what might have been," she lectured herself and turned to go back to the house. When she turned, her gaze fell upon a rosebush she had planted near the kitchen door. *Maybe I should have dumped the basin on my roses,* she thought. *The blood might have nourished the soil.* She permitted a little chuckle for her thought and started toward the door, but paused again when something across the valley caught her eye. Shielding her eyes with her hand, she stared toward the hills on the far side, making out two horses. As they got a little closer, she could see that there was one rider, while the second horse was pulling a travois. It was not an uncommon sight. Many of their Indian patients were transported to her father's clinic by travois.

I'd best go tell father that another patient is coming, she thought, although she hesitated a few moments longer. There was a familiar look about the rider on the lead horse, and she continued to stare hard in an effort to get a better picture. It didn't appear to be an Indian. A few moments more and she suddenly felt a tiny flutter in her heart. "John Ward," she uttered, barely above a whisper. Although still over a hundred yards away, there was no mistaking the solid, wide-shouldered form of the deputy marshal.

With no further hesitation, she immediately turned on her heel. Without pausing as she passed the pump, she set the basin down and hurried into the kitchen. "Dad," she called out as she breezed through the kitchen, untying her apron as she walked, "someone's coming." She didn't wait to find out if her father had heard her, going straight to her room.

"Who is it?" Dr. Summerlin called back from the front room.

"Looks like John Ward," Lucy answered from her room. "He's hauling somebody on a travois." To herself, she muttered, "Damn, damn, damn," as she fussed with her hair in a frantic attempt to put some semblance of order to her rebellious tresses. *He would have to come this morning when I've just washed my hair and can't do a thing with it.* Smoothing it down as best she could, she decided it would have to do. A long, scrutinizing look in the mirror caused her to frown as she examined each familiar line and wrinkle. She then heard her father greeting their visitor from the front porch, so she gave each cheek a pinch and offered one little sigh in memory of her youth.

"Well, John, looks like you've run down another outlaw," Dr. Summerlin called out in greeting.

"Howdy, Doc," John returned. "Not this time. This is a friend. Got shot up pretty bad last night. There's two slugs still in him—name's Two Buck."

John dismounted while Dr. Summerlin stepped off the porch and walked around to the travois. While the deputy stood silently by, the doctor examined the two bullet wounds in Two Buck's chest.

"He's a good man, Doc. I'd be obliged if you can patch him up."

After a brief examination, Summerlin stood up straight and gave Two Buck his prognosis. "Well, young fellow, I guess if you're still alive after bouncing across the hills on that travois, then you've got a pretty good chance of making it. Let's carry you inside."

Eyes wide open, but saying not a word, Two Buck lay still while John and Dr. Summerlin lifted him up from the travois. With John at his shoulders and the doctor at his feet, the injured man was carried toward the porch. Lucy stepped out on the porch and held the door for them. "Hello, John," she said as he passed by her.

"Miss Summerlin," John replied politely, briefly exchanging glances with her before turning away lest she might think he was staring.

"Miss Summerlin," she clucked impatiently. "I

swear, John, you can call me Lucy, for goodness'
sakes."

"Yes, ma'am, Lucy," he replied meekly. *Why,* he
wondered, *do I turn into a complete fool every time I
see her?*

"I'm gonna need your help, honey," Dr. Summerlin
interrupted. "Let's get him on the table and get that
shirt off of him. Better pump some water into that
basin so we can clean him up a little. John, you can
wait in the kitchen if you want to. Make yourself at
home. There's some coffee on the stove that's probably still got some kick to it."

"Much obliged," John mumbled, suddenly aware of
Lucy Summerlin's eyes upon him. The lady had a way
about her that made him feel self-conscious. Once
Two Buck was settled upon the table, John turned to
make a hasty retreat to the kitchen. Going through the
doorway, he glanced back once more only to meet
Lucy's gaze again. He looked quickly away, still
afraid she might think him too bold.

In the kitchen, he found the coffeepot sitting on the
edge of the stove just as the doctor had said. Looking
around in the cupboard, he found a cup and filled it
with the black liquid. One sip and he almost walked to
the back door to spit it out. He appreciated strong coffee as much as the next man, but this had no doubt been
sitting there since early morning. The thought occurred
to him that maybe Doc required coffee stronger than
sheep dip to bring him down off a drunk. He had noticed an Indian woman and a young boy riding away

from the clinic. Lucy might have found it necessary to sober her father up so he could doctor the boy.

Thoughts of Lucinda Summerlin caused him to reflect upon the strange effect the woman had upon him. Lucy was a fine-looking woman, tall and strong—no nonsense about her, either. She was not what he would call a beautiful woman. *How many women were who lived in this wild country?* But he would bet she had been a handsome young girl in her day. *Hell,* he thought, *she still cuts a fine figure.* He thought about that for a second before admonishing himself for wondering about things that were none of his business. It occurred to him then that he never considered himself a lonely man until he was in her presence.

His mind still on the doctor's daughter, he absentmindedly took another gulp of the coffee. "Damn!" he blurted. "I ain't man enough to drink this stuff."

It was over an hour before the door to Dr. Summerlin's surgery opened and the doctor came out. Going straight to a lower cupboard, he took out a bottle and a glass, poured a drink, and downed it before bringing the bottle to the table. Only then did he acknowledge John's presence. Settling himself wearily into a chair, he sighed, "I'm too damned old to do this work anymore. I swear, whiskey is the only thing that keeps me going."

"What about Two Buck?" John asked. "Is he gonna make it?"

"Who?" Summerlin replied, pouring himself another drink. "Oh, the Indian. Yes, he'll live. You can take him out and get him shot up again. But not for a couple of weeks."

Lucy came out of the room then, carrying another basin full of bloody water. She paused when she saw John sitting there drinking coffee. "Are you drinking that awful stuff? It's been on the stove since before sunup."

John grinned. "I made some fresh. I hope you don't mind."

"In that case," she said, smiling back at him, "I'll have some, too, as soon as I get rid of this." She paused again before reaching the back door. "Your friend is resting easy right now, but he won't be ready to ride for a week or so."

"Much obliged," was all John replied, but he was thinking that he could not afford to wait around for Two Buck to heal. As much as he had come to like the young Cherokee, and even though Two Buck was desperate to rescue Lilly, John still had no intention of letting Boot Stoner's trail grow cold.

When Lucy returned, she poured herself a cup of coffee and sat down opposite John. After a couple of sips of the dark liquid, she complimented him. "Well, John Ward, I have to say you make passable coffee." She cocked a mischievous eye at her father, who was lost in his postoperative balm. "When the doctor makes coffee, he uses more beans than water."

"Yes, ma'am, I know," John said, having recently sampled some of the doctor's brew. There followed a rather awkward silence between them before he finally asked, "Is there some place around here where

Two Buck could lay up for a while till he gets his strength back?"

"He can stay in the spare room till he gets on his feet. I thought you might be staying with him," Lucy replied, obviously disappointed. Then, with a quick smile to hide her feelings, she said, "We thought we might have some company for a few days."

"I wish I could, but I was chasin' a murderin' half-breed when Two Buck got himself shot. I need to get back on his trail just as quick as I can. I'm afraid he might have already given me the slip. I'm much obliged to you for takin' care of Two Buck. I'll see that you get paid for the doctorin' and his keep."

"Well, there's no use starting out this late in the day. You might as well stay for supper. It's probably been a while since you've had a decent meal." She paused to fix him with an impish smile. "I don't suppose you've gotten yourself married since we saw you last."

John shook his head. "No, ma'am, I doubt if anybody'd have me. I thank you for the invitation, but I really oughta get started back. I reckon I'll look in on Two Buck for a minute, and then I'll be off."

"You'll be missing a good supper. Lucy's a damn good cook." This was the first comment from the doctor for quite some time.

"Yes, sir, I know she is, but I don't wanna put you folks out any more than I already have." The desire to stay and visit Lucy Summerlin for a while longer was strong, but he couldn't ignore his responsibility for the capture of Boot Stoner.

"Well, suit yourself," Lucy said curtly, having become impatient with him.

After looking in on his wounded friend, John unsaddled Two Buck's horse and turned it in with the doctor's horses. He was checking Cousin's girth strap in preparation to leave when Lucy came out of the kitchen with half a cake of cornbread wrapped in a dish towel. "Here," she said, "this is left over from earlier. There's no telling when you'll stop to eat."

"Well, thank you, ma'am," he said, and turned to put it away in his saddlebag. When he turned back to face Lucy, it was to find her gazing intently into his face. It was an expectant gaze and he sensed that he was called to respond somehow, but he was dumbfounded as to the nature of that response.

After a long moment with no response from him beyond the blank expression of confusion on his face, she shook her head in exasperation. "I swear, John Ward, sometimes I wonder if there's anything going on inside that head of yours." She stepped back, leaving him to puzzle over her remark. "Take care of yourself," she said, and turned to leave. She took no more than three steps before spinning on her heel. Stalking back up to him, she reached up and planted a kiss on his lips. It was quick, but firm, as if she meant business. Then, without another word, she turned and marched to the kitchen, leaving him mystified and mesmerized. *Maybe that will make him think about something besides chasing murderers and thieves,* she thought.

He watched her until she disappeared into the house and the door had closed behind her. His mind revolving in a whirlpool of bewilderment, he could still feel the burn of her lips upon his. He had a feeling that the sensation would dwell in his mind for a long time, giving him something to puzzle over until he could sort out the confusion it generated. He found it hard to believe that a fine-looking woman like Lucinda Summerlin could possibly have any affection for a weather-beaten range rider like himself. He didn't remember climbing up into the saddle, and was mildly surprised when Cousin broke into a lope passing the doctor's front gate.

Inside the house, Dr. Summerlin greeted his daughter. "I saw that little farewell through the window," he said with a slight chuckle.

"You did?" She flushed, then shrugged, unconcerned. "I guess he's still trying to figure out what happened. He's so damn smart in some ways, and so dumb in others." She glanced at her father's face, which was still bearing an amused grin. "Hell, Papa, I'm not getting any younger." She had waited for John Ward to notice her for two years, and she *was* getting older. She wondered what on earth he was waiting for. She was certain that he had special feelings for her. She had often seen it in his face, as well as his instant embarrassment when she caught him looking at her. *The big dumb clod,* she thought. *He'd better speak up soon or to hell with him.*

With a shake of her head and a long, tired sigh, she turned back to her father. "I expect I'd better throw some supper together. You'd best get some food in your stomach to mix with the whiskey you've already downed today. I'll look in on John Ward's Indian friend after supper."

Chapter 7

Lilly waded out into the river up to her knees, her legs numb in the chilly water, her skirt tied up around her waist. Shivering, she slowly lowered her bottom into the water, being careful not to let her skirt fall. Some thirty yards behind her on the shore, Boot Stoner sat by the fire, rolling himself a smoke. He would be satisfied for the night now, permitting her to sleep unmolested. Her mind long since adapted to the half-breed's use of her body, she no longer tried to resist his assault. It had become almost mundane as she lay waiting for him to reach his satisfaction. She had learned early on that to protest and resist only brought physical pain to accompany the ordeal.

At this point in the shallow river, she was almost a third of the distance across. With Boot lounging by the fire, she could easily push out into the deeper water and swim to the other side. She would be gone before he even took notice of her absence. There was no thought of escape, however. She had resigned herself to the fact that she was now simply Boot's property, like his horse or his rifle. What good would a few hours of freedom do, anyway? He would only come after her, and the punishment would be far worse than before. Even if she did manage to evade him, where would she go? The only place she had relatives was Low Hawk, and that was a long way away from this river on the Kansas border.

"Hey!" A roar came out to her from the riverbank. "Get your lazy behind outta that water. I'm hungry."

She responded to his command immediately, wading ashore and hurrying up to the fire. Standing before the fire, she rubbed her legs vigorously with her skirt in an effort to dry them, all the while being careful not to expose too much of her legs so as not to arouse his interest again.

She need not have worried. Boot's mind was on another passion. In a talkative mood, he proceeded to voice his intentions while she prepared his meal. "If Billy was right, Oswego can't be far from here. We oughta make it before noon tomorrow." She worked away in silence while he talked. He didn't expect conversation from her. " 'Course, Billy Sore Foot and Henry Dodge was both born liars, but if what they said was true, that store in Oswego might be easy pickin's."

"No more flour," Lilly said, holding up the empty sack for him to see, her voice submissive as if it were her fault.

"We'll stock up tomorrow," Boot cheerfully replied, his spirits up with the prospect of a plum ripe for the picking. His mind skipped back to another subject then, one that concerned him, even though he would not admit it. "What do you know about this lawman that took a shot at me the other night?"

She looked up from her cook fire to meet his intense gaze. "John Ward?" she replied with a shrug. "He stopped at my father's house several times."

"*My* father's house," Boot immediately corrected. "Wendell Stoner weren't your daddy. This John Ward—what's he supposed to be, some kinda big-dog lawman or somethin'?"

"I don't know. They say he will never stop until he gets his man."

Her answer angered him. "I'm damn sure not afraid of John Ward, or any other two-bit lawman. I hope to hell he does keep comin'." He fumed for a few moments more before saying, "He won't follow us in Kansas, anyway."

Doug Fannin gazed fondly at the carved nameplate that resided on the right-hand corner of his desk. JAMES DOUGLAS FANNIN it proclaimed. Given to him by his wife, Joyce, when he finished law school, it had never graced the desk of a practicing lawyer. Instead, Doug, as his friends called him, decided his fortune lay in the field of trade, and the new frontier. In the summer of 1865, he journeyed west until he reached the little settlement of Oswego in Kansas Territory. Seeing potential for the little town nestled in a crook of the Neosho River, he decided to plant his roots right there. Due to his shrewd business sense and a fair-dealing attitude, the trading post he established soon became a thriving store that did business with settlers and Indians alike. These were thoughts that occupied his mind on this spring morning in May, thoughts interrupted by a call from the front of the store.

"Doug," his wife called, "there's a man outside that wants to talk trade with you."

That usually meant a man with no money, a poor farmer in hopes of trading worthless possessions for needed staples, or maybe an Indian hoping to acquire tools or utensils. At any rate, it was certain to be of no gain to Douglas Fannin and family, for Doug was a kind man and his trading often amounted to little more than charity. With a sigh of resignation, he got up from his chair and started toward the front of the store.

Upon first glance at the customer awaiting him outside, Fannin sensed a feeling of caution. The man was a lean, rawboned individual, dark of complexion—Fannin guessed a half-breed—wearing a smirk of contempt. There was a young woman with him, a girl really, he decided on second glance. Riding two horses, they had two mules on a lead rope, packed with an odd lot of household items. When Fannin walked past his wife, he said, "Honey, go in the back room and tell Ed to come out here."

"Good afternoon to you, friend," Fannin greeted the man cordially in spite of his initial assessment of him. "What can I do for you?"

"I got some things I'm lookin' to trade," Boot

replied as he sized Fannin up. Without taking his eyes off the merchant, he nodded toward the pack mules.

"Looks like you brought a whole household on those mules," Fannin said.

"Yeah, it does, don't it?" His tone was almost surly.

Fannin was somewhat puzzled at the man's attitude, considering he should be currying his favor. "What are you looking to trade for?" he asked.

"I don't know"—Boot shrugged—"a gun, some ammunition, some whiskey maybe."

"I don't sell whiskey," Fannin came back, "or guns either, but I do carry some cartridges and shotgun shells."

"Is that so?" Boot replied, not really caring. He had no plans to trade anything, anyway. "Well, I'll just go inside and see what you've got. You can take a look through them packs to see if there's anything you wanna swap for."

Fannin glanced up at Lilly, who was still seated on her horse. He was about to ask if she would like to dismount when Ed appeared in the doorway. "You send for me, Mr. Fannin?"

"Yes, Ed, go on back inside and help this gentleman." Ed Swadley was not endowed with an especially active brain, and Fannin didn't expect him to help a customer with anything, since he was barely able to help himself. Fannin had given the simple man a job, another of his charitable acts. It primarily consisted of cleaning the store and outhouse. He had, in fact, sent for Ed simply because he didn't want Joyce to be alone in the store with a man who looked capable of violence.

Predictably, Ed responded with, "Help him do what?"

"Nothing," Fannin replied in exasperation. "Just go on back in the store while I look through these packs."

Confused, Swadley shrugged. Just then, Boot turned to go inside, coming face-to-face with Fannin's bumbling employee. "Well, I'll be danged," Ed blurted. "Boot Stoner."

"Shut your mouth!" Boot hissed. "Do like he told you." Both men were equally surprised. Boot looked back to see if Fannin had heard the exchange, but the storekeeper was already on the other side of one of the mules, giving no indication that he had.

Stumbling along before Boot, Swadley asked, "When did you get out?" He almost tripped on the door sill as a result of the shove helping him along.

Once inside, Boot looked quickly around to make sure no one else was in earshot. The store was empty except for the two of them, Joyce Fannin having gone into the office. When he was satisfied no one could hear, he lit into Swadley. "What the hell are you doin' here?" Ed Swadley was perhaps the last person he had ever expected to encounter, especially in a settlement like Oswego. A petty thief and pickpocket, Swadley was known to him in prison, but not a man Boot would associate with, even there.

"I work here," Ed answered. "Mr. Fannin gimme a job."

"Is that so?" Boot growled. He was on the verge of

threatening him to keep his mouth shut when it occurred to him that he might make use of the simple-minded man. Changing his tone, he said, "So you work here, do you? What does he pay you?"

"Fifty cents a day," Swadley replied.

"Fifty cents a day," Boot repeated. "How'd you like to go partners with me and make you some real money?"

Ed's eyes lit up at that. While in prison at Little Rock, he had never had the guts to approach Boot Stoner lest the fearsome half-breed slit his throat. "You mean I could ride with you?"

"Yeah, you could ride with me," Boot replied, making a halfhearted effort to hide his disgust for the half-wit. "All you gotta do is make sure that back door ain't locked when he closes up tonight. You can do that can'tcha?"

"I don't know, Boot. He don't let me lock up. He puts a padlock on both doors and carries the key on him."

"What about the windows?"

"He locks 'em and latches the shutters."

Losing his patience, Boot growled, "Well, god-dammit, you oughta be able to sneak around behind him and unlock a window."

Ed thought about that for a moment before his eyes brightened and he answered, "Yeah, Boot, I bet I could do that."

"One of them in the back, away from the street," Boot felt it necessary to say. Ed looked puzzled, but Boot didn't have time to explain before Fannin walked in. "Don't let on you know me," Boot whispered. He received a large, exaggerated wink of the eye in reply.

"Ed, you can go on back to cleaning up the storeroom now," Fannin said as he came in. Directing his comments toward Boot then, he said, "Mister, I didn't see a whole lot of things I could sell in your packs. Some pots and pans and some blankets and tools was about all I could use."

Boot cocked his head around to look directly at the storekeeper, a hint of a smile on his face. "Well, that's all right. I didn't see nothin' in here I wanted, anyway." He turned and left the store.

"Well, wasn't he the odd one?" Fannin commented to Ed, who was still standing there. He shook his head and sighed. "I'm just as glad he decided to leave. He had a mean look about him." He smiled then, and added, "He didn't have anything of value that I could see, anyhow, nothing but well-worn household goods." He walked to the door then to take another look as Boot and Lilly slow-walked their horses down the dusty street. "Yes, sir, Ed, there's some strange folks who pass through here."

"Yes, sir," Ed replied, following with a foolish grin. "I'll get to that storeroom now."

It was well past dark when Boot guided his horse up to the back of Douglas Fannin's store, with Lilly following close behind. He had no sooner dismounted than a figure emerged from the shadows by the corner of the stockroom. "It's me! Ed Swadley!" Ed blurted

as Boot's pistol was trained on him in a flash. Like a
faithful dog, the simpleminded thief had been waiting
for Boot's return.

"Well, you almost got your ass blowed away," Boot
returned crossly. Holstering the pistol, he told Lilly to
get down off her horse. Turning back to Swadley, he
asked, "Which one of them winders did you fix?"

"Well, see," Ed began, "that's just it, Boot. I didn't
get to unlatch any of 'em. I was goin' to, but Mr. Fannin, he run me out before he locked up."

"Why you dumb . . ." Boot started. "Hell, then
what good are you to me?" He considered putting a
bullet into Ed's skull right then, but he had further use
for him. Disgusted, he pushed past the bewildered
simpleton. Walking up to the back door, he tried it
several times, even though the padlock was plainly
visible. "There's a choppin' ax packed on one of them
mules," he said to Lilly. "You go fetch it while I take
a look to see if there's anybody around. He moved up
the side of the store, keeping to the shadows, until he
reached the front of the building. There was a saloon
about seventy-five yards up the street, and the sound
of piano music and boisterous voices drifted on the
chill evening air. Other than that, the town was quiet.

When he returned, walking back along the opposite
side of the building, Lilly was waiting with the ax.
Boot grabbed it and shoved it into Ed's hand. "Chop
me a hole through that door," he ordered.

Ed did as he was told. "Mr. Fannin ain't gonna like
this," he said as he buried the blade deep in the door.

"Whadda you care?" Boot smirked. "You're ridin' with me now."

"Yes, sir," Ed said, remembering then, "I shore am!" With the enthusiasm generated by that thought, he set into the door with a vengeance.

The door was stout, but it had to eventually yield to Ed's determination, and finally, one last blow splintered the timber next to the hinges and the door sagged open. "There she is," Ed panted triumphantly and pulled the broken door back on its lock.

Boot entered the darkened storeroom. He took two steps inside and had to strike a match to see his way to the door that connected the room to the store. "Another damn locked door," he complained. "But at least the hinges are on this side. Find me somethin' to knock these hinge pins out with."

"Best keep to this side with that there match," Ed said while he groped about for a tool on the workbench.

Boot was about to ask why when he turned to hold the lit match toward the other side of the small room and discovered several cases of dynamite stacked against the wall. "Jesus!" he gasped, drawing the match back so quickly that it almost went out. "Damn you. Why didn't you tell me there was dynamite in here?" When Ed was unable to come up with a reason, Boot grumbled, "Get that damn door off the hinges."

Once inside the store, Boot wasted little time in ransacking the shelves for anything that appealed to him. Hesitant about lighting a lamp, the three of them groped around the shelves, the two men gathering up ammunition, knives, and tobacco, and Lilly, at Boot's direction, collecting what foodstuffs she could find. "Hell, that's all I can pack on them mules," Boot finally announced, and grabbed Ed by the sleeve. "Where's he keep the money?"

"There's a drawer under the counter," Ed replied reluctantly. He had hoped Boot would forget about the cash money, so he could take it when Boot's back was turned.

Boot picked up a crowbar from a shelf of various tools and made short work of the lock. Opening the drawer, he was disappointed to find no more than fifty-five dollars in currency. "Damn," he swore. Looking at Ed, he demanded, "Is this all there is?" Remembering how Billy Sore Foot and Henry Dodge had bragged about the rich pickings waiting in Douglas Fannin's store, Boot felt cheated. He had expected several hundred. Angry, he picked up a shovel and threw it across the room. "I know that son of a bitch has got more money than this," he snarled.

"Most of the time he takes it home and puts it in his safe," Swadley volunteered.

"Well, maybe we oughta go and pay him a visit," Boot said while filling his pockets with the contents of the cash drawer. "Lilly," he called, "finish up them packs." Hearing voices, he stepped to the front window and peered through the shutters. The voices he had heard came from the last stragglers from the saloon down the road. He stood watching while a couple of men made their way unsteadily along the middle of the street. As they were opposite the front door of the store was the moment when Ed Swadley dropped a large glass container of peppermint sticks. The crash of glass on the plank floor was plainly heard by the two drunks, causing them to pause and stare at the store for a few moments before exchanging words that Boot could not make out, but could well guess. When they promptly turned around and scurried off down the road again, Boot swore, "Damn you, Swadley. You've give us away."

Thoughts of a safe filled with money at Fannin's house had to be abandoned. There was no time now before who knew how many would come running to investigate the mysterious noises coming from the store. Boot was furious. His anger was directed at the clumsy Swadley, but also at Fannin for the simple reason that his plans had been thwarted. "Get in the saddle, Lilly," he ordered. She immediately obeyed.

"I'll get my horse," Swadley said, and started for the door.

Falling in behind him, Boot said, "You ain't gonna need no horse." A second later, Ed exhaled forcefully as Boot's knife plunged deep into his side. Too stunned to react to protect himself, he simply stood there while Boot's other arm locked around his throat, holding him while he withdrew the knife and thrust it in again. Two times more the slender blade struck deep inside his body before Ed slid limply to the floor.

"You dumb turd," Boot growled contemptuously. "You cost me money." He hurried to join Lilly out back, but when passing through the storeroom, he saw one last way to take out his anger against Fannin.

Acting quickly, he hazarded another match. Busting the lid of a crate, he took out a stick of dynamite. Yanking the fuse from one of the other sticks, he tied it to the one in his hand, making a longer fuse. Hurrying back inside, he placed the dynamite in Swadley's hand and lit the fuse. "Here's your share of the goods, *partner*," he snarled, and made a hasty retreat, pausing only to pick up a couple more sticks of dynamite. "These might come in handy," he said.

Outside, he ran for his horse. With one foot in the stirrup, he yelled, "Ride!" They galloped away into the darkness. In a matter of seconds, there was a sudden explosion, sending flaming timbers shooting up into the darkness, and the night sky lit up the tiny settlement behind them. Startled, Lilly's horse skidded sideways, almost throwing her from the saddle. She grabbed the saddle horn and held on as her frightened mount charged after Boot, whose wild and eerie laughter, ringing out in the night air, would remain in her memory for quite some time after.

It was a town still devastated that greeted John Ward two days later. Walking Cousin slowly up to the charred ruins of Douglas Fannin's store, John could only assume that the wreckage was most likely associated with the man he trailed. There was a man standing in the middle of what apparently was once a store, pulling splintered timbers aside and poking under piles of debris. John stepped down from the buckskin.

"If you were looking to buy supplies," the man said, "I'm afraid you're a little late."

"I expect I might be lookin' for the man who did this," John replied. "At least, that would be my guess."

"Who might you be?" Fannin asked.

"John Ward."

Fannin dropped the smutty timber he was holding and walked out of the wreckage. "Are you a lawman?"

"Yes, sir," John said. "From Fort Smith."

"Fort Smith? Arkansas? Do you know you're in Kansas Territory?"

"I reckon," John replied. "I've been trailin' an outlaw from south of here in the Nations, a half-breed. His name's Boot Stoner. Has a young girl with him. And I'm bettin' this is some of his work."

"I wish to hell you had been here two days ago," Fannin said.

"Yes, friend, I wish I had, too."

"It was the man you're after, all right," Fannin continued. "Half-breed, had an Indian girl with him. Couldn't have been anybody but him. He acted mighty strange. Said he wanted to trade. Then, after he looked around in the store, he said there wasn't anything he wanted, and left." He wiped the smut from his hands with a bandanna. "It was him, all right. We thought at first he got blown up with the building. There were pieces of some poor soul scattered about the place. Turned out it wasn't him, though. We found a belt buckle like one my hired man wore. It was driven halfway into a solid timber, and he hasn't been seen since. His name was Ed Swadley. We buried as much of him as could be found. What I can't figure out is how he happened to be in the store." He shrugged and shook his head. "Maybe poor Ed stumbled on him robbing the place, and tried to stop him. I reckon I can build the store again," he mused, now mostly to himself. "I was planning to tear it down sometime, anyway, and build a bigger one." He paused a moment. "Why in God's name did he blow the damn place up? Why didn't he just take what he wanted and leave?"

"Hard to say," John said. "Seems he's carryin' a powerful hatred for just about the whole world." Looping the buckskin's reins over the hitching post, the only thing left standing after Boot's departure, he started looking around the area for tracks that might tell him where the renegade had headed. Fannin resumed his search through the ruins of his store.

It took some time and careful examination of the ground because of the multitude of tracks left by the town's curious after the explosion, but he finally settled upon a trail left by two horses leaving the back of the store. They led off to the east, and were a day or two older than most of the other tracks. He returned to the hitching post and stepped up into the saddle. With a brief farewell to the disgruntled storekeeper, he rode out of Oswego. About a mile out of town, he came to a creek. Close to the bank, in a wide patch of switchgrass, he discovered multiple tracks and droppings that told him Boot had left the two mules there while he raided Fannin's store. Certain now that he was on the proper trail, he nudged Cousin for a little increase in speed. Crossing the creek, he followed the tracks east toward Missouri.

Chapter 8

The cash in Boot Stoner's pocket was beginning to burn against his thigh, and he was itching to spend some of it on some strong spirits, and maybe a little gambling. His last drink had been with Billy Sore Foot, and there was no whiskey among the goods he had taken from Fannin's store. He was developing a craving for a little fun when he led Lilly and the pack animals down into the Joplin River valley.

He halted the horses after rounding a bend in the river to discover a cluster of shacks in what appeared to be a mining camp. Looking the assembly of structures over, he determined all but one were living quarters for the miners. The one remaining was built larger and a bit more substantially. Boot was certain it must be a saloon. "I need me a drink," he announced, and jammed his heels into his horse's sides.

Pulling up again before crossing a narrow creek that emptied into the river a dozen yards away, he sat there for a moment or two studying a roughly carved sign that proclaimed the camp to be JOPLIN. The proclamation was wasted on both Boot and Lilly, for neither could read. Finally, he grunted his indifference and prodded his horse toward the building in the center of the settlement. As was the case regarding the sign at the creek, he could not identify the individual letters in the crudely painted sign nailed over the door of the building, but he recognized the familiar arrangement of them to mean saloon. Tying the horses at the rail, he opened the door and stepped inside. The fumes that greeted his nose told him that he was in the right place. He stood in the doorway for a moment, looking the room over while he waited for Lilly to catch up. Small and dark, but large enough to offer a short bar on one side and three tables near the back, the saloon was windowless except for one shuttered opening beside the door. Consequently, it was dark and dusky. What scant light there was came from two kerosene lamps, one at each end of the bar.

Two men sat at one of the tables, playing two-handed poker. They both looked toward the door when Boot entered, followed by Lilly. A third man got up from a chair at the end of the bar and shuffled casually over behind it. "That there gal looks Injun to me," the bartender said in greeting, "and I can't sell no likker to no Injun."

"I didn't hear nobody say she wanted likker," Boot snarled in reply.

The bartender studied his customer for a moment longer in the dim light before commenting, "You know, you don't look exactly all white to me, either."

Boot's eyes narrowed in a deadly frown. He brought his rifle up level with the bar and said, "This Winchester says I'm damn sure white enough to drink in this pigpen." He slapped some hard cash on the bar and said, "Now suppose you pour me a drink."

In that moment, the bartender realized he had picked the wrong half-breed to hassle. "Whoa, mister!" he exclaimed, taking a step backward. "I didn't go to rile you. Sure, you can have a drink, no hard feelin's." In his haste to comply, he wasted a generous amount on the bar around the glass.

The slight altercation at the bar attracted the attention of the two card players at the table. The two ten-dollar gold pieces Boot slammed on the bar were of special interest, prompting one of the men to rise from his chair and approach the bar. Boot cocked a suspicious eye toward the man and stood ready to act.

"I'm Reese Freeman," the man said. "Don't pay no mind to Barney there. He don't mean no harm." He favored Boot with a wide grin and tipped his hat to Lilly before continuing. "I don't believe I've seen you around here before." He cocked his head at the bartender. "That sure is a helluva way to welcome a stranger, Barney." Back to Boot, he said, "Why don't you come on over and set down with Jake and me, and I'll buy you another drink?" He stepped aside and gestured toward the table and the man identified as Jake. "Me and Jake was just playin' a little poker to pass the time. Maybe you'd care to play a few hands—just friendly stakes, you understand."

A thin smile appeared across Boot's face. Gambling

appealed to him, especially since he was secure in the knowledge that, if he lost, then the winner was dead sure of getting bushwhacked on his way home. "Yeah, I'll play some poker," he said. He started toward the table, then paused long enough to send Lilly to sit on a stool in the corner of the room.

As could be expected, Boot's luck was strong in the beginning, and he won four of the first five hands. There was a great deal of friendly banter while the cards were dealt, all of it generated by Reese and bouncing off of a stoic Boot Stoner. The whiskey glasses were never allowed to go dry, and Barney brought a fresh bottle to the table before nonchalantly slipping out the side door. The flame in the lamp on the end of the bar flickered slightly from the draft when he opened the door a few minutes later, followed in by a buxom lady wearing a long kimono, the top of which was unbuttoned almost to her navel. She sashayed casually over to stand behind Boot.

Boot paused to look the woman over, then returned his attention to the card game. It struck him that he was the only one playing with hard money, while Rafe and Reese bet with paper. He voiced his concern. "This place looks like a mining camp to me. Ain't you got any hard money?"

Reese laughed. "It is a mining camp," he said. "But there ain't no gold. It's a lead mine." He winked at the woman behind Boot's chair. "You wouldn't think too kindly of us if we was to bet with lead dollars." Boot merely grunted in response.

Eager to get a share of Douglas Fannin's gold dollars, the woman placed a hand on Boot's shoulder. "Hey, darlin', my name's Rose. You might wanna spend some of that money to have a little fun."

"I might," Boot replied, "when I get done here."

Rose bent low over him, causing her gown to gap even more, and placed a hand on his thigh. "I can guarantee you a good time," she whispered, and planted a wet kiss on his mouth.

Boot grinned. "I bet you could," he said, and rested a hand on her generous backside.

She gave him a playful slap on the hand and stepped away. "Naughty, naughty," she teased. "No free samples."

While Reese and Jake chuckled patiently at the interruption of the card game, there was a converse reaction from the spectator on the stool in the corner. When she witnessed Rose's advances upon Boot, and Boot's obviously welcome reception, a hailstorm of confusing and conflicting thoughts went racing through Lilly's mind. She had been long battered and abused by the cruel half-breed, and her young brain had been sufficiently broken that she could no longer remember what life was like before becoming Boot Stoner's property. Confronted with the seductive performance of the saucy but overripe saloon whore, she momentarily lost all sense of reality, seeing it as a direct threat to her rightful position. A rational person would find it difficult to explain what took place next.

Still taunting playfully, Rose took a step back toward Boot and puckered her full painted lips as if to tempt him with a kiss. Boot started to grab her again, but before he could raise a hand, Rose's head was suddenly jerked back and she screamed in pain. Her face twisted in surprise and agony; she tried unsuccessfully to maintain her balance. With a handful of dyed black hair and a knee in the woman's back, Lilly hauled back on the unfortunate whore's neck until Rose had no choice but to collapse. Flat on the floor now, Rose struggled to free herself and retaliate, but Lilly was upon her like an irate wildcat defending her young. Still clutching the handful of hair with one hand, she pummeled and kicked the screaming predator unmercifully.

It had happened so fast, and so unexpectedly, that the spectators to the assault were stunned into paralysis for a few moments, and none more so than Boot Stoner. At first he was amused by Lilly's reaction to the advances of the other woman. Then the thought of her presumption angered him, and he was the first to take action to stop the attack. Without a word, he got up from his chair and delivered a hard right-hand punch that knocked Lilly across the room. Following the stunned Creek girl, he struck her again when she tried to scramble to her feet. She crumpled against the wall and stayed there.

"That goddamned Injun bitch!" Rose screamed as she staggered to her feet. Seeing Lilly totally subdued, she thought to extract further retribution from the now defenseless girl. One look from the cruel eyes of the angry half-breed stopped her before she took another step.

A sudden pall fell over the dark room while the startled spectators waited to see what was going to

happen next. For a few extended moments, there was
no sound in the saloon except the pitiful whimpering
of the injured whore. All eyes were on the half-breed
as he stood glaring back at them, his rifle in both
hands now. Reese sought to ease the tension. "Nothing but a little whore fight. Let's have a little drink and
get back to the card game." He didn't like the look in
Boot's eye, and he feared that he might lose the
money he and Rafe had invested to set the half-breed
up for the fleecing. The thought of those ten-dollar
gold pieces rolling out of town was almost more than
he could bear.

"I'm done playin' cards," Boot said. With one hand,
he reached down and dragged Lilly to her feet. "Go
get on your horse." With a cut lip and a swelling red
lump beside her eye, she dutifully followed his orders.

"Ah, don't go lettin' this little scuffle rile you,"
Reese pleaded. "Hell, we was just gettin' started good,
and you're ridin' a pretty good lucky streak."

"I'm done playin' cards," Boot repeated. Then, before Lilly reached the door, he stopped her. "Lilly,
rake that money off the table."

Seeing that the game was up, Jake protested, "Now
wait a minute, friend. You can't quit while you're way
ahead without givin' us a chance to get even. That
money stays on the table." He glanced at Reese for
support. "We ain't gonna let you walk outta here with
all that money." Seeing the way things were going,
Rose made a sensible decision and slipped out the
side door to the spare room.

Lilly quickly swept the money from the table into

her skirt. She recognized the cold, almost lifeless look
in Boot's eyes as he stood there motionless, his rifle
held loosely before him. She had seen the same look
moments before he murdered Jacob Mashburn, and
again just before the slaughter at Billy Sore Foot's
shack. She hurried out the door.

"You drank up a helluva lot of whiskey that ain't
been paid for," Barney interjected from the bar.

Without turning his head, Boot replied. "I put two
ten-dollar gold pieces on the bar when I came in.
That'll take care of any likker I drank." His main concentration was on the two men he had been playing
cards with. Neither wore a pistol, but he suspected
there might be a derringer in an inside coat pocket of
either or both. "I'm leavin' now, so I expect all three
of you best get over in that corner so I can keep an eye
on you." He brought the rifle up to emphasize his instructions. Seeing no recourse but to obey, all three
shuffled over to stand in the corner while Boot backed
cautiously toward the door.

Inside the spare room, Rose inspected the damage
done to her hair and face. Forgetting the sensible decision she had made in retreating, she became more
and more angry as she stared into the mirror. She
stalked back to the door and pressed her ear against
the crack to listen, just in time to hear Boot order the
men to move to the corner of the room. Her gaze fell
upon the shotgun Barney kept propped against the
wall beside her, and she decided to take matters into
her own hands.

On the other side of the door, Boot continued to

step backward toward the front door, keeping his eye riveted to the three watching anxiously from the corner. He had just moved past the side door when one of the lamps on the end of the bar fluttered from a sudden draft. Without hesitation, he wheeled around and fired. Rose dropped the shotgun and fell back on the floor. Instantly, he wheeled back to cover the three men. "Who wants to go next?" he said with a smirk. No one moved.

Once outside the saloon, he wasted no time in making a hasty getaway. Lilly was seated in the saddle, holding his reins. He jumped in the saddle and they galloped away, weaving their way through the assembly of shacks and tents of the miners. Behind them, Lilly could hear shouts of alarm from the three men, now outside the saloon and running after them. They soon left them in their dust.

Following the river, Boot drove the horses hard until they came to a shallow ford. Crossing over then, he drove them on until he was forced to let them rest. Selecting a copse of poplars and oaks, he led the horses in among the trees and dismounted. There had been no sign of anyone chasing them, even though they had been slowed considerably by the pack mules—so much so that Boot decided he was tired of bothering with them. "Ain't nobody chasin' us," he said. "Make me some coffee. After that, you can go through them packs and get out anything you need for cookin'. I'm cuttin' them mules loose. I'm tired of foolin' with 'em."

Lilly proceeded to go through the mechanical

movements required to gather wood, build a fire, and
boil a pot of coffee for him. But her mind was else-
where, hovering between the reality of her present
state and that of a mere few weeks past. What had
happened to her that had caused her to attack the
woman in the saloon in what could only be described
as a jealous rage? She had actually fought to defend
her claim as victim of a man who had savagely beaten
and raped her. Now that fact came down hard enough
on her to cause her to question her sanity, and she was
suddenly shocked with the reality of her situation. She
could no longer surrender to her status as his piece of
property. The incident in the saloon made her realize
how debased she had become and how hopeless her
future would be. It would be better to be dead. Her decision was made at that moment to attempt escape, no
matter the cost.

After resting the horses, Boot took the bridles off
the mules and set them free. In the saddle again, he led
out toward the south, planning to cut back to the west
before reaching the Boston Mountains. Lilly followed
dutifully. Looking back over her shoulder, she could
see the mules tagging along behind them. Boot figured that his greatest safety would lie in Indian Territory where, except for the rare individual like John
Ward, lawmen hesitated to venture. Before he went to
prison, there were several spots along the Cimarron
that served as outlaw havens. Perhaps they were still
in existence.

They made another five miles before approaching
darkness dictated the need to select a campsite. In a

country of gently rolling hills, there were many likely spots to choose from. Boot picked one by a narrow stream. Without being told to, Lilly immediately began setting up their camp and building a fire. While her thoughts dwelled upon her resolve to escape her evil master, Boot's were of a smug and self-satisfied nature. Thinking back now with a chuckle, he amused himself with the image of an infuriated Lilly, furiously kicking and scratching the woman in the saloon. He had broken the Creek girl's spirit. Of that there could be little doubt. These thoughts served to trigger his lust, and he availed himself of the pleasures of his property. Lilly submitted to his pawing and thrusting impassively. When he was satisfied, he rolled away from her and went to sleep, knowing that she would be there when he awakened.

Following her usual practice, she went to the stream to cleanse herself when he was through with her. While she bathed in the clear, cool water, she was startled for a few moments by sounds in the brush on the other side of the stream until she realized what had made them. The mules had continued to follow along behind them. She looked back at the sleeping man by the fire to see if he had heard. Her question was answered by a loud snore.

Moving about as quietly as she could manage, she saddled her horse and packed the few things she felt she needed, all the while watching Boot for any signs of waking. If he awoke, there would be no explanation that would satisfy him to explain why she had saddled her horse. Knowing that to be true, she took the risk of tiptoeing back to his blanket to lift his pistol from the holster. If she was discovered trying to escape, she vowed to defend herself. Bending over the sleeping man with the pistol in her hand, she hesitated for a brief moment. The temptation to kill him was strong, but her fear of the man was such that she could not pull the trigger. What if the gun misfired? What if there was no bullet in the chamber and he was awakened by the click of the hammer on an empty cylinder? She had witnessed his rattlesnake-quick reactions. He would be on her in a split second. Rather than risk failure in the deed, she resigned herself to simply fleeing and hoping that he would lose interest in following her after a while.

When all was ready, she led her horse quietly out of the camp, across the stream, and into the hardwoods along the bank. In an attempt to slow his pursuit, she took Boot's bridle with her, and threw it into some brush about fifty yards away from the camp. Once that was done, she paused to listen. There were no sounds, save that of an owl's low hoot floating softly on the night air. With one deep breath to steady her already frayed nerves, she climbed up in the saddle and pointed her horse toward the dark silhouette of the mountains to the south. Her thought was to first attempt to lose him in the mountains. After that, the only place she knew where she might be safe was with her people in Low Hawk. It would be a long journey, but there was nowhere else a young Creek girl could go, especially one who had been ruined.

Chapter 9

The buckskin moved at a comfortable pace that effectively chewed up the miles, a pace the broad-chested horse could maintain for hours on end. It was for this and other reasons that John Ward rode a buckskin. The breed had more stamina than most others, more determination, harder feet, better bones, and a willingness to stand up to tests that might cause other horses to back down. John needed a strong horse. He was a big man.

Passing through patches of heavy sedge two feet tall, John Ward followed an obvious trail that never veered from an eastward course. It was late in the spring now. Already there were signs of budding on the sage. In spite of being in Kansas Territory, and soon to be in Missouri, if the trail continued east, John gave no thoughts toward the matter of jurisdiction. As long as he had a warm trail, he would follow it to the end, no matter where it led. Considering the manner of man he pursued, however, he was mildly surprised that Boot had not fled back to Indian Territory where there was a scarcity of law enforcement.

A day and a half after leaving Douglas Fannin's store in Oswego, John came to the mining settlement proclaiming itself to be Joplin. As he walked Cousin slowly through the camp, he was conscious of the stares of the occasional miner, receiving a nod from one or two, as they looked upon another suspicious stranger. Had he known the circumstances that prompted the cool reception, he would have understood the absence of a friendly greeting.

The trail so easily followed from Oswego was now obliterated among the many tracks in the mining camp, so he guided Cousin toward the one larger structure near the center of the community. It was typical, he thought, that the one commercial business in the entire camp was a saloon. Dropping Cousin's reins loosely across the hitching post, he stepped up on the low stoop and went inside.

Coming in from the bright sunlight, he had to pause inside the door for a few moments, waiting for his eyes to adjust to the dim interior of the bar. After a brief period, he made out the form of the bartender sitting in a chair at the far end of the bar. There was no one else in the room.

"What'll it be, mister?" Barney Pollard uttered unenthusiastically while getting up from his chair.

"I reckon I could use a glass of beer," John allowed, pointing to a large wooden keg behind the bar.

Barney took a glass from the shelf behind him, blew the dust out of it, and filled it from the tap.

"We're gettin' to be a regular tourist stop," he said when he set the glass on the bar. "You're the second stranger we've had in two days. Make that three if you count the Injun girl."

"Is that a fact?" John replied. "It just happens I'm lookin' for a man and an Indian girl."

Barney's eyebrows immediately lowered into a frown. "I hope to hell they ain't friends of yours," he said.

"Hardly," John said.

"Good," Barney came back before John had a chance to explain, " 'cause you're too damn big to throw outta here."

"This man," John continued, "was he a half-breed? Name of Boot Stoner?"

"That's the one, all right. As mean a son of a bitch as I've ever seen. He hit this place hard, I'm tellin' you."

"What happened here?"

Barney jerked his head back as if recoiling. "He shot a whore, he did." Nodding his head up and down vigorously for emphasis, he added, "The only whore in this camp." Pausing to see if John appreciated the seriousness of that, he then asked, "Why are you lookin' for him? Are you a lawman?"

"I'm a deputy marshal outta Fort Smith. He's left a string of murders across Oklahoma and Kansas, as well as one family in Arkansas."

"Saints preserve us!" Barney gasped. "I reckon we was lucky he didn't shoot nobody but Rose."

"Don't sound like Rose was too lucky," John said dryly. "Don't you have any law in these parts?"

"Oh, we sent for the sheriff over in town—that's about a mile away. He came over and stood around a while before he said the half-breed was too long gone. There wasn't much he could do about it."

John gave that a moment's thought. "How long has Stoner been gone?"

"Since last evenin'."

"Do you know which way he headed?"

"Sure," Barney replied. "He took off through the south part of the camp. If we go outside, I can show you exactly."

"Much obliged," John said, and swallowed the last gulp of beer. He started toward the door with Barney right behind him. Opening the door and squinting into the bright sunlight, he couldn't help but remark, "You know, if you'da built some windows in this place, a man wouldn't go blind goin' in and out."

"I reckon," Barney said. "I didn't build the place. It started out as a storeroom. 'Course most of my customers is half blind by the time they walk outta here anyway."

Outside, Barney pointed out the path Boot took when he galloped away. John thanked him and climbed aboard Cousin. As he was riding away, Barney called after him. "That son of a bitch stole money from me, too. Maybe if you catch him, you could get it back for me."

"Maybe," John replied without turning to look at the bartender.

He was anxious to pick up Stoner's trail, knowing now that he was less than a full day behind. It took some time, however, to pick out the tracks he searched for among the many around the camp. Before, he could distinguish the mule prints from the horses', making the trail easier to follow. Unfortunately, there were as many mule tracks around the mining camp as horses', maybe more. Consequently, he followed a couple of false trails before settling on the one he felt certain was that of Boot Stoner, the girl, Lilly, and their two pack mules. He had closed the gap between himself and the bloodthirsty outlaw. Of that, he was certain, but there was still a lot of ground to make up.

Boot Stoner woke up hungry and chilly. The fire had died out to nothing more than a few live coals. His immediate reaction was anger, and he rolled over on his side, intending to give the slumbering Creek girl a kick. Lilly was not there. He assumed that she had re-treated to the bushes to relieve herself. Angry that she had not built up the fire before tending to her physical needs, he yelled out for her. "Lilly! Get your lazy ass back here and make me some coffee!" Expecting an immediate rustle of bushes signaling the girl's response to his command, he began to fume over her disobedience. Throwing his blanket aside, he stormed up from his bed with the intention of administering the punishment she deserved.

Stalking toward the path she had chosen the night before to answer nature's call, he yelled out her name again. Still there was no answer. After a few moments more of silence, the fact that she might have fled occurred to him. Beyond anger, he stamped about in the brush, searching, knowing as each second passed that the girl was not there. *She was gone!* The thought infuriated him so that her recapture dominated all other thoughts. Then another thought occurred that caused him to panic. *The horses!* He turned around and ran back to the stream where the horses were hobbled. Much to his immediate relief, his horse was still grazing near the water's edge. Across the stream, the two mules were contentedly munching on fresh shoots of spring grass, but Lilly's horse was gone.

"Damn mules!" he swore. He picked up a stone and threw it at the nearest mule, having to vent his anger on something. The unsuspecting animal jerked sideways when the stone struck its flank and moved a few yards away before resuming its grazing. "You think you can run from me?" he roared, looking at the mule, but directing his wrath toward the missing Indian girl. Searching along the stream bank then, he found tracks pointing south.

Forgoing breakfast, he rolled up his blanket and picked up his saddle, furious in his eagerness to pick up Lilly's trail. When he reached up to take the horse by the bridle, there was no bridle. Confused at first, for although the horses were hobbled, he had left the bridles on, his anger now reached the point of rage. "That Creek bitch!" he cursed. "She's as good as dead." Fuming and cursing, for he assumed Lilly had taken the bridle with her, he took a length of rope and fashioned an Indian bridle with two half hitches in the middle, looped around the horse's lower jaw. The horse was not pleased with the strange rope around its jaw, and tossed its head repeatedly in protest. Boot responded with a sharp crack across the animal's face with his rifle barrel. The horse, subdued for the moment, allowed Boot to throw the saddle on.

In the saddle then, Boot kicked the horse in the flanks and jerked on the rope reins. Finding the rope an irritation, the horse renewed its protest, proceeding to wheel around and around in a circle when Boot attempted to guide it with a pull in one direction. After a furious battle between man and horse, and a severe beating with a tree limb, the horse finally accepted its new bridle. Under way at last, Boot set out after Lilly nearly blind with rage. Crossing the stream some fifty yards south of the camp, he failed to spot the bridle hanging from the lower branch of a sweet gum tree. As before, the mules tagged along behind until Boot turned in the saddle and fired several pistol shots at them. Neither mule was hit, but they wisely dropped back, deeming it sensible to trail the irate half-breed from a greater distance.

Rugged and foreboding, the Boston Mountains loomed up before the desperate Indian girl. A land of steep slopes and deep river valleys, rocky cliffs and forests thick with red oak and hickory, as well as the ever-present pine, her mountains were the highest of the Ozark Plateau. Birthplace of the White and Buffalo Rivers, the harsh area had served as hideout for

more than one gang of bushwhackers and rebel guer-
rilla bands during the War Between the States.

Nearing exhaustion, Lilly pushed her weary horse
onward. She would not permit the horse to rest until
she was safely into the slopes at the base of the mountains. Riding without pause throughout the night, and
now until dusk of the following day, she, like her
mount, was in dire need of food, water, and rest. On
foot now, she led the drained animal up into a ravine
where a trickle of water from an underground spring
bubbled up between the roots of a large oak tree. This
would have to do until her horse had rested enough to
carry her higher up into the mountains.

Using her knife, she carved a hole in the earth
around the roots of the oak to form a small basin for
her horse to drink. After pulling the saddle off, she
used the saddle blanket to wipe some of the sweat
from the horse's back while the grateful animal drank
from the basin. Unable to keep her mind from the
image of the cruel face of Boot Stoner, she could not
resist the constant urge to look over her shoulder, expecting the savage half-breed to suddenly appear. Although her rational mind told her that it was unlikely,
if not impossible, for Boot to have caught up to her,
she feared he was possessed of such evil medicine that
he could summon dark spirits to help him. With
thoughts like these to haunt her, she resolved to move
farther into the mountains as soon as her horse was
rested. As for herself, she would remain vigilant, re-
serving her time to rest until after she had found a
place she felt was safe. She knew he was set upon re-

turning to the Nations, and when she first fled from
her captor, she had hoped that he would not feel it
worth his time to follow her. Deep inside, however,
she feared he would come after her, if only to kill her.

Not willing to risk a fire, for fear the smoke might
be spotted, she made a meal of some dried meat taken
from Fannin's store. There seemed to be an abundance
of small game in the hills about her, so she was confident she would be able to find food once she found a
safe place to hide. She had her flint and steel to make
a fire, and she could fashion a snare from the short
length of rope on her saddle. Fighting the almost over-
powering urge to close her eyes for a few minutes'
rest, she ate her beef strips while constantly watching
her back trail.

As soon as she felt her horse was rested, she left the
ravine and pushed on, following a narrow valley that
appeared to lead deeper into the towering mountains.
After riding for approximately two hours, she found
that the valley broadened into a wide meadow leading
up to a river that flowed through the mountains. The
other side of the river was bordered by lofty cliffs of
limestone that reached straight up for hundreds of
feet.

Pausing at the edge of the river to let her horse
drink from the clear, cool water, she peered ahead, as
far down the river as she could see. The setting sun
was now at her back as her eyes followed the river's
course to the east. Soon it would be dark. Again, unable to resist the urge, she looked back along the way
she had come, but there was no sign that anyone other

than herself was in the valley. It was time to think about making camp for the night.

Thinking the riverbank was too exposed, even at night, she followed the river farther east until she came to a creek. With darkness almost upon her, she followed the creek back into the hardwood forest for several hundred feet before selecting her campsite. After hobbling the horse by the creek, she gathered enough dead limbs to build a small fire. By the time the flames were healthy, darkness had descended upon the quiet watercourse, draping a deep black shroud around the tiny glow of her fire. Finally, too weary to worry about Boot Stoner for the moment, she finished the rest of the dried beef and was sound asleep within seconds.

Burley Chase sat down and slid to the bottom of the steep slope on his behind. Upon reaching the bottom of the wooded draw, he got to his feet and, with one casual swipe of his hand, brushed the dead leaves from his seat. All the while, his eyes searched the faint trail that had led him down the mountainside to the creek. She was a fine-looking doe. Burley had spotted the four deer when they began to move just after first light. He hadn't approached quietly enough, so they scattered when they heard him in the trees above them. He wasn't particularly proud of that, but he had his mind set on venison, so he gave chase. Forgetting the others, Burley went after the doe. She looked fat and sassy.

She had run about fifty yards along the slope before

stopping to see if anything was after her. Burley almost got within range to take a shot at her, but she turned and descended the steep slope to the creek bottom. He had no choice but to try again. He could have taken a long shot, but cartridges were precious, and hard to come by. He could not afford to waste them. "I'm gettin' too damn old to run a damn deer down," he complained as he crept along the creek bank.

"I know you're in here, darlin'," he murmured. "I can feel you." Carefully placing one foot at a time, he inched his way closer to a thicket of laurel. Suddenly he saw slight movement of the branches on the other side of the creek. Instantly he dropped to one knee, thinking he had stumbled upon one of the other deer, for he was certain the doe had not crossed over. Peering intently at the thicket, he decided to forget the doe and take the closer shot. There was just a brief glimpse of brown hide showing through the leaves, and he figured the shot would not be there for long. He raised his carbine and sighted on the target. *Wish I could see a little more of the damn thing,* he thought, *so I'd know whether I'm shooting the ass end or the head.* As his finger poised to squeeze the trigger, the bushes parted a little and a head pushed through. But instead of a deer, it was a horse's head.

Burley froze, afraid to move. Startled to find a horse in this part of the mountains, his initial thought was that it was ridden by a lawman, possibly looking for him. After a few moments stalled by indecision, he deemed it in his best interest to immediately withdraw. Stepping carefully and quietly, skills acquired out of necessity to survive in this mountain wilderness, he made his way back up through the hardwood forest to a sandstone ledge from which he could watch the creek below him. He decided it best to get a look at the intruder to see if, in fact, there was any threat to him.

It had been years since he had taken refuge in these mountains, and Burley had lost count of the seasons that had passed. The rest of his gang of bushwhackers had long since returned to their homes after the war, seeking amnesty, or had moved west. A few had been caught by the federals while trying to buy supplies in the settlements. Burley had chosen to live off the land. He was an outlaw. Of that there was no denial. But he had not started out that way. Joining a group of guerrillas led by Jack Wheeler, Burley, like most of the others, had sought to punish the Yankee troops who invaded his homeland. As the war wound down, however, the gang turned toward attacks on civilian targets with no military significance. It had become a matter of survival, and the raids became more and more justifiable in their minds. Before they were finally dispersed, Bloody Jack Wheeler's name became synonymous with bushwhacker and was despised by Reb and Yankee alike. Two months after Lee's surrender, Bloody Jack was shot in the head by a farmer who caught him in his barn stealing chickens. It was a somewhat less than glorious demise for a group of men claiming to proudly fight for the Confederacy.

Burley figured his family and friends had long since given him up for dead, and that was the way he wanted it. Fearing a prison cell, he preferred to live out his years here in the mountains. This intruder today was not the first to venture into this wilderness. There had been others, hunters and trappers, most just passing through. Burley had managed to stay out of sight until they had gone. And none had stumbled upon his cave under the waterfall. But he had almost blundered into this situation today, and at this point, he didn't know if it was one man or a posse. So he waited and watched.

The sun made its initial appearance for the day before Burley detected any further movement in the trees by the creek. Minutes after the morning sunlight penetrated the leaves of the hickory and oak, a person appeared briefly by the creek bank. "Well, I'll swear . . ." Burley muttered. It looked like a woman. Moments later, he changed his mind. "A girl," he said to himself. "An Injun girl." Peering as hard as he could in an effort to see through the trees, he looked for her companion. Surely she was not alone up here in the mountains. Try as he might, however, he could not see anyone else.

Deciding that even if there was someone with her, they did not pose any threat to him, he determined to take a closer look. Backing down from the ledge, he worked his way across the slope until he found a place where he could get a broader look at the creek bank. Parting the juniper leaves before him, he peered through to discover a scene he found most surprising. There was no one with her, just one young girl with one horse, and she looked to be trying to rig a snare by the creek bank. *I'm damned if I know what she thinks she'll catch with that,* he thought, shaking his head in disbelief. *Well, ain't none of my affair,* he thought, and prepared to retreat to his cave, the deer hunt having been effectively canceled for the morning.

He picked up his carbine and took a step backward, preparing to leave, but something about the girl made him hesitate. *What in the world is an Indian girl doing here in the Boston Mountains,* he wondered, *by herself, this far from the Nations, where she most likely came from?* She looked to be about the age of his daughter when he had left wife and family to join Bloody Jack Wheeler. That thought proceeded to tug at his conscience a bit as he watched Lilly's wasted efforts with her snare. Annie, his daughter, used to catch rabbits with a snare. He had a sudden attack of melancholy when he thought about how long it had been since he had seen her. "Damned old fool," he muttered. "I'm probably gonna regret this." He started to make his way down toward the creek.

Lilly withdrew to a position a few yards away from the rope snare she had fashioned. There were squirrels skittering among the trees above her head, but none seemed the slightest bit interested in the scraps of dried beef in the rope circle on the ground. She knew the rope was really too big and clumsy, and she needed better bait, but the beef was all she had, and she was depriving an already empty stomach of that in the desperate hope that a curious squirrel would investigate. She was on the verge of giving up when she heard a faint rustle of leaves above her on the slope. A moment later she froze at the sudden sound of a voice.

"You won't likely catch no squirrel with that thing," Burley called out, "and there ain't no rabbits up this high that I've ever seed."

In a panic, Lilly almost stumbled and fell as she ran to her horse and fumbled in her saddlebag for the pistol she had taken from Boot. Figuring on the possibility of that reaction from the startled girl, Burley moved a few yards over to a clump of laurel surrounding a stout hickory trunk. He watched carefully as Lilly, her hands trembling with fear, took cover behind her horse, aiming the pistol at the bushes from which his voice had come.

"Little lady," Burley called again, causing the frightened girl to whirl around and point her pistol at a different clump of laurel, "I don't mean you no harm. You ain't got nothin' to fear from ol' Burley." When there was no immediate response from the girl, he asked, "You speak American?"

"I've got a gun," she announced, in case he had not noticed, her voice quaking with fear. "What do you want?"

"Me?" Burley replied. "I don't want nothin'. It looks to me like you're the one needin' help." There was a momentary standoff with neither party knowing what to say. Burley almost wished that he had not decided to speak to her, but he made another attempt. "Are you lost? 'Cause you look lost to me."

"No, I'm not lost."

"Well, this ain't the road to nowhere. Where are you headed?"

Lilly hesitated a moment before answering, "Low Hawk."

"Low Hawk?" Burley echoed, somewhat baffled. "You mean Low Hawk over in the Creek Nation? This sure ain't the blame road to Low Hawk." Certain that the Indian girl was, in fact, very much lost, and frightened as well, he decided he'd best see if he could help her. "Listen, I'm comin' out, and we'll talk. I ain't gonna do you no harm. You can hold on to your pistol if it'll make you feel better, but don't go pointin' the blame thing at me. All right? I'm comin' out."

Remaining behind her horse for protection, Lilly jerked the pistol around to aim at a sudden parting in a clump of laurel ringing a large hickory tree. Out in the open stepped a short gnome of a man, no taller than Lilly herself. With a protruding stomach paunch, he was almost as big around as he was tall. With a face flushed red from years of cold wind and hot sun, and partially covered with dirty gray whiskers, he presented a picture that was far from menacing. Lilly let the pistol drop to her side. Dressed head to toe in animal skins, the workmanship decrying expertise with a sewing needle, Burley Chase stepped into Lilly's life. The very appearance of the man disarmed her. She found it impossible to see him as a threat to her.

"Burley Chase is my name," Burley volunteered cordially as he strode up to the creek bank.

"Lilly," she responded.

"You say you're goin' to Low Hawk?" She nodded.

"Well, how on God's green earth did you wind up here in the mountains? Low Hawk's over a hundred miles from here, yonder way." He pointed southwest. "Where'd you start out from?"

Lilly turned and pointed north. No longer feeling a need to protect herself from this comical figure of a man, she stuffed her pistol back into the saddlebag and came out from behind her horse. Burley looked her up and down thoroughly, which prompted him to ask his next question. "You in some kinda trouble?" Thin and drawn, the girl looked quite the worse for wear.

Lilly was tempted to take advantage of the man's apparent charitable nature toward her, but a mental picture of the cruel, avenging half-breed caused her to hesitate. Boot Stoner might or might not be on her trail, but chances were that he was, and it would be a cruel act on her part to involve this innocent stranger. Harmless or not, Boot would not hesitate to kill this cherubic figure in buckskins. With these troubling thoughts in mind, she answered Burley. "Someone is after me—someone who is very dangerous and might kill anyone who helps me."

"Blame!" Burley exhaled softly. "Who'd wanna . . . I mean, what did you do?" The girl hardly looked old enough to have done anything to warrant such reaction from anyone.

"I ran away," Lilly answered. Then, in childlike fashion, she poured out her story, although she had thought not to involve him. She told of Boot Stoner's sudden appearance at her adoptive parents' home, and the horrors that followed.

Listening with wide-eyed astonishment and open sympathy, Burley was touched by the girl's words. He could not keep the picture of his own daughter out of his mind while Lilly told of the abuse she had endured and the slaughter she had witnessed. "You think he'll come after you?" Burley asked. When she nodded sadly, he made up his mind. "Well, young lady, maybe you was lucky I found you. I've been hidin' out in these here mountains for a good many years, and ain't nobody found me yet. You come on back to my cave. That devil ain't gonna find you there." He paused, noting her hesitancy. "I've got food aplenty, and you can rest up awhile." He grinned then. "'Course I coulda offered you some fresh venison, if I hadn't run up on you."

She desperately wanted to take him up on the offer, but she still felt concern for his safety. "I'm afraid Boot will find me, and it would be bad for you," she said.

"He ain't gonna find my place," Burley boasted. Then, trying to ease her mind, he joked, "Hell, I'll be lucky to find it again myself." He stood waiting for her answer. She so desperately wanted help that she finally agreed to accompany him, feeling a sudden release of tension as soon as she said yes. "Good," he said. "You just get your horse and follow me. It might be best if you lead him." As soon as she was ready, he led off up the slope.

It was a trek of no more than three miles, but on

foot it seemed a great deal longer. Crossing over the river—Burley said it was the Buffalo—they made their way underneath steep cliffs of limestone before coming to an opening little bigger than a crack. Lilly would not have noticed it at all, since it was well disguised by a dense patch of wild holly. Burley cautioned her to follow directly in his footsteps so as not to disturb the foliage. When she had led her horse through the opening, Burley went back and made sure the branches were not broken or leaning awkwardly to indicate someone had passed through them.

Following a narrow game trail, they climbed for what seemed hours to Lilly, causing her to marvel at her round little guide's stamina. Finally, they came to a waterfall, high up on a mountain, that fell two hundred feet to a rocky stream below. There was a dingy gray horse tethered by the bank of the stream. "Welcome to my abode," Burley said with a wide grin and an exaggerated gesture.

Except for the gray mare by the stream, Lilly could see no signs of a camp. She expressed that observation to Burley, and he nodded smugly before explaining. "My camp's inside, behind the waterfall. That's why nobody can't find it."

"What about your horse?" Lilly asked. "Anybody can see your horse."

"I bring her in the cave at night, or when I think somebody might be close abouts. Wait. I'll show you." Childlike in his eagerness to show off his primitive dwelling, Burley hurried up to the base of the waterfall. The mare issued an inquisitive whinny that was returned by Lilly's horse. "See," Burley said, "Sadie'll let me know if anybody's comin'."

Forgetting Boot Stoner for the moment, Lilly could not suppress a smile as she followed the elfish little man as he stepped from rock to rock in the surging stream of clear water. When they reached the other side, she dropped her horse's reins, confident that it would be content to graze unfettered. Standing before the waterfall, Burley paused long enough to let Lilly take a good look at it. "Ain't no way you can tell there's a cave behind that water unless you was to get right up against the cliff beside the fall. That's the way I found it. Before that, I passed by this waterfall two or three times when I was ridin' with Bloody Jack Wheeler. I never seen it." He paused to read her reaction. "I reckon you've heard of Bloody Jack's gang." She shook her head. Disappointed, he went on. "No? Well, I reckon you are a mite young to know about such things." He beckoned for her to follow.

Inside, just beyond the sheet of falling water, they entered a small cave about the size of a large room. Still, there were no signs of a camp there other than several piles of horse droppings. Burley went directly to a small opening at the back of the cave and, turning sideways, squeezed through. Lilly, without the restrictions of Burley's generous stomach, passed through easily to find Burley waiting for her in a huge, cavernous chamber perhaps three times larger than the outer cave. Here, in the dim light, she saw the evidence of more than eight years' existence of the self-imposed hermit. Lilly stopped to take it all in: his bedroll spread neatly against one wall, a fire pit near the back wall, various pots and pans stacked to one side of a wood pile. Next to the cooking utensils, there were several large parfleches, which she would later find to contain dried meat.

Watching her reaction, Burley proudly pointed out, "There's a natural smoke hole above the fire pit, right through solid rock. The ceilin' on this cave is a flat slab of rock, layin' across what I reckon was a gulch a long time ago. Now it's filled in around it with trees and stuff. The hole lets in a little light. If it weren't for that, you couldn't see a blame thing in here without a torch." She nodded, having already wondered why she could see this deep inside the cliff. "One time, about a year ago, a dead tree came down on the ridge above us—fell right smack across my smoke hole. I didn't even hear it fall. But pretty soon the cave started fillin' up with smoke, till it plum run me out." He chuckled as he related the incident. "Me and Sadie had to go up on the ridge and move the blame tree. While I was at it, I drug another one over so's I had a log on both sides of the hole. Now a whole passel of trees could fall across it and they wouldn't stop up my smoke hole."

Realizing then that he was rambling continuously, he said, "But I'm just runnin' off at the mouth. Let's see about fixin' you up with somethin' to eat. I reckon I've just been too blame long without somebody to talk to besides Sadie."

In short order, Burley stirred up the coals in the fire pit and had a fresh blaze going. He took several strips of dried venison and one chunk of smoked turkey from the parfleches and placed them in a pan to warm them. "This'll do for right now," he explained. "Tonight, we'll have us a stew. I'll catch us a squirrel or maybe a possum. Stew up a possum with some greens from the stream and some of them roots that look like turnips, and you got yourself a fine supper. All the comforts of a home in the settlements—I do miss coffee, though." He stopped to remember the taste. "I make my own coffee—make it outta acorns. Don't taste the same." He shook his head regretfully.

After the meal of dried meat, Lilly tried a cup of Burley's acorn brew. It was much too bitter for her taste. Burley laughed at the face she made when she tried to drink it. "You have to get used to it, I reckon," he allowed, and finished it for her. "You rest here while I take care of your horse. Then I'll be gone for a spell while I find somethin' for supper. You can use my bedroll if you wanna." It hit her then that she was near exhaustion. When Burley left the cave, she took a closer look at his bedroll. One look was enough to convince her that she would be more comfortable just curled up by the fire.

Chapter 10

John Ward stood staring down at the remains of a small campfire in a grove of poplars by the river. He extended one foot and poked around in the ashes with the toe of his boot. From all appearances they had not lingered long at this camp, judging by the amount of ashes. He looked around the little clearing again, somewhat puzzled by the two piles of items left behind: some cooking utensils, clothing, tools, blankets, and other items, as well as the packs that had held them—enough to furnish a household. Lying near the piles were two bridles. For some reason, Boot had decided to cut his pack mules loose. This notion was confirmed a short time later when he picked up their trail out of the camp. Tracks of the two horses alone led off toward the south. A short distance farther on, the tracks were joined by the tracks of the mules. John pictured the two mules tagging along behind Stoner and Lilly even though they had been freed.

He followed the tracks for about five miles or so

before finding another camp by a small stream. This was where they had stopped for the night. This was evident by the size of the fire and the disturbed leaves and grass where their bed had been. Horse droppings, the little bit of grass that had been grazed, broken branches; everything pointed to an overnight stay.

It was getting late in the day. There would be little more than an hour left before darkness would force him to make camp. Boot had chosen a good campsite, and John hesitated over a decision to use it himself, or push on for an hour or so before darkness stopped him. The buckskin seemed to be trying to influence him to stay. The horse sauntered over to the bank of the stream and began feeding upon the tender shoots at the water's edge. "All right," John said, "we'll make camp here."

While he made coffee, he considered the manner of man he trailed. Judging by the direction the outlaw had now turned, John had to speculate that Boot was gradually circling back toward the Nations. He would know that for sure if Boot took a turn back toward the west before reaching the mountains. He felt confident that he was gaining on Boot. Each campsite he found told him so. But he was still not satisfied with his progress. It seemed that every day Boot was not caught provided the potential for another poor soul being murdered. He was already losing track of the number of days he had been on the half-breed's trail, arriving at the scene of one massacre after another, and always at least one day behind. It was beginning to try John's usual patience.

While thinking about the man he chased, he also paused to puzzle over Lilly. It was especially disturbing to him to recall the Joplin bartender's account of the shooting there. According to him, Lilly had attacked the woman called Rose in a jealous rage over the woman's flirtatious attention to Boot. That didn't fit with the picture he had of Lilly. The young Creek girl had been like a daughter to Wendell Stoner. It was hard to accept the fact that she might be a willing accomplice to Boot Stoner. During John's occasional visits to the trading post, Lilly had always demonstrated affection to both Wendell and Morning Light. It just didn't seem right that the shy young girl would go bad, and willingly ride with the likes of Boot Stoner. It was troubling, but he would be aware of the need to keep one eye on Lilly when he caught up with Boot. These thoughts were heavy on his mind when he drifted off to sleep.

He was awakened by a sharp clap of thunder, followed moments later by a driving rain that fairly soaked him before he could get his slicker from his saddlebags. Cursing loudly while fumbling with the oilskin slicker to keep it from flapping in the wind, he gathered his weapons and blanket in a losing effort to keep them dry. Crouching up under a low oak, he tried to fashion a tent with the slicker while the lightning flashed and the rain poured down in torrents. The storm had taken him totally by surprise, as storms this time of year had a habit of doing. There had been no sign of an approaching storm the day before. It irritated him that he had not seen it coming. Disgruntled, but knowing there was nothing to be done about it, he sat under the tree and waited for morning.

With the arrival of first light, the storm had passed over, leaving broken tree limbs and leaves scattered about that spoke of the ferocity of the wind. The little stream had swollen to twice its original size. And most devastating of all was the absence of tracks. Boot's trail had been washed away by the storm.

He spent some time searching the area where he had discovered the trail the night before, in hopes that the rain had not erased every single track, but his search was in vain. Although he found some tracks, they were scattered—some horse, some mule, but none in a pattern that would signify a definite trail. Knowing only the general direction Boot had started out, he was left with no choice but to set out in the same direction, and hope to pick up tracks farther on. Without taking time for coffee or breakfast, he saddled Cousin and, with a soggy blanket rolled up behind him, rode off through the trees toward the distant hills. He would ride until the sun climbed a little higher in the sky before stopping to dry his gear and make coffee.

After stopping just before noon, he was back in the saddle and on his way once more, riding blind, for there were no tracks to be found. It was difficult to believe that the storm had smoothed out every track, so he had to assume that Boot's trail was either to the east or west of him. Following the hunch that Boot would eventually cut back to the west and head for Indian Territory, John decided to continue riding south, and hope to pick up Boot's cross trail.

Some two miles short of the rugged Boston Mountains, his hunch appeared to have borne fruit. Riding between two hills, he crossed over a trickle of a stream and paused to let Cousin drink. While he waited, his eye caught sight of a clearly defined hoofprint in the sandy shoulder of the stream. He immediately dismounted to look for more. Looking closely at the print, he determined that it was from one of the mules. Evidently they were still following Boot and Lilly. The hoofprint was pointing west, crossing his trail. Needing at least one more for confirmation, he walked carefully along the bank, his eyes searching the ground. Suddenly, there it was! A second print, also that of a mule, and pointing west, like the first. This seemed to be confirmation, but he stopped to debate it in his mind before committing. There was no print from a horse, and there were only two mule prints. He squinted his eyes and looked to the south, where there were no tracks. Then he considered his hunch that Boot was heading back to Indian Territory. He decided to follow the tracks. He stepped up in the saddle and turned Cousin's head to the west. With no other tracks to follow, the only option was to follow a hunch. With one last look toward the mountains to the south, he uttered, "Hell, I'd just be wastin' time wanderin' around in those mountains lookin' for a trail."

Burley Chase knelt before the fire, tending a frying pan containing strips of fresh-killed venison, the meat courtesy of the doe he had hunted two days before. "She shoulda knowed I'd be back for her," he bragged

as he turned the strips over with a fork. Lilly had offered to cook the meat, but he insisted that she was his
guest, and as such, it wouldn't be polite to let her do
the cooking.

After some solid food and two nights' sleep, she
was at the point where she could put Boot Stoner out
of her mind for long periods of the day. She felt safe
for the first time in weeks. And Burley was obviously
pleased to have her company. She studied the round
little man's face as he knelt over the fire, and she
could not picture him riding with a gang of bushwhackers. Bright blue eyes that seemed a contrast to
the bushy dark eyebrows fairly sparkled with good
humor when he talked about his days with Bloody
Jack Wheeler. The thick gray bush that served as a
beard bore traces of acorn coffee and was comple-
mented by gray tufts of hair protruding from each
nostril. It was a picture that fascinated the slender
Creek girl.

For his part, Burley was thoroughly enjoying the
company. The Indian girl did not, in fact, talk a great
deal, but Burley hardly noticed, as he was so busy carrying the conversation without her help. Her presence
served to demonstrate to him just how lonely he had
been for human company, and he found himself thinking about risking a trip back to find his wife and
daughter. Maybe he might even offer to go back with
Lilly. But thoughts of Union patrols searching the
countryside for outlaw bands like the one he had ridden with still caused him to hesitate. His existence
was a lonely one, but certainly preferable to living out

his years in a prison cell. Besides, he had been a hermit for so long now that he wasn't sure he would even be able to leave the security of his mountain cave. Maybe it was best that he didn't realize exactly how many years had passed since he had made his home here, and that Union patrols had long since given up looking for holdouts like Burley Chase. For the time being, he was content to enjoy Lilly's company. It would be best for the girl to linger here awhile in case the crazy savage who was after her was, in fact, looking for her in these mountains.

As each day passed, Lilly gradually lost more and more of the fear that had driven her so desperately. Burley was a kind man, very much like Wendell Stoner had been, and she felt safe in the cave behind the waterfall. Thoughts of reaching her aunt and uncle in Low Hawk were still present in her mind, but the urgency was no longer dominating her every moment. Burley was obviously happy to have her stay as long as she wanted.

"It's a right nice evenin'," Burley said. "If you wanna, we can take our supper outside by the waterfall. Might be nicer than settin' in this cave."

The suggestion appealed to Lilly. They had eaten outside the night before, and it was a pleasant setting indeed. The cave felt safe and secure, and she was thankful for it at night. But she didn't like the feeling of being inside the ground during the day.

Outside, the air was fresh and crisp. Spring in the mountains lagged behind the lower climates, but it was finally showing signs in the budding trees and bushes. Soon the foliage above the waterfall would be thick with leaves that would screen any animal from sight. On this early spring day, however, the trees had not filled in to that point, and if Burley or Lilly had chanced to glance up toward the top of the waterfall, they might have noticed the solitary figure standing there.

He stood motionless, watching for a long time. The beauty and tranquillity of the setting escaped his twisted mind as he took time to gloat over having found her. The fury that had built up in him over the last several days was pacified by the prize of finally tracking her down. He gazed with contempt at the fat little man sitting cross-legged before her, and eagerly awaited the pleasure to be derived from his slaughter.

Boot had almost given up on his search for Lilly, having lost her trail several times before stumbling onto it again. He had found her tracks at the creek when she had joined someone else, an occurrence that had infuriated him. But he lost their trail when they crossed the river. So for a day and a half after that, he had roamed the mountain, looking for some sign until he decided it was useless to continue. And then he heard a single shot from a carbine on the far side of the mountain. He followed the sound, and searched again until he found the spot where a deer had been killed. It was easy to follow the trail from there. And now, there they were, trapped in a box canyon with no escape. He could feel the adrenaline pumping in his veins as he anticipated the pleasure of the reunion.

*   *   *

Lilly finished her supper of fresh venison and took her plate to the edge of the stream to wash it. Bathed in the afterglow of the setting sun, she lingered there for a moment more to watch the last rays of sunlight filter through the mist at the base of the waterfall. Suddenly she felt a chill race along her spine when she heard the whisper of an owl's wings passing directly over her. This was a bad sign, and she sensed something wrong. When she looked up to find the owl, her gaze drifted to the cliff high above her, and the solitary figure standing there. Dismissing it as a shadow, she shifted her gaze again, looking for the owl, but her gaze was instantly drawn back to the figure.

It was him! For a moment, her heart stopped, then resumed its beating with a rapid pounding in her breast that threatened to explode. She rocked back on her heels. The plate, forgotten, dropped from her hand and drifted a few yards downstream before settling to the bottom. Unable to speak, she simply stared at the apparition for long moments, praying desperately that it was no more than that, a ghost, conjured in her mind, and would disappear as suddenly as it had come. Paralyzed by her fear, she could not move until Boot suddenly made a move, releasing her from the spell. She screamed as he pulled his rifle up and aimed.

Startled by the girl's sudden scream, Burley tried to scramble to his feet. In the next instant, a shot rang out, the bullet catching Burley in the shoulder. The impact of the slug spun him around sideways, causing

Boot's second shot to pass harmlessly by his chest. "Run!" Burley yelled as he lunged to his feet. The two of them ran for the waterfall, just managing to disappear behind the cascading water before two more shots ricocheted off the cliff wall behind them.

Puzzled by the flight to the waterfall by the pair below him, Boot stood waiting for a minute, expecting them to show on the other side of the water. When they did not, he figured there had to be a cave behind the fall. Although the thought served to irritate him, he was smug in the knowledge that they were still trapped. Keeping his eye on the waterfall, he led his horse as he began to work his way down the side of the cliff on foot. He had found her, and she was going to learn a harsh lesson for trying to escape from him. The thought brought a thin smile to his face.

Inside the cave, Burley and Lilly hurried past the horses in the outer chamber and through the narrow opening to the larger cave. His brain in confusion, Burley immediately grabbed his rifle and, with blood running down his arm, knelt down and trained it on the passage between the two chambers. Lilly ran to him to try to tend to his wound. "Boot!" she kept repeating as she fumbled with his shirt, attempting to clean the wound.

"Was that the son of a bitch?" Burley asked, his voice shaking, his face grimaced with pain. "He blame-sure put a hole in my shoulder."

Fighting her emotions, Lilly tried to stop Burley's bleeding, still unable to speak beyond repeating, "Boot! Boot!"

Seeing the young girl's panic, Burley tried to calm her, even though he was close to that state himself. "We're all right," he assured her. "He's got to come through that openin' to get to us. And if he does, I'll pepper his ass good." Gradually, the glaze of fear left Lilly's eyes. "Are you sure that's the man chasin' you?" Burley asked again. He asked the question with the thought in mind that the shots had been fired at him.

"I saw him," Lilly replied. "He was standing at the top of the cliff, just looking down at us."

"Well, like I said, he's got to come through that crack to get at us, so we'll just wait and see what he does." Seeing the panic about to reappear in Lilly's eyes, he tried to reassure her. "We've got food and a little bit of water. We can hold out for a good spell, and from what you've told me, he ain't hardly the patient kind." Reading her face again, he added, "And don't worry about this wound. I'll be all right." He managed a smile for her, then turned his full attention to the opening.

Moving with the utmost caution, Boot Stoner worked his way down to a point next to the stream, where he paused to take a long look at the sheet of water dropping from the cliff he had just left. It was impossible to see any outline of a cave, if in fact there was one. He had to also allow for the possibility that there was nothing more than a hollow behind the fall and that they might be waiting in ambush. Leaving his horse by the stream, he moved quickly to the other side and dropped to one knee, again waiting and listening. The light was fading fast, so he deemed it best to wait a few minutes more until darkness started to set in.

He managed to wait for a while, but being a man who had never known patience, he started creeping toward the fall before a hard dark set in, his rifle ready to return fire. But there were no shots as he approached the wall of the cliff. He slowly edged along behind the curtain of crashing water until he came to the opening to the cave. Dropping immediately to the ground when he heard movements inside the dark opening, he peered into the cave, searching for a target. Still there were no shots to greet him.

He lay there for a few moments, his eyes gradually adjusting to the darkness. As he stared, the moving objects slowly took shape, and he realized then that they were horses. Beyond them, a faint light revealed a narrow opening in the back wall. Moving up beside the opening, he hesitated to expose himself long enough to look inside, so he took his hat off and placed it on the end of his rifle barrel. Staying close to the wall, he held the hat out in front of the opening. It was immediately knocked off the rifle with a bullet hole through the crown, just as he expected.

"Lilly!" he roared. "Come outta there and I won't hurt the old man."

Inside, Burley shook his head at Lilly. To Boot, he yelled back, "Tell you what—why don't you just come on in?"

"Lilly, if you don't come on out," Boot returned, "I'll kill the old man." He waited a moment. "If you come on out now, I won't hurt you. But if you don't, I'll make you wish you never was born."

"You can go to hell," Burley answered. "She ain't comin' out."

Burning with rage over the apparent impasse, Boot took a few steps away from the wall, enough to give him an angle to shoot through the opening without exposing himself. The sudden explosive combination of gunfire and startled horses reverberated around the outer cave as he pumped half a dozen shots through the narrow passage. His fury demanded some restitution, even though he knew there was very little likelihood he would hit anything. He listened as the sound of ricocheting bullets came back to him from inside. On the other side of the opening, Lilly and Burley hugged the wall on one side as Boot's slugs found purchase in the hard clay and rock of the inner chamber.

When the noise caused by Boot's frustrated barrage died away, and the only sound was that of the two horses as they bolted, frightened, through the waterfall, Boot waited and listened. After several tense moments, he called out again. "This is the last chance I'm givin' you. Come on outta there." No reply came back to him this time. All was silent in the cave.

On the other side of the passage, Burley motioned for Lilly to keep silent. "Let him think he mighta hit somethin'," he whispered. Then he sat with his back against the wall and his rifle aimed at the entrance, hoping Boot would become impatient enough to come in.

Seconds ticked away. Boot knelt, glaring at the narrow opening, his frustration growing with each moment. Still there was no sound from inside the cave. *I might have hit one of them,* he thought, *maybe both of them.* He thought it over, considering the odds of charging through the entrance, blazing away. *And they might just be playing possum, hoping I come through that opening.* The more he thought about it, the bigger the likelihood seemed that they wanted him to come in. He had to admit that they were at an impasse. They couldn't come out, and he couldn't go in after them. Then another thought occurred to him, one he had forgotten about.

Remembering, he chuckled to himself. "I got just the thing to take care of them two," he said. Running back to his horse, he reached into his saddlebags and retrieved the two sticks of dynamite he had taken from Fannin's store. Hurrying to return to the cave, he quickly crawled up beside the opening. Placing the sticks near the foot of the narrow entrance, he lit both fuses, waited for a brief second to make sure they were lit, then ran back outside. Giving the explosives plenty of room, he passed behind the sheet of falling water and ran toward his horse.

There was a muffled thump, as though some supernatural giant had pounded the earth with a heavy hammer, followed by a deafening roar, and a thick black cloud mushroomed out of the mouth of the cave. The cloud of smoke and dirt infused with the waterfall, the water flattening it to spread across the meadow, where his horse was tied.

Feeling the ground tremble beneath his feet, Boot stood transfixed for a long moment, in awe of the magnitude of the explosion. Then, delighted with the apparent results, he made his way back into the cave, holding his bandanna over his mouth and nose as he moved through the thick black haze. Reaching the back wall of the outer chamber, however, he found that instead of blowing a hole in it, the dynamite had caused the dividing wall to collapse, effectively sealing off the entrance completely. "Damn!" he swore. Taking out his knife, he made a few futile stabs at the wall of dirt and rocks in a desperate attempt to dig a hole through. He soon realized that it was impossible, and his anger threatened to choke him.

Reeling with frustration, he backed away a few steps to glare at the wall he had created. Gaining some measure of control over his emotions, he took a calmer look at the problem. "All right," he conceded. "I can't get in, but by God, they can't get out." Stepping back closer to the wall, he yelled, "I told you to come outta there, you coyote bitch. Now you're in the ground for good. I bet you wish you was with ol' Boot now."

Inside the earthen tomb, Lilly crawled on hands and knees, trying her best not to breathe in the thick, dirty air that filled the chamber. Faint sounds of Boot's ranting from outside came to her, but she could not make out the words. Her concern was for Burley. The round little man had not called to her after the explosion, and the air was so thick with dirt and smoke that she could no longer see him. Making her way across the littered floor of the cave, she found him. Half his body was buried under a massive mound of dirt and rock, and his eyes stared unseeing into hers. She at once recoiled in horror, then reached out to touch him. There was no response, only the cold, sightless stare.

Panic-stricken at first, realizing she was sealed in this silent tomb, she backed away from the body and sat weeping on the floor. Her confusion lasted for only a short while before her will to survive returned to calm her. Her one chance for escape came to her then—the smoke hole. In frantic eagerness, she crawled over to the fire, still glowing with dying coals. Looking up to the top of the cave, she could just barely make out the small opening some twenty feet above her. From the floor of the cave, she found it hard to judge if she could squeeze her body through it. The problem was secondary to the question of whether or not she could climb up the back wall of the cave to reach the hole. She told herself that, if she could somehow reach it, she would damn sure find a way to squeeze through it.

The problem facing her at the moment was the lack of light in the cave, the only source being the fire— and it was dying. She considered building it up again, but that would make it too hot for her to climb up the wall behind it. There was no time to waste on building a fire, anyway. The faint light coming through the smoke hole was already growing dim.

She gathered the few things she could carry for her survival, knowing that if she reached the hole, she was not coming back down. She bundled them up in one of Burley's shirts and tied them with a rope. The free end she tied around her ankle and prepared to ascend the wall.

There was little effort required to reach a stone ledge about six feet above the fire pit. After that, there was a long expanse before reaching a narrow rocky shelf. Standing on the ledge, she went to work with her knife, carving out hand- and footholds. It was not easy, and she almost decided it was impossible, but when she thought of the alternative, she forced herself upward, inch by painful inch. By the time she reached the rock shelf, she was climbing in almost total darkness, feeling her way up the wall, holding on with one hand while digging hand- and toeholds with the other.

Straining to get both feet on the shelf, she felt her strength draining away, and a new feeling of panic began to overcome her. She thought that if she could just get her feet up under her, she could rest for a moment. This was when she felt a faint whisper of fresh air upon her face. It was enough to encourage her to continue climbing, for she knew she was getting close to the opening. Reaching deep inside her frail body for strength, she pushed upward, digging each handhold, until finally she reached up and felt the edge of the opening.

Flushed with the excitement of reaching the hole, she pushed her body up high enough to clear it with her head. A new sense of panic struck her. The hole was not big enough to get her shoulders through! Immediately, the blood in her veins turned to ice when it seemed apparent that she was doomed to die in the tomblike chamber. Just managing to hold her body against the wall of the cave with one hand and her feet wedged in the tiny footholds was almost more than she could do. But knowing that she could not remain in this position forever, she tried to enlarge the opening with the one free hand she could risk. The edges of the hole were solid rock, and she remembered then that Burley had explained that the flat ceiling of his cave was a rock slab.

Feeling her self-control slipping away, she looked down at the tiny glow of the fire some twenty feet below her. She had a sudden impulse to simply let go. Then she fought back against the feeling of doom, telling herself that she would not die in this cave. With a new determination, she crouched low enough to pull her head back down. Then she extended her free hand up through the hole, and with her chin tucked tightly against her breast, thrust upward with her legs as hard as she could. Her body was wedged into the narrow opening, seemingly stuck. Though awkward and painful, she laboriously forced her foot up to the next foothold, jamming her body even tighter in the unforgiving passage. Once again she strained against the opening, her shoulder throbbing with pain and threatening to break. Trying with all her might to extend her trailing shoulder in an effort to make her body smaller, she pushed and pushed until she feared her rib cage was going to cave in. It was no use. She could not make herself any smaller. Now, effectively stuck, unable to go up or down, she feared this was going to be the place of her death. Resigned to her inevitable ending, she felt her pounding heart slowly settle into a normal rhythm, and she exhaled in a great sigh of surrender. As soon as she did, she felt her body slip a fraction of an inch. Reacting instantly, she pushed up with her legs, mustering all the strength she could, and suddenly her hand grasped a limb. She remembered then that Burley had dragged a couple of logs over on each side of the opening. With a good firm hold on the limb, she pulled herself up until she felt the skin being scraped from her trailing arm as her shoulder moved upward. Suddenly her shoulder was free and she pulled her arm up until it was out of the opening, and she was now free from the waist up. Her heart pounding again, this time from joyous excitement, she placed her hands on both sides of the hole and drew her lower body up. When at last she swung her feet over the top of the hole, she pulled her possessions up, and then lay exhausted beside the log on one side of Burley's smoke hole.

She did not rest there long. Thoughts of the unfortunate little man buried beneath the rubble below her caused her a few moments of grief before the brooding image of Boot Stoner descended upon her mind. As if to remind her of her peril, a bright three-quarter moon stared down at her like an unblinking eye in the dark heavens above the trees. On her knees at once, she peered over the log to see where she had emerged. As best she could determine, she was about halfway up the slope rising to the top of the waterfall. Looking all around her, there was no sign of anything but the dark trees and underbrush, but she still felt an urge to run before Boot suddenly appeared. With her few belongings and Boot's pistol, she started making her way down the mountain. On foot now, and not certain if she was even fleeing in the right direction, she set her determination on Low Hawk in the Creek Nation.

Chapter 11

Satisfied that Lilly was as good as dead, sealed in her earthen tomb, Boot spent the rest of the night camped by the waterfall. It was a disappointment to have been cheated of the personal restitution he so desired. Lilly was his property, and he regretted the loss of satisfaction he would have enjoyed in rendering her punishment. There was nothing he could do now but feel smug in the knowledge that she was dying a slow and terrifying death under the ground.

There were few thoughts spent on the nameless little man who had perished with her, other than the pleasure it would have been to squash him like the bug he resembled. There was a bright side to the event. Boot had gained two horses, although one of them looked too old to be of much value. With the morning light, he rounded up the two. They had not strayed far from the waterfall. He would take them back to Indian Territory and sell them.

After tying his horses on a lead rope, he returned to

the cave under the waterfall to make sure there was no sign of survival of the two trapped behind the wall of debris. With his ear against the wall, he listened for sounds of digging from the other side. Again, he took his knife and tested the wall. Now that the smoke and silt had dissipated, he could see that the narrow opening that had been there had collapsed upon itself, leaving nothing but solid rock between the two chambers. "Ain't nobody diggin' their way through that," he chortled. Then he yelled out, "Can you hear me, Lilly? Ain't nobody diggin' outta there." He threw back his head and laughed. "No, hell no," he added. Then a worrisome thought struck him, one he had not even considered. _What if there's a back entrance to the cave?_ The simple possibility of it caused him to scowl once more, and he knew he must have the answer.

Outside the cave, he stood back and stared up at the top of the fall and the slope down the side of the mountain below it. He tried to estimate the probable point on the slope that would be right above the inside chamber of the cave. Then he looked around himself at the steep cliff on one side of the fall. From where he stood, there was only one way to get back on top of the mountain, and that was the way he had come down the night before. Wasting no more time, he started back up the mountain, leading his three horses.

At the top of the fall, he glanced briefly up at the peak before crossing over the rushing stream and descending through the trees. His eyes sharply scanning back and forth, he searched for any sign of movement. All seemed quiet and peaceful in the hardwoods as he continued downward. His eye searched for a mound or depression that might indicate the opening for a tunnel. There was none, only the vine- and brush-tangled undergrowth and the trees. Finally reaching a point that he considered too far down the slope, he stopped to decide whether or not to search any further.

Looking back up the mountain, he felt a confusion of emotions. On one hand, he felt a certain smugness over knowing there was no way out for the slender Creek girl. On the other, he was almost disappointed not to find a back door to the cave. He still resented the fact that he was deprived of dealing with Lilly and her new friend personally. Seeing two trees that had apparently fallen to lie side by side across a rocky flat, he walked over and stepped up on one of the logs to take one last look up the mountain.

A casual glance down between the logs seized his attention. At first, it appeared to be the home of some burrowing animal, but it was a fairly large hole, although nowhere big enough for a bear. The longer he gazed at it, the more it intrigued him. He stepped down between the logs to take a closer look. He immediately felt his muscles tense. The leaves around the hole had been disturbed, as if someone had lain there. The more he measured the hole with his eyes, the greater he considered the possibility that a slender girl of Lilly's size might have been able to squeeze through it. "The little bitch!" he hissed, somehow knowing that what he was thinking had actually occurred. Dropping to his hands and knees, he tried to look inside the hole. There was nothing but darkness, but as he continued to peer into the empty darkness, he thought he saw a tiny red glow. After a while, he determined the glow to be the dying coals of a fire. It was not a tunnel he was peering into, but a hole. And the floor of the cave was far below it.

Certain now that the picture he formed in his mind was most likely what had actually happened, he looked more carefully around the hole for confirming signs. On the other side of the log he had stood on, he searched the ground. She had not left much to find, but there was enough to tell him that she had fled down the mountain. *There's only one ending to this story,* he thought as an evil smile creased his scowling features. He started down the mountain after the fleeing Creek girl.

Able to pick up a print here and there, where leaves had been disturbed, or her foot had slid in loose gravel, he followed the trail down through the forest. Hampered by having to lead three horses, he was concerned that she might have been increasing the distance between them. And even though he was not sure when during the night she had escaped, he was confident in the knowledge that he would easily overtake her once the slope was gentle enough to ride. Close to the bluffs of the river, however, his confidence disappeared when he suddenly realized that he had found no sign of her trail for more than fifty yards. Cursing her deceptiveness, he fumed while he wasted time scouting back and forth along the bluffs in search of her tracks. His one thought was that he must find where she had crossed the river, or he might never find where she came out on the other side. After an hour of searching all along the bluffs, he was forced to admit that he had lost her. The thought was sufficient to cause him to roar out his frustration and anger, his voice echoing back from the limestone bluffs.

Her heart pounding with the fear that he might start toward her hiding place at any second, Lilly lay concealed in a pine thicket barely one hundred feet above him. Like a frightened rabbit with a fox on the hunt, she trembled in her terror, afraid to move a finger lest he detect the motion.

Exhausted by her efforts to escape the cave, she had made it almost to the river before having to stop. Being careful to hide her trail, she had cut back to a pine thicket where she lay down on a bed of pine needles to rest. With no intention of doing so, she had fallen asleep only to be awakened by Boot's voice reverberating up the mountainside, venting his anger. Now forced to wait until he had gone, she lay on her bed of pine straw, terrified that he might do a more thorough search of the mountainside. When he finally gave up his search and went down to the river, she scurried out of her hiding place and ran in the direction opposite to the one he had taken. Her thought was to find the hidden opening in the cliff where she had followed Burley up from the river.

*   *   *

John Ward cursed himself for being a fool. He swung a leg over and stepped down from the saddle. Dropping Cousin's reins to the ground, he walked over to the brow of the hill from which he had a broad view of the Grand River valley. There below him, happily grazing on the new spring grass, were the two mules. Boot Stoner, Lilly, and their horses were nowhere in sight. He had realized that he was following the mules alone a couple of miles back when he reached a point where the tracks were clear and undisturbed. But he followed them up anyway—just to see the clear evidence of his stupidity, he supposed. *So much for following hunches,* he thought. The discovery was a setback, but he still felt strongly that Boot would return to the Nations. He was bound to show up somewhere, so John was just going to have to keep looking. With nothing to go on at that moment, he decided to push on across the Grand—the Neosho as he still called it—and maybe check on the welfare of Two Buck. He wasn't that far from Red Bow and Dr. Summerlin's clinic. On the way, he could check in with the Cherokee Lighthorse and his friend Jim Big Crow over in Tahlequah. It was beginning to look like he was going to need help finding Boot Stoner, and if he showed up anywhere in the Cherokee Nation, Jim's scouts would likely get word of it. John wouldn't admit it, even to himself, but it also served as a legitimate reason for going a bit out of his way to visit Dr. Summerlin's clinic. As much as he tried to stifle them, thoughts of Lucy Summerlin frequently returned to distract him, especially at night by his campfire. He could still feel the warm softness of her lips when she had startled him with that quick kiss as he was leaving. "Foolishness!" he suddenly blurted to Cousin. "It didn't mean anything to her. She was just teasin' me." The words were meaningless, for deep in his serious mind he could not help but wonder what she might think if he expressed his real feelings for her.

"John Ward," Jim Big Crow called out in greeting when he glanced up to see who was approaching the cabin that served as Cherokee police headquarters. Seated in a chair, leaning against the outside wall of the cabin, Jim had been enjoying a cup of coffee while soaking up some early springtime sun. When he recognized the big lawman from Fort Smith, he let his chair settle back down to the ground and got to his feet. "What brings you out this way?"

"Mornin', Jim," John returned. "I just rode over to see if you were workin' or just sittin' around on your ass." He favored his friend with a wide grin and stepped down from the saddle.

Jim returned the grin. "Damn, John, that's a mighty hurtful thing to say to a man who was about to offer you a cup of coffee. Besides, I just got back this mornin'—had to go over to Fort Gibson to help the soldiers find a young Cherokee boy that stole one of their horses." He shrugged it off and changed the conversation. "What are you doin' over this way?" he repeated.

"Hopin' you can give me a little help," John replied. "I've been trackin' Boot Stoner all over hell and back, and I lost him somewhere over near the Boston Mountains. I thought maybe some of your boys might have heard something. I've got a strong hunch he'll show up back in the Nations somewhere."

"I heard you was on his tail," Jim said. "We ain't seen hide nor hair of him around these parts, but I'll let you know if we do." He opened the door and held it for John. "Come on in, and I'll get you that cup of coffee."

The visit with Jim Big Crow lasted for over an hour. John recounted the bloody trail left by Boot Stoner, and his subsequent flight through parts of Kansas and Missouri before he gave John the slip. Now, John admitted, he had nothing to go on but a hunch. He told Jim that he wouldn't even rule out the possibility that Boot might return to his father's trading post on the Grand, and that was going to be his next stop on his way to Red Bow. They parted with Jim promising to see if any of his men had a notion where the half-breed might have gone.

Approaching Wendell Stoner's old place from the south, John paused to consider the horse tied in front of the two-cabin trading post. The horse looked rather poor and neglected. John was sure it was not Boot's. Still a hundred yards away, he watched the cabin for a few minutes longer to see if there was anyone about. Before long, he saw two children appear from the cabin behind the store. Both boys, they were playing a game of chase. *Looks like somebody's moved into Wendell's old place,* he thought. *I don't know if that's a good idea or not.* If Boot did return, for whatever reason, he would not likely greet them kindly.

When John was within thirty yards of the cabin, a lone Indian man of perhaps thirty-five or forty appeared in the doorway. He stood there for a few moments to judge the nature of the visitor. Although he had never seen John Ward, Nathan Smoke recognized the big lawman from descriptions he had heard. He went outside and took a few steps to meet him, wondering what business the deputy marshal had with him.

"Howdy," John offered in greeting.

"Howdy," Nathan Smoke returned guardedly. "Mr. Stoner dead, Morning Light dead. All gone."

"So you moved into Wendell's place," John said.

"All gone," Nathan repeated. "Nobody live here now. I take him. I hurt nobody."

"That's all right with me," John assured him. "I didn't come here to cause you trouble, but I expect I oughta warn you that somebody might show up here that could make it hot for you. I'm lookin' for Boot Stoner. He might show up here again, might not, but if he does, it could be dangerous for you and your family." He paused to look toward the open door of the store. "How many people livin' here?"

Feeling more hospitable now that he knew he was not in trouble, Nathan said, "My wife and children." He turned and pointed to Wendell's old living quarters behind the store. "My brother and his wife and children live there."

John considered that for a moment. "What's your name?"

"Nathan Smoke."

"Well, Nathan, I don't know where Boot Stoner is right now. Don't know if he's headin' back here or not. But if he does, I'd advise you to get out of his way. He's on a killin' spree, and he might not like it if he finds somebody in his old home."

Nathan nodded thoughtfully. "My brother and me, we are not afraid of Boot Stoner."

"Well, that's mighty admirable, but I'd still recommend gettin' your women and children outta his way. He kills everybody that gets in his way."

"Thanks for the warnin'," Nathan said, "but we're okay."

John nodded with a finger to his hat brim. "I'll be on my way. Good luck to you folks." He nudged the buckskin into motion, then called back as he was leaving, "Tell your brother the sun reflects back off of that rifle in the window."

Lucy Summerlin sat up straight in her chair, straining to identify the lone rider topping the rise some four hundred yards to the south. Curious, but not overly so, she watched the rider's hazy form in the evening dusk as she sipped her coffee. In a few moments more, however, something about the figure in the saddle caused her to slide up to the edge of her chair, frowning in an effort to see more clearly. More seconds passed before she was sure. Then she got to her feet and fled from the porch. "Damn . . . damn . . . damn," she mumbled. "Why does he always come when I look like a tired old scrubwoman?"

"What did you say?" Dr. Summerlin asked as his daughter breezed through the room. Still seated at the supper table, although the dishes had long since been cleared away, the doctor was indulging in his evening toddy.

"Nothing, Papa," she answered as she went straight to her room. Then, as an afterthought, she informed him, "Somebody's coming—looks like John Ward."

Her father grinned, amused by his daughter's flustered reaction to the deputy's arrival. He tossed his drink down, got up from the table, and proceeded toward the front porch to greet their visitor.

"Well, Mr. Ward," Dr. Summerlin called out cordially, "didn't expect to see you so soon. Come to check on the patient?"

"I reckon," John answered. "How's he doin'?"

"Tolerable, I guess," Summerlin replied with a chuckle. "But he doesn't seem to take to recovery very well. He's healing just fine if he would just give it time." He watched John dismount, then said, "You're a little late for supper, but I expect Lucy could rustle up something if you're hungry."

"What can Lucy do?" his daughter interrupted, appearing in the doorway at that moment. "I heard my name being volunteered for something."

Before she could get through the door, a voice right behind her yelled out, "Is that you, John Ward?" And Two Buck charged through the door, almost knocking Lucy off balance. He stormed out on the porch, although still on rather shaky legs, a wide smile displayed across his face.

"Damn . . ." Lucy blurted before she could recover to quickly force a smile. "You need to be more careful, Two Buck," she said sweetly. Her father chuckled, still amused by the change in his daughter's appearance that had taken place in the last few seconds. Careful to avoid meeting his gaze, she turned her face to John. "Well, hello again, John."

"Miss . . . Lucy," he stammered, wondering why he instantly felt embarrassed in her presence.

"You get Boot?" Two Buck blurted. Before John could answer, he asked, "You find Lilly?"

John glanced at Lucy and smiled when she shook her head, exasperated with Two Buck's lack of manners. "No," he answered patiently, "I didn't catch up with him, and I haven't found Lilly."

Two Buck looked puzzled, wondering why the lawman had come back before catching Boot Stoner. "You come back for me?" he asked. "You need my help, right?" Then a frown crossed his face. "You're not givin' up on chasin' him, are you?"

"No," John replied. "I haven't given up, but I lost him north of the Boston Mountains. I followed a trail that turned out to be the wrong one. I'm pretty sure he'll eventually head back to the Nations, though. I'll pick up his trail again."

"Maybe Lilly got away from him," Two Buck said, a hopeful gleam in his eye.

"I'm afraid she's still with him. At least, when they left Missouri she was." Maybe he should have told

Two Buck that Lilly had apparently taken to Boot, but he didn't have the heart at this point. That could wait until Two Buck was a little steadier on his feet.

"I'm ready to ride," Two Buck declared.

"Might be best for him to rest a couple more days," Dr. Summerlin interjected.

Two Buck started to protest, but Lucy, who had been waiting none too patiently, interrupted. "Take him, please," she insisted, the exasperation clearly evident in her tone. "He's just about driven us crazy ever since you left. We had to hide his boots to keep him from trying to saddle his horse and go looking for you."

"They did, John Ward. They hide my boots," Two Buck confirmed with a pitiable frown upon his broad face.

Dr. Summerlin shook his head slowly, remembering. "I can't recall a patient so all-fired anxious to commit suicide. He had lost so much blood that he was too weak to sit up in the bed. Two days later, he wanted to leave. I should have let him go if he was in that much hurry to die."

"I'm all better now," Two Buck insisted.

John cocked his head in the doctor's direction. "What do you think, Doc?"

"Probably wouldn't kill him," Summerlin said. "But he'd best get one more night's rest."

"Can you stay one night?" Lucy asked, half expecting him to say no. "You're probably hungry. I'll fry some potatoes and side meat, and make a pot of coffee." She raised an eyebrow, threatening. "If I go to the trouble, you'd better not ride off somewhere before it's done."

"No, ma'am," he said meekly. "I'll just go put my horse in the corral."

They all sat down at the table with him while he ate, anxious to hear details of his search for Boot Stoner, especially Two Buck. John patiently answered all their questions until Lucy scolded, "For goodness' sakes, let the poor man eat before the food gets stone cold." Two Buck let up on him a little after that, and even agreed to go back to bed when Lucy promised that she would return his boots in the morning. After Two Buck turned in, Dr. Summerlin lingered awhile longer before excusing himself for the evening, claiming to have some medical texts he wanted to study. Lucy knew her father never referred to medical journals, and hadn't for years, but she appreciated his gesture.

"I thank you for goin' to the trouble to feed me supper," John said after the others had left them alone. "Maybe I could help you clean up some of these dishes."

"Why, that's a right nice idea," Lucy responded cheerfully. "I'll just sit down and drink that last bit of coffee in the pot and watch you do the dishes." Seeing the instant look of mild shock on his tanned face, she laughed, unable to maintain the ruse. "I'm only joking. Sit down there at the table and I'll pour the last of this coffee for you." She emptied the pot in his cup. "I wouldn't trust you with my good dishes, anyway."

Sheepishly, he did as he was told, realizing the

woman was teasing him. Feeling like a bungling oaf, he glanced up at her smiling face as she emptied the pot. "I expect I should go on out to the barn and make my bed, and not interrupt your evening any more than I already have," he said, hoping she would protest. She did.

"It's early yet, and I don't get a chance to talk to anyone but Dad very often," she said. "So I guess you're stuck with keeping me company for a while."

She finished the last of the dishes while he sat watching. When he downed the last of his coffee, she took his cup and washed it. All done, she suggested that it might be pleasant out on the porch. Both parties were thinking about the parting kiss between them on his last visit, but both carefully avoided reference to it.

There were two chairs on the front porch, but he chose to sit down on the step. She sat down beside him. "It is a beautiful evening," she said, breaking a silence of almost ten minutes. When he merely mumbled an agreement, she made another attempt to stimulate conversation. "So, John Ward, tell me about yourself. All I know is that you seem to wander all over Indian Territory all the time. Do you even have a home?"

He hesitated for a long moment, realizing that he didn't have much to tell. He had never spent much time thinking about the lonely routine that passed for his life. Now that she asked the question, it struck him how dreary it must seem to someone like her. "There ain't much to tell," he finally began. "I reckon most of my life is spent in the saddle, chasin' after some scoundrel or another. I don't know if most folks would call it a home, but I do have a place down on the Poteau River, below Fort Smith. It ain't much more than a shack, but it's a place to stay when I'm not workin' for Judge Parker."

"I declare, John, I do believe that's about the most conversation I've ever heard from you at one time."

He blushed. "I reckon I have been rattlin' on a bit," he said. He wanted to ask her about herself, if she ever thought about getting married, but he was afraid she might think him too bold if he did. For that reason, he was startled speechless for a moment when she spoke again.

"I've never heard you say one way or the other. At least I've never heard you mention a wife or family. Have you ever been married?" She watched him carefully as he thought about his answer. For a man reputed to be so fearsome to the many outlaws who sought refuge in the untamed wilderness of Indian Territory, John Ward more closely resembled an embarrassed schoolboy at this moment. She knew he had feelings for her. It was obvious in his manner. Neither he nor she was getting any younger. In her mind, it would be a good union for both of them. If that was the case, she reasoned, why didn't he act on his feelings? Unless, she hedged, she had misjudged his interest in her.

"Nope," he answered when he could speak again.

"Me either," she said. *There,* she thought, *I've laid it right out there for him. If this doesn't give him an idea, then I might as well give up.*

Like a tongue-tied child, he was afraid to open his mouth, afraid that he was reading too much in what was probably an innocent remark. So he declined to take the opening she had provided. Instead, he sat silently contemplating the toes of his boots until the void became awkward.

"Well," she finally sighed, "I guess it's time to turn in for the night." A little irritated, and slightly embarrassed at what she considered outright aggressive gestures on her part, she got to her feet. "Good night, John," she said, and went inside, leaving him sitting on the step. *I guess I was wrong about him,* she thought, *but damned if I'm going to ask him to marry me.*

He didn't leave right away, but sat there wondering if he had said something to make her angry. She seemed to have left abruptly for no reason at all. Although she had gone, he could still feel the closeness of her body. It troubled him. He would like to tell her that he thought about her all the time, but he didn't know if he had the right to. If he were to openly express his feelings for her, it might strain the friendship of both her and her father. *Hell,* he thought, *maybe I can talk to her again in the morning.*

He was awakened early the next morning by the sounds of someone moving about in the barn where he had made his bed. He sat up to find a lantern glowing in the dark two-stall stable and Two Buck saddling the horses. "Two Buck, what the hell's goin' on?" John asked.

"Almost sunup," Two Buck replied. "We better get goin' if we're gonna find Boot Stoner."

John sat up straighter and looked toward the open end of the barn. It was still pitch-black outside. "Almost sunup?" he echoed. "Hell, it's still the middle of the night." He fished his watch from his pocket and held it up toward the lantern. "It's still about an hour till sunup," he said, then held the watch to his ear to make sure it hadn't stopped.

"Maybe," Two Buck replied without pausing. "We'd best be ready to go. I saddled your horse for you."

"I can see that," John said, a little disgruntled by Two Buck's insistence. "I expect we could have a little coffee before we start out in the middle of the night."

"Dr. Summerlin and Miss Lucy ain't up yet. If we be real quiet, we can get goin' without wakin' them up."

"Why, that wouldn't hardly be the proper thing to do," John said, "ridin' off without so much as a thank-you." He did not care to give the real reason for wanting to wait until the doctor and his daughter were up.

"It's all right," Two Buck assured him. "I told Dr. Summerlin we was gonna ride out real early."

"Dammit!" John blurted out before reining his temper in. "I've got to see the doctor before I can leave." On the spur of the moment, he came up with the best reason he could. "I've got to get his bill for treatin' your wounds so I can take it to Fort Smith."

Two Buck's face lit up with a broad smile. "It's

okay. I've got his bill. He stuck it in my boots last night."

John's frustration mounted to the point where he was tempted to tell the impatient Cherokee that he couldn't go with him, but he didn't have the heart. The young man was obviously about to burst at the seams in his desire to make up for wasted time. After a few moments to reflect upon his conversation with Lucy the night before, he told himself that there was really nothing more to say in the light of day. She had to know that he had special feelings for her. If there was some serious interest on her part, she certainly would have told him so. With a leaden heart, he finally shrugged and said, "Well, since I'm wide-awake already, we might as well get started."

He pulled his boots on and rolled up his blanket. While Two Buck waited anxiously, he checked Cousin's girth strap and led the buckskin out of the barn. Two Buck followed. Outside, he looked toward the east, where there was now the faintest hint of light. With a slight shake of his head and a soft sigh, he stepped up in the saddle and nudged the buckskin gelding with his heels. Passing the house, he saw that the windows were dark, and there was no smoke in the chimney. There seemed no point in waking the household. He regretted the missed opportunity to see Lucy one more time, but, he decided, it might be best. He might have said something to make a fool of himself.

The two riders crossed the little stream that emptied into the Verdigris above the house, unaware of the lone figure that came out on the porch after they passed. With a robe pulled around her shoulders, Lucy stood watching until the broad-shouldered form in the saddle faded into the coming dawn. With a sad feeling of resignation, she turned and went back inside.

Chapter 12

Nathan Smoke was awakened by a sharp crack of thunder that sounded like it was almost right on top of him. Wide awake at once, he listened to the sounds of the storm outside as he lay in his bed, staring up at the dark ceiling. In the next instant, lightning flashed, illuminating the inside of the cabin for a long second. Like the flash that had awakened him, it was followed almost immediately by the crash of thunder. It was close, he thought. He looked over at his wife, still sleeping soundly in spite of the noise. He smiled to himself. He would have to tease her in the morning about her failing hearing.

Lying there, counting between the flashes of lightning and the following thunderclaps to determine if they were getting closer, he thought he heard a horse snort and blow. Thinking his pony had somehow gotten out of the corral, probably scared by the storm, he slipped out of bed and went to put the animal back.

When he opened the door, it was almost as black outside as it had been in the closeness of the cabin. The rain was pelting the bare baked ground so hard that the drops spattered against his bare legs. Expecting to find the frightened pony outside the door, he was surprised to find nothing there. He was certain he had heard the horse, but thinking he must have still been half asleep, he started to return to his bed. As he turned, another bolt of lightning lit up the yard around the cabin, revealing a solitary figure at the corner of the building. Nathan's heart almost failed him, for he was certain he was looking into the face of an evil spirit.

Seemingly oblivious to the rain pelting down upon him, Boot Stoner stood watching the startled man standing in the doorway. It was only for a moment, however, for Nathan stumbled backward in an attempt to flee, causing him to fall on his back. Before he could get to his feet again, Boot was standing in the door, his rifle aimed at the fallen man.

"Who the hell are you?" Boot demanded.

"Nathan Smoke," Nathan replied, his voice quaking with fear. "Wendell Stoner don't live here no more. He's dead."

"I know that," Boot snapped. "Who said you could use this house?" By this time the sound of voices had awakened Nathan's wife, and she started to ask what was wrong. "Shut up!" Boot commanded. "Get up and light a lantern."

Still quivering, Nathan pleaded, "Wendell Stoner was my friend."

"I say who can live here and who can't. I got a good mind to shoot you for trespassin'." He waved his rifle over at Nathan's wife. "Fix me somethin' to eat." Pausing to make sure she acted at once on his command, he then looked back at Nathan. "The girl—Lilly—is she here?" Nathan shook his head solemnly. "Who's in the store?" Boot demanded, nodding toward the adjoining cabin.

"My brother, his wife and children."

"Go get 'em," Boot said, "and no tricks or I'm gonna put a big hole right between your woman's eyes."

Boot pulled a chair over to the corner of the room and sat down with his back to the wall. He held his rifle across his lap and watched Nathan's wife as she scurried about in an effort to find something for him to eat. A few minutes passed. Then Nathan came back through the door, followed by a bedraggled man and his wife, still blinking the sleep from their eyes.

"I thought you said there was kids," Boot said.

"They're still asleep," Nathan replied.

"You're Boot Stoner, ain't you?" Nathan's brother, Lester Chases Rabbits, blurted. "I remember you before they sent you to prison." Already warned that Boot Stoner was in Nathan's house, his brother attempted to lower the notorious half-breed's guard by making conversation—hoping Boot wouldn't notice the .44 handgun he had slipped inside the back of his waistband. "Yes, sir, that was a pretty bad deal you got, sendin' you off to . . ."

"You know the girl that was livin' here with my pa?" Boot interrupted.

"Yes, sir, Boot, sure do," Lester was quick to answer. "Lilly was her name."

"Where is she? You seen her around here?"

"Why, no," Lester answered. "Word is that you took her off with you after you shot . . ." He caught himself before continuing. "I mean, after you left here." He glanced nervously at his brother, and placed his hand on his hip with a casual move he hoped would go unnoticed. Boot's eyes never wavered from his face, encouraging him to continue. "I expect if you're lookin' for Lilly, she most likely went back to her folks in Low Hawk, in the Creek Nation."

Boot's gaze shifted to Nathan and then back to Lester. "Low Hawk, huh?" He considered that possibility for a moment.

Detecting a possible distraction, Lester decided to make his move. Very casually, he removed his hand from his hip, and let it drop to his side. He hesitated for a brief second, calculating his odds. Boot made a motion as if to get up from the chair. Lester decided to act, and made a sudden move to grasp his pistol. It had barely cleared his waistband when Boot leveled his rifle and cut him down with a slug in his chest. His pistol clattered to the floor as he dropped at his wife's feet.

Amid the screams of the women, Boot stared at Nathan, a smile slowly forming on his face, challenging the Cherokee to retaliate. Knowing such a move would mean his own death, Nathan wisely backed away. Boot glanced down at Lester's wife, now wailing hysterically as she knelt beside her wounded husband. Looking back at Nathan again, he asked, "Is that right? Does Lilly have folks in Low Hawk?"

Afraid that his answer might be his last act on earth, Nathan slowly nodded his head, then waited for the bullet. Boot's bloodlust had been satisfied, however. He took the food that had been prepared for him and left the mourning family to grieve. "I'm comin' back here," he threatened. "I better not find you here when I do."

John Ward reined Cousin back and waited for Two Buck to come alongside. The young Cherokee had not complained during the entire day's ride the day before. But on this morning, he appeared to be wilting a little in John's opinion. The question in the lawman's mind now was whether or not Two Buck could keep up the pace. "How're you makin' it?" John asked when Two Buck caught up.

"Good," Two Buck was quick to reply. "Don't worry about me. I'm gettin' stronger every day."

John shook his head. "I shoulda left you back in Red Bow," he grumbled, and started to nudge Cousin. Two Buck stopped him and pointed to a rise some three hundred yards ahead. Topping the rise was a horse pulling a travois, with what appeared to be two children on the horse's back and three adults walking beside them.

John and Two Buck rode forward to meet them

and, upon approaching, recognized Nathan Smoke and his family. When he saw who it was, Two Buck rode out ahead. "Nathan," he called out, "what has happened?"

While Nathan related the encounter with Boot Stoner, John took a look at Lester lying on the travois. The wound looked pretty bad, as bad as Two Buck's had been, and the grieving party was still a full day's ride from the doctor's office at Red Bow. Speaking wildly and rapidly in Cherokee, Nathan told Two Buck about Boot's sudden appearance, and how the evil half-breed had ordered them out of the cabins.

"Is he still there?" John interrupted to ask.

"No, gone now," Nathan replied. Then, lapsing back into Cherokee, he told Two Buck that Boot was looking for Lilly, and had most likely gone to Low Hawk to look for her there.

With an anxious look, Two Buck relayed Nathan's words to John. "She's got away from him!" he exclaimed. "I knew she would. And now that devil's after her again. We've got to hurry."

John did not linger after learning that. They wished Nathan and his family well and set out for the Creek Nation. Once again, John Ward was no more than a day or two behind the murdering half-breed. By nature a patient man, he was beginning to feel a sense of anxiety over his inability to finally close the gap between himself and the bloodthirsty fugitive. He took a close look at Two Buck, trying to evaluate the young man's progress in his recovery and wondering if he could keep up with the pace John prepared to set. Two Buck looked pale and weary, but there was a determination in his eyes that seemed to refute what John was thinking.

As if reading John's thoughts, Two Buck said, "I'm going to Low Hawk, John Ward."

John nodded. He knew it would be with him or on his own. "All right, then, let's get goin'. We oughta make the Arkansas by sundown."

Close to total exhaustion, Lilly climbed to the top of a low ridge that paralleled a slow-moving stream. Seeming to have spent her last bit of strength, she sat down at the crest of the ridge and stared out across the grassy flat before her. *Low Hawk.* She could scarcely believe her eyes, but there it was, an isolated settlement of no more than a half dozen homes, scattered at odd distances around one general store. Her body, weary from walking for the most part of four straight days, crossing rivers and hills, was at the point of collapse. Footsore and hungry, having survived on little more than one rabbit and one squirrel—both shot with Boot's pistol—she sat there a while, gazing at her journey's end. Though only three hundred yards away, she wondered if she could force herself up on her feet once more. Then, at the thought of what might lie behind her, she turned to look over her shoulder, fearing that she might see Boot.

With renewed determination, motivated by fear, she struggled to her feet. On legs that seemed to be on the verge of failing, she descended the ridge, crossed the stream, and trudged toward a grove of cottonwood trees on the far end of the settlement. She had been to her uncle's cabin on many occasions before her parents were killed. They had offered to take her in after the tragic accident, even though they had no room for guests in their tiny shack. It had seemed a lucky coincidence that Wendell Stoner had been visiting friends near Muskogee and, hearing of the young girl's plight, had volunteered to bring Lilly home to live with him and his wife.

Now with renewed hope, Lilly's heartbeat quickened as she crossed a small stream, pushing through a tangle of bushes and vines to reach the clearing where her aunt and uncle had built their home. Once clear of the bushes, her brief excitement of a moment before was replaced by a sudden despair. She stood looking at a weathered and rotting shack, obviously vacant for quite some time. Her aunt, Blue Woman, was gone.

Despondent, feeling totally defeated, she dropped down on the ground and wept. She could think of no one who might help her other than her aunt and uncle. Her determination gone, she surrendered to the hopelessness of her situation. Boot would find her. He would always find her. It was useless to run any farther, so she lay back on the ground and closed her eyes, halfway expecting him to be standing over her when she opened them again.

While she lay there, her brain dizzy with fatigue, she thought of poor Burley Chase, who had been so willing to help her. She knew she was responsible for

his death, and she ached in her grief for him. Then she
thought about her time with Boot, and what she could
expect when he caught her. *It is better to be dead,* she
thought. And then she became angry with herself for
giving up, so she struggled to her feet and willed her
weary body toward the little store in the center of the
settlement. Surely someone there would know where
her aunt and uncle had gone.

"My Lord in Heaven!" Jonah Feathers exclaimed
upon glancing up to see the bedraggled young girl approaching his store. "What happened to you, child?"
Not remembering having seen the girl before, he
called back over his shoulder, "Ruth, come out here."
Then he stood gaping, hands on hips, wondering
what to make of the half-starved Indian girl, now
within a dozen yards of the door and staggering
drunkenly. From the sunken-eyed look of despair in
the thin face, he knew that he had best have his wife
talk to her.

Ruth Feathers, a full-blooded Creek, appeared in
the doorway just as Lilly stopped before Jonah. The
obviously distressed young girl said nothing at first,
shifting her gaze from Jonah to settle on his wife.
When she spoke, it was a simple question. "Blue
Woman?"

"Blue Woman?" Jonah repeated the question, confused. He knew a Creek woman named Blue Woman.
She was the wife of Tom Talltree. "Whaddaya mean?"
he blurted. "You lookin' for Blue Woman?"

Lilly nodded. Ruth, who had been studying the

desperate young girl intensely, interrupted her husband. "She's looking for her aunt, Jonah." She stepped forward and took Lilly's hand. "I didn't recognize you at first, but you're Walking Owl's daughter, aren't you?" She turned to her husband again to remind him. "Her folks were killed a few years ago, drowned in the Canadian River." Back to Lilly then: "Ain't that right, honey?" When Lilly nodded again, she continued. "I'm sorry. I can't recall your name, but I remember you now—went to live with a family in the Cherokee Nation."

"Lilly," was the simple reply. Then, with haunting eyes searching from one face to the other, she asked, "Do you know where I can find my aunt?"

"Sure we do," Ruth responded at once. "They built a new place over on Black Rock Creek. Jonah'll take you over there. But first, I need to fix you something to eat. You poor child, when did you last eat?"

Not waiting for Lilly to answer his wife's question, Jonah butted in. "What happened to you? How come you're back here? Did you run away from them folks that took you in?"

"They're dead," Lilly answered, and seeing the shock in both faces staring at her, she related the tragic homecoming of Boot Stoner. She told them of her captivity and her subsequent escape, embellishing as little as possible, ashamed to tell all the details of her time with Boot.

"Oh, you poor child!" Ruth exclaimed when Lilly had finished telling her story. "Let me get you something to eat, and then Jonah can hitch up the wagon and take you to your aunt. It's about two miles from here, and you don't look like you can walk another step."

They sat Lilly down in a chair behind the counter and bade her to rest while Ruth fried some corn mush and beans, the quickest thing she could come up with. Feeling she was safe for the moment, Lilly relaxed, and was soon dozing sitting up in the chair. "That poor thing," Ruth commented to Jonah. "No soul on this earth should have to go through what she's gone through. Just look at her. She's already asleep."

"That child might still be in for some bad times. I heard some talk about Boot Stoner already. He's been on a killin' spree over in the Cherokee Nation. I didn't know he'd murdered his own parents, though."

Ruth frowned as she considered what Jonah said. "You think he would try to follow her in the Creek Nation?"

"Maybe not," Jonah replied. "Maybe he won't wanna risk gettin' your people stirred up against him, but from what it sounds like, he's a crazy son of a bitch."

Ruth let Lilly sleep until her food was ready, then awakened her. "You need to eat something, child." Still drowsy, Lilly let herself be led into the kitchen behind the store and sat down at the table. She needed no encouragement to eat. Half-starved, she devoured the meal. When she had cleaned the plate, she made motions to wash it, but Ruth stopped her. "You just sit there. I'll take care of this, and my husband will hitch up the wagon."

Lilly sank back in the chair gratefully. When Ruth turned around after washing the plate in the dishpan, the exhausted girl's head was down on the table. Ruth stood, hands on hips, watching her for a few moments before calling to her husband. "Jonah, never mind hitching up the wagon. Let's pick her up and carry her in on the bed. You can take her over to Tom's in the morning."

Lilly slept through the afternoon and the night that followed. Her mind, free of fear for the time being, insisted upon time to rest and recover. Ruth felt certain she could not have awakened her even if she had tried. When morning came, Lilly woke up to the sound of bacon sizzling and the aroma of fresh-brewed coffee. Bolting upright with a start, she looked around her frantically, not sure where she was. "Well, look who's awake," Ruth greeted her. "Good morning, sleepy-head. Feel like something to eat?"

As she looked around, Lilly at once felt confused. There was but one bed in the room, and she realized that she had occupied it. "I'm so sorry," she started to apologize. "I didn't mean to fall asleep."

"Nonsense, child," Ruth said. "You needed to sleep."

Still at a loss, Lilly asked, "But where did you sleep?" Then she spied a couple of quilts rolled up against the wall. "I took your bed!" Lilly exclaimed, alarmed.

"Don't you worry your head about it," Ruth insisted. "Now, if you're ready for breakfast, there's a basin of water by the pump, and the outhouse is back of the barn."

Tom Talltree followed his mule to the end of the row and turned the animal to start back up the next row. He had placed a large rock on the plow to make it bite in the hard soil, and he leaned heavily on the handles in an effort to help it dig in. It had not been an easy transition to make a farmer out of Tom, but there was little choice if he and his wife were going to have food to eat. He had grown up in the white man's world, knowing of his Creek heritage only through the tales of his father and grandfather. Those stories would die with him, for he and Blue Woman had no children. It was just as well, he thought, for this life in the Creek Nation was a hard path to walk.

He was nearing the end of the second row when he glanced up to see a horse and wagon approaching from the bend in the road. He recognized the portly figure of Jonah Feathers, but not the woman sitting in the seat beside him. It was not Ruth; this person was much smaller than Jonah's wife. He stopped the mule at the end of the road and waited. Glancing toward his cabin, he saw that Blue Woman had heard the wagon and had come to stand in the doorway.

"Hey-oh, Tom," Jonah called out as he pulled up at the end of the garden patch Tom was plowing. "I got somebody here that's come to see you."

"Lilly?" Tom responded, recognizing his brother's child.

Recognizing the girl at the same time her husband did, Blue Woman hurried out the door to greet her niece. "Lilly!" she exclaimed. "Is that really you?"

"It's her, all right," Jonah answered for her.

"What's wrong, child?" Blue Woman asked upon taking a closer look at her niece, lines of distress evident in her weathered face. Although Lilly was much improved after a long rest and some solid food, her emaciated appearance caused her aunt immediate concern. Blue Woman's first thought was that Lilly had known abuse at the hands of her adoptive parents. "What have they done to you?" Blue Woman implored.

Reading her aunt's meaning, Lilly was quick to explain that she had suffered no harm by the hand of Wendell Stoner. She climbed down from the wagon seat into her aunt's embrace. She explained that she had not run away from Wendell and Morning Light, but from their savage son.

Jonah Feathers watched with keen interest as Lilly told of her escape from the evil half-breed, observing the concern registering in Tom's face. The thin, somber-faced Creek farmer was already thinking of the possible trouble the runaway girl might visit upon his household. Though eager to help the young lady in distress when she arrived at his store, Jonah was just as eager to be done with her. He didn't bother to get down from the wagon, offering only a simple line of conversation to his neighbor. "Looks like you're tryin' to get your spring plowin' done, Tom."

"Yes, tryin' to," Tom replied, not really interested.

Like Jonah, he had heard of Boot Stoner's rampage in the Cherokee Nation.

"Well, I'd best get back to the store," Jonah said. "Good day to you folks." With that, he turned the horse around and left them to care for their niece, unaware of the storm that was about to hit the tiny settlement of Low Hawk.

Chapter 13

Oblivious to the rain beating against his face like tiny stinging insects, Boot Stoner pushed steadily through a driving thunderstorm. Brilliant flashes of lightning lit up the bluffs before him for brief seconds and illuminated the cruel anger in his face, anger that drove him well past sundown and into the night. Unconcerned for the welfare of his horses, he had not stopped for food or rest the entire day. Only the Arkansas River stopped him now, further fueling his anger. In his mind, he had been wronged, betrayed by the slight Creek girl, and the lust for vengeful punishment for such a crime was the one driving force in his mind.

Running high from spring rains, the Arkansas was too risky to cross in the dark, in the midst of a violent storm, and with animals already weary from the day's travel. Obsessed as he was to get to Low Hawk, it was obvious even to him that he could lose horses and gear if he attempted to cross over that night. Cursing the night and the storm, he reluctantly sought shelter among the trees along the bluffs of the river.

The storm passed during the early hours of the morning, and the new day broke bright and clear. It would have been a refreshing and cheerful sight to most people, but no such potential resided in Boot Stoner's dark mind. Anxious to get under way again, he saddled his horse, then paused to examine the two he had picked up at the old man's cave. The dun that Lilly had ridden seemed in good shape, but the old horse that had belonged to the man was showing its age after being pushed so hard the day before, and was standing with its head down and ears drooping. The very sight infuriated Boot. It suggested that the aging horse would be a source of irritation, and Boot had no capacity to tolerate irritation. With no hesitation, he cocked his rifle and dropped the unfortunate animal with a bullet in the head. There was no thought toward simply setting the horse free, as he had done with the mules. The mere fact that the aging horse could not stand up to his cruel pace struck Boot as an affront to him personally. The chore taken care of, he stepped up in the saddle and started out along the bluffs, looking for a likely place to cross over into the Creek Nation.

Only one full day's ride from the bend in the Arkansas where Boot Stoner crossed over, an uneasy homecoming was taking place in the home of Tom Talltree. "What are we going to do about her?" Tom asked Blue Woman when she came to the garden to bring him water.

Puzzled by the question, Blue Woman responded, "What do you mean? She is our niece, your brother's child. We will take care of her."

"There is barely enough for the two of us," Tom insisted. "How can we take her in?"

"Lilly is a bright girl. She can help you in the garden and help plant the corn. She can help me in the house."

Tom frowned at the thought. The scarcity of food was not what was really bothering him. "What if this Boot Stoner is still chasing her? What if he comes here looking for her?"

Blue Woman hesitated for a moment, considering the likelihood. When she answered, it was with determination in her voice. "Then we will hide her, and tell him she is not here. And he can go look for her somewhere else." There were still some lingering feelings of guilt on Blue Woman's part that Lilly had been sent away to live with strangers when her parents were killed, instead of being cared for by members of her family.

Tom shook his head slowly as he considered his wife's comments. He had serious doubts that the problem could be handled that easily. "I don't know," he said. "It's bad business, that Boot Stoner. From what the girl says, he's left a string of dead people everywhere he's been." He looked at Blue Woman and shook his head again. "I just wish she had lit somewhere else."

Blue Woman expelled a long, troubled sigh. "Tom," she stated earnestly, "we can't send her away, not again. We're all the family she's got." She picked up the water bucket and turned to retrace her steps to the house. Tom stood still for a while longer, watching his wife walk away. Maybe he was worrying uselessly. Boot Stoner might not even care enough about Lilly to go to the trouble of searching for her. Not many people knew where Low Hawk was, anyway. Still, he was not comfortable thinking about the possibility of a visit by the half-breed Cherokee.

Foreboding thoughts, initiated earlier in the garden, were still fresh in Tom's mind at supper time. Although Blue Woman did her best to put a cheerful face on the meager meal, it was obvious that her husband was still in a brooding mood. "Look who's up and feeling fit, Tom," Blue Woman greeted her husband when he came to the table. "Lilly helped me fix supper. She knows her way around the kitchen." Her comment caused Lilly to blush.

"Well, it all looks good enough to eat," Tom responded, doing his best to summon a portion of the cheerfulness demonstrated by his wife.

The meal was taken in almost total silence, with an occasional comment from Blue Woman the only interruption. Though she made no reference to it, her husband was stoically quiet, a practice atypical for one who was usually so talkative. When she sought his gaze, he avoided her eyes, his own focused upon his plate. She knew he was still brooding over their guest.

Supper finished, Tom got up from the table and went out on the front porch to smoke. Lilly helped Blue Woman clear away the dirty dishes and pans, and then excused herself to retire to a corner of the front room, which had been divided off to make her a bedroom. After Lilly went to bed, Blue Woman joined her husband on the porch. "You are very quiet tonight," she said as she pulled the other chair over to his side of the porch.

Tom shrugged indifferently. "There was nothing I wanted to talk about," he said.

"It still bothers you," she stated, her voice low so that she would not be overheard inside.

He didn't respond right away, letting his reply build up in his mind. "She brings danger to our home," he finally replied. "She has no right to bring this down on us."

"Keep your voice down," Blue Woman warned. "She will hear."

He did as he was told, but it was too late. The tiny house, still warm from the kitchen stove, had caused Lilly to abandon the idea of sleeping. She decided to seek the comfort of the porch with her aunt and uncle, and was at the door in time to hear Tom voice his concerns. Undetected by the two on the porch at that point, she backed away and returned to her bed.

The fear she held for Boot Stoner had never left her mind completely, but it had faded to the point where she was free of it for extended periods in the last couple of days. It was much like the time she spent with Burley Chase before Boot found her there. Now that fear returned to torment her once again, for, after hearing her uncle's comments, she knew she was not welcome there. She must run again.

Lying awake in the little corner that served as her bedroom, she waited until Tom and Blue Woman went to bed. Still she waited, until the soft drone of Blue Woman's snoring reached her ears. Moving as quietly as she could manage then, she got up and gathered the few belongings she had brought with her from Burley's cave. The only thing she took from her uncle was the blanket on her bed. She reasoned that they would gladly give her the blanket in exchange for her departure. Moving silently through the tiny cabin, she paused briefly before their bedroom to make sure they were not awake. Then she lifted the latch on the door and let herself out. The night air was chilly, so she wrapped the blanket around her shoulders as she stood trying to decide which way to go. East or west, north or south, it made little difference. She had no destination in any direction, nowhere to seek refuge, so she stepped off the porch and started walking along the creek, not really caring in which direction she went.

Jonah Feathers stepped up on a chair in order to reach a bolt of calico on the top shelf. His customer, Bonnie Rainwater, watched his efforts with intense interest. Neither she nor Jonah heard the stranger step silently through the open doorway. "Is this the one you want?" Jonah asked as he pulled the bolt of cloth from under several others. When he turned to hear her response, he was so startled that he dropped one end of the bolt, causing it to fall against the side of the chair, almost overturning it. One glance at the menacing figure standing by the door told him that he had come face-to-face with Boot Stoner.

Jonah had never seen Boot before, never been given a description of the renegade half-breed. But he knew without a doubt that he was now staring into the cruel eyes of the savage responsible for the long string of murders in Indian Territory. Puzzled by Jonah's sudden distress, Bonnie Rainwater turned to follow the direction of his wide-eyed stare. Like Jonah, she was instantly alarmed. Though she knew nothing of Boot Stoner and Lilly, she recognized evil in that pitiless face. Instinctively, she immediately backed away until stopped by her shoulder blades striking the side wall.

Amused by the reactions of the storekeeper and his customer, Boot stood, feet widespread, a full cartridge belt wrapped around his lean belly, with a twelve-inch skinning knife sheathed in a leather scabbard and a Winchester rifle cradled in his arms. The most frightening aspect of this sudden apparition, however, was the total lack of mercy in the dark face. He said nothing while he watched Jonah disentangle himself from the chair and the bolt of cloth.

Doing his best to gather his wits once again, Jonah attempted to regain some measure of composure. "Good mornin'," he squeaked, before finding his voice again. "I'll be with you just as soon as I help this lady with some cloth."

"I'm lookin' for somebody," Boot said with no regard for the lady or her cloth. "A girl. She came this way. Lilly's her name. Where is she?"

Jonah hesitated, weighing his answer. He could not, in all good conscience, tell Boot where Lilly was, but he feared to remain silent in case it might cause him grief later on. "Lilly?" he finally stuttered. "I don't know no Lilly that lives in Low Hawk. What's her last name?"

The question caused Boot to hesitate for a moment. He almost said Stoner, since his father had taken the girl in. Irritated by the storekeeper's response, he snapped, "I don't know her last name. Have you seen her or not?"

"I can't recall seein' no strange girl around here," Jonah replied. He glanced nervously at Bonnie, still plastered against the wall. Boot followed his gaze. Jonah silently thanked God that he had not gotten around to telling Bonnie about the sudden appearance of Walking Owl's daughter, Lilly. "Anything else I can help you with?"

Boot stared at Jonah for a long moment while he considered whether or not the storekeeper was telling him the truth. "How many houses in this place?" Boot demanded.

"Half a dozen right around Low Hawk," Jonah answered. "A couple more over on Black Rock Creek. There's a bigger town ten or twelve miles from here. Okmulgee—maybe that's where she went."

Boot turned abruptly and walked outside. Looking to the north, he focused his gaze on the closest house.

Bonnie Rainwater reacted immediately. She ran to the door after him. "My house! My house!" she cried. "No girl there." What she said was not entirely true. There were two small boys at home as well as her twelve-year-old daughter, and she feared for her daughter's safety. What if this madman would be satisfied with just any young girl?

"Is that so?" Boot replied. "Well, I reckon I'll just have to see for myself." He stepped up in the saddle and started toward Bonnie's house, with the terrified Creek woman running after him.

Although relieved to see the menace depart, Jonah knew it was probably not the last he would see of him. After his face-to-face confrontation with the notorious outlaw, he did not doubt the evil Boot Stoner could bring to the entire community of Low Hawk. The foremost thought in his mind at this point was to send for the Creek Lighthorse. The Creek Nation was divided into six districts. There were one officer and four privates stationed in Okmulgee, the headquarters for this district, which was ten miles away. "Ruth!" Jonah called out. When she came from the kitchen, he told her of Boot's visit. "Here," he said, handing her his shotgun. "You keep this handy in case he comes back. I'm gonna run over to Henry Red Shirt's and send his boy to fetch the police." Seeing the distress in her eyes, he said, "I'll be right back."

Concerned that Boot might happen to look back and see him running for help, Jonah slipped out the back door. Crossing the creek by the footbridge, he ran as best a man of his heft could toward a weathered frame house a quarter of a mile away. Finding Henry and his thirteen-year-old son in the yard, Jonah, out of breath and gasping for air, explained his unlikely mode of travel. After hearing Jonah's account of Boot Stoner's visit, Henry immediately sent his son galloping toward Okmulgee.

While the young Creek boy was dispatched to bring help, Boot Stoner stormed through Bonnie Rainwater's house, tossing tables and chairs aside as if Lilly might be hiding behind or under them. Surprising a startled young girl in the kitchen, he grabbed her by the arm and stared into her face for a long moment. The terrified girl screamed, causing him to draw back his hand, threatening to strike her. She immediately froze. Snarling in disgust, he cast her aside just as her mother ran in behind him, pleading for his mercy.

His search fruitless, he went out the back door, only to confront the girl's father running from the barn. Certain his wife and daughter had been attacked, Billy Rainwater charged into the intruder. With reactions quicker than most, Boot drew his rifle up to fire, but decided not to waste the bullet. Instead, he stepped aside and administered a sharp blow to Billy's skull with the rifle barrel. Billy dropped like a heavy sack of potatoes, stunned. Boot stood over him for a few moments, waiting for him to move. When he did not, Boot grunted in disgust and returned to the front yard to retrieve his horses.

Leaving a mother and daughter crying over an

injured father, and two small boys hiding in the barn, Boot rode away, determined to search every cabin in Low Hawk. He felt certain that Lilly was hiding somewhere in the little settlement. It just made sense. Where else would she go? Still lingering in the back of his mind was the suspicion that the storekeeper had lied when he said he hadn't seen Lilly. *I may have to settle with him before I leave this stinking hole,* he thought. *If I don't find the bitch pretty soon, I'll go back and beat the truth out of that fat son of a bitch.* Boot was rapidly forming a hatred for the entire community of Low Hawk.

Like a crazed bear bent on destruction, Boot went from house to house, ransacking his way through room after room, leaving terrified residents in his wake. By nightfall, word had reached the remaining two households of the one-man tornado that was methodically wreaking havoc upon the community. The occupants of one of the houses, an old couple, chose to flee to the house of their neighbor, George Longpath. George, however, was not one to run before a confrontation with danger.

Giving his wife his pistol, George sent her, the children, and the old couple to hide in the barn. When they were safely away, he loaded his double-barreled shotgun and took a position by the front window of his house, determined to defend his home.

Almost an hour passed before the evil horseman appeared on the path to George's front door. Riding slowly up the path toward the darkened house, Boot pulled his horse up short and took his time looking the place over. There was no sign of anyone about, no lamps lit, no smoke from the chimney, yet Boot sensed someone watching him. A moment more passed, and then his suspicions were confirmed.

"That's far enough, mister," George called out from the darkened cabin. "You can turn right around and git off my property."

"Send Lilly out here and I'll do that," Boot called back.

"There ain't nobody named Lilly here," George said, "so git movin', else I'll let you have both barrels of this shotgun."

"All right, then," Boot replied, but made no move to leave. He had suspected a gun was aimed at him even before George threatened him. He glanced at the barn, dark like the house. *I bet there's more than a horse or a cow in that barn,* he thought. Then he announced, "I'm leavin'," and turned his horse around. Walking the horse slowly, the dun following along behind, he gradually faded into the deepening night. When he was confident the man inside the house could no longer see him, he cut back to circle around behind the barn. All the other people had stood by like frightened cattle while he ransacked their homes. This was the first place, other than the first house he searched, where someone was willing to stand up to him. Consequently, it was easy for Boot to figure this man had more reason to fight, someone to protect— someone like Lilly.

Inside the house, George stared out the window, trying to penetrate the darkness. It didn't figure that

Boot would give up that easily. George moved to a side window and stared out at the yard. Then he went to the back door, carefully lifted the latch, and peered out into the backyard. Nothing. Perhaps the murdering savage had passed him by. He knew he could not take any chances, however, so he went back to his station by the front window.

Inside the barn, Sarah Longpath sat watching the house through a crack in the door. She was barely able to make out the form of a man on horseback seeming to talk to her husband. With the pistol in her lap, she strained to hear what was being said, but it was too far away. Behind her, sitting in terrified silence, were her two children and her neighbors, White Bear and his wife, Walks All Day.

"How long do we have to stay here, Mama?" her youngest asked.

"Till your father calls us back," Sarah answered. "Just sit quietly and wait."

"Come sit beside me," Walks All Day said, reaching out toward the youngster. "I am old. You can help me keep warm."

"I can't see," the child complained. "It's too dark in here. Mama, why don't you light the lantern?"

"Yeah, Mama, why don't you light the lantern?" The gruff voice came from somewhere in the darkness, like the chilling voice of an evil spirit, freezing the occupants of the barn.

Only for a moment was Sarah Longpath stunned into immobility. She grabbed the pistol from her lap and spun around. With no visible target, she fired anyway, aiming toward the place from which she thought the voice had come. The thick darkness was split momentarily by the muzzle flash. Unfortunately for her, it pinpointed her position, and in the next instant a rifle slug tore into her breast, killing her instantly.

The next few moments were filled with the horrified screams of the children and the old woman. Into their midst, like a demon from the dark, the belligerent half-breed dropped from the short hayloft above them. White Bear attempted to stand up to him, and received a rifle butt to the head as reward for his bravery. Walks All Day rushed to her husband's aid while the children bolted for the door, flinging the barn door open in their desperation to escape. Boot snapped his head around quickly when they ran, but elected not to bother with them when he saw that Lilly was not with them.

Turning his attention back to the two who remained, he grabbed Walks All Day by the back of her collar and dragged her away from White Bear. The old man was sitting up now, but clearly was still rattled and confused, a result of the blow to his temple. "Where is the girl?" Boot demanded as he turned the old woman around to face him. When she did not answer, he grabbed her by the throat and tightened his grip. "Where's Lilly?" She tried to tell him she did not know, but his grip on her throat steadily tightened until she could not speak. Annoyed by her seeming refusal to tell him, he clamped down hard on her throat until she finally fainted away. He let her drop then, and she fell across her husband's lap. On his way out the door of the barn, he paused to take a close look at Sarah's body, just to make sure it was not Lilly.

Shocked by the gunshots from the barn and the screams of the children, George Longpath was jolted into action. He ran out the back door to find his children running toward him, screaming in terrified panic. "Git in the house!" he ordered, on the verge of panic himself. He had suddenly found himself in the middle of a nightmare. Determined to stand his ground and protect his family before, he was now totally unnerved and hesitant to enter the barn—even to save his wife. He was unaware of the draining of blood from his knuckles as he gripped the shotgun so tightly that his hands were losing feeling. He made up his mind to charge the barn when suddenly Boot stepped outside to face him. Confronted with sudden death, George tried to react, but his hands were so numb with fear that he couldn't even feel the shotgun. The ruthless half-breed pumped two shots into him before he could raise his weapon waist-high. Boot laughed out loud when George's last feeble effort pulled the trigger and sent a shotgun blast into the side of the house.

Boot strode straight for the house, confident that no one remained save the two children. As he stepped inside the back door, he heard the children go out the front. Hurrying through the house, he stepped out on the porch to watch then as they fled for their lives down the path on which he had first approached the house. He grunted once, amused at the sight. Then he went back inside to see what he could find to eat. He had been wrong. Lilly was not there, but he was still confident that she was hiding somewhere in the settlement. It occurred to him that maybe he should stay put, and let the people come to him. "I'll let 'em know where to find me," he said, chuckling.

Chapter 14

A sizable crowd of frightened and disoriented residents of Low Hawk gathered in Jonah Feathers' store, seeking refuge in the safety of numbers. The question before them was what to do about the monster who had torn through the community like a rabid wolf. There was scared talk floating about, but there were also irate voices demanding a stop to the maniac's plundering and killing.

Henry Red Shirt was one who spoke for immediate action instead of waiting for the Creek police to come. "If we wait for my son to get back with the police, this mad dog may murder more of us. I say we get what weapons we have and go after this killer."

"Who is this woman he looks for?" someone asked. "Does anyone know where she is?"

"It's Lilly, Walking Owl's daughter," Jonah Feathers answered. "She came back, looking for her aunt and uncle. I took her over there yesterday."

This quieted the crowd for a moment. Then someone asked, "Why didn't you tell him that? Then maybe he wouldn't have terrorized the rest of us."

"She was runnin' from him," Jonah replied. "Didn't seem right to tell him where she was."

"Maybe not," someone else spoke up. "But now we got us a problem we have to take care of. I stood by, like the rest of you, and didn't do nothin' when he went through my house. I ain't exactly proud of that. But he can't fight us all if we stick together. I say to hell with waitin' for the police. Let's go find the bastard and hang him."

There followed a noisy reception for his suggestion among the men gathered there, with most in agreement. Most were already armed with old shotguns, pistols, or single-shot rifles. "All right," Henry Red Shirt said. "We need to find out where he is right now." Before anyone else could comment, the Longpath children ran into the store, breathless from running. The tale the children told of the murders of their parents brought an upswell in the already rising emotions of the mob. Some of the women quickly took charge of the children and hurried them into the kitchen.

"Is he still at your place?" Jonah Feathers asked as the children were led away.

Someone on the porch outside the door answered for the children. "He's there all right. Come take a look." When those inside filed out the door, he pointed in the direction the two children had just come from. There, off to the west, the moonless black sky was aglow with a cloud of flames.

"Lord have mercy," Jonah gasped. "We better get movin'." The quickly formed posse moved out, a conglomeration of horses and wagons, some riding mules, in the direction of George Longpath's house. Most of them had no real stomach for the chore that had to be done, but were going because it was the right thing to do. More than a few hoped deep down that they would be too late to catch the renegade, and find that he had left Low Hawk.

"Hurry," Walks All Day pleaded with her husband. White Bear tried to get to his feet, but the blow to his head had made him dizzy and nauseated. Each time he struggled to a standing position, he had to drop to his knees again to vomit. Still Walks All Day implored him to try. "Hurry," she repeated. "He will be back to kill us."

Her pleading was in vain, for Boot came back to the barn before the old couple could reach the door. Upon seeing their efforts to escape, he trained his rifle on them. "You ain't goin' nowhere. I might need your worthless old bones." It might prove worthwhile to retain an ace in the hole, he figured. Spying a coil of rope on a post, he bound them both, hands and feet, and tied them to the post.

After turning George Longpath's livestock out, Boot put his two horses in the barn. Then he stood outside for a few moments admiring the towering blaze from the house. "By damn, that'll bring 'em," he uttered. Smiling to himself, he turned about and returned to the barn. Instead of going back inside, he climbed up and positioned himself on the roof. From there, he had a clear field of fire over the entire clearing around the burning house. His wait was not long.

With Henry Red Shirt leading, the posse stopped short of the path leading to the house. Though long on purpose, the men of Low Hawk were reluctant to charge straight into the clearing without knowing what might await them. Some suggested making an effort to save the house, but were soon overruled, the reason being the house was already too far gone. "Well, what are we gonna do?" someone asked.

Since there was no sign of anyone about, Henry eased off his reins and let his horse inch closer to the burning structure. The others crowded close in behind him. The posse halted again when they discovered George Longpath's body lying in the yard between the barn and the house. "Poor George," Jonah Feathers lamented.

"Where's Sarah?" someone wondered aloud.

"Let's look in the barn," Henry said, and guided his horse toward the one remaining building.

Pulling up before the front of the barn, they were startled by the sudden appearance of Boot Stoner. Springing to his feet, Boot stood above them on the roof, his rifle aiming down at the leaders of the posse at point-blank range. To a man, no member of the posse was willing to make a move, knowing the penalty would be instant death.

"Nice of you folks to make a call," Boot slurred sarcastically. "Now I'm gonna tell you how things are gonna be around here." He paused to see if any of the mob was brave enough to make an attempt to surprise him. No one dared at first. He started to continue when young Ben Highwalker decided to take the risk. Before he could raise his old Springfield rifle hip-high, Boot knocked him out of the saddle, cocked the Winchester, and trained it once again on the group. "Anybody else?" Boot asked. There were no takers. "All right," he continued. "Here's the way things are. I know somebody here is hidin' the Creek girl named Lilly. She's my property, and I've come to get her." He motioned toward the burning house behind them. "That's the first one. I'll burn every last one of you out if you don't hand over the girl."

"Ain't none of us knows anythin' about the girl," Jonah lied. Encouraged by the possibility to deal with the renegade, he was encouraged to speak. "Least-ways, she ain't here, and that's the God's honest truth. Why don't you just move on? You've done enough killin' here."

"You take me for a fool?" Boot roared back. "She's here, and I'll burn this town to the ground if I don't get her back."

Feeling a tad bolder now, Jonah responded, "There's a lot more of us than one man can handle. We could spread out and make it pretty hot for you."

"Is that so?" Boot sneered. "Well, how you gonna back away from here right now before I start shootin'?" The question caused a sobering thought to flash through all their minds as they stood exposed at point-blank range. Their consternation caused Boot to grin. "The ones of you that do get away without gettin' shot might not wanna be shootin' at this barn, since I've got that old man and his wife tied up in there."

"White Bear," someone whispered, "George's young'un said they was hidin' in the barn with 'em."

"White Bear, huh?" Boot snarled. "Well, White Bear and his ol' lady are settin' in a pile of hay with a lantern right beside 'em. I can see 'em through a hole in the roof. One shot from me and the whole barn will go up." The part about the lantern and the hole in the roof was pure fabrication, but it served Boot's purpose. "Now there ain't nothin' to keep me from knockin' half of you bastards outta the saddle right now. So how about it? Bring me the girl, or there ain't gonna be no Low Hawk after tonight."

Struck with the sobering realization that they had allowed themselves to ride right up under him, and knowing that his was not an idle boast, a clammy fear gripped the entire posse. Each man couldn't help but wonder if he would be one of the lucky ones to escape the repeating rifle in a sudden dash for safety. Jonah Feathers knew that it was time for negotiation. "All right," he said. "If you'll hold your fire, and let us back off, we'll bring you the girl. Fair enough?"

"I thought so." Boot smirked. "Make it quick. I'm runnin' low on patience." He watched with amused interest as the posse wasted no time in backing away.

Once they had retreated beyond the glow of the firelight, the posse crowded together to question Jonah. "You plannin' to go over to Tom Talltree's and fetch the girl back here?" Henry asked.

"I don't know," Jonah confessed. "I didn't see how to tell him anythin' else to keep from gettin' half of us shot. He had us dead to rights."

"I say give him the damn girl," a voice from the back of the pack said. "He's done killed enough of us already."

The comment started a heated discussion, divided between those who favored concession and those who still wanted to fight. While they argued, Boot climbed down from the roof and slipped into the trees behind the barn where he could watch without being seen. "Why ain't Tom here?" Henry Red Shirt voiced. No one could answer for sure, but it was assumed that he simply had not heard what was going on. His new house was a considerable distance from the others, and there was a high ridge between there and Low Hawk. They had just about decided to go in search of Lilly when out of the darkness rode Captain Jack Wildhorse with two privates from the district police.

With great relief, Jonah and Henry turned the problem of the renegade half-breed over to the Creek Lighthorse. "You got a fair piece of work ahead of you, Jack," Jonah advised. "He's a wild-hog killer, and he's holed up on top of the barn."

"Boot Stoner," Wildhorse said. "We heard about him from the Cherokee Lighthorse. A deputy marshal has been trying to track him down, but he ain't been able to corner him."

"John Ward?" Jonah asked.

"That's what I heard."

"I wish to hell John Ward was here now," Jonah said.

Jack did not take offense. He was well acquainted with the lawman from Fort Smith. "Well, don't worry. Me and my boys will take care of Mr. Stoner."

"He says he's got White Bear and his wife tied up in the barn," Henry said. "That's the only thing that kept us from going after him," he added.

Jack nodded thoughtfully. "That makes it a mite more hairy. We'll just have to be careful if the shootin' starts." Wasting no more time, he directed his men, sending one to each side of the barn. "Watch yourselves," he warned. "This boy is supposed to be a real killer."

Waiting long enough to give his men time to get in position, he then rode his horse up to the edge of the firelight from the smoldering flames of the house, and dismounted. Pulling his horse around so that it stood between him and the barn, he called out to the fugitive. "All right, Stoner, this is Captain Jack Wildhorse of the Creek Lighthorse. We've got you surrounded. There ain't no way out of that barn except through us, so you might as well come on out peacefully."

A long moment of silence followed, and then it was shattered by a single rifle shot. The crowd of onlookers was stunned by the sudden appearance of a black bullet hole in the lawman's forehead. Jack stood there for a frozen moment, then keeled over backward. He had made a fatal mistake in assuming Boot was still on the barn roof.

Though frozen, horrified for a moment, the spectators

scattered for cover in the next instant. Wildhorse's two men immediately started firing at the barn with no visible target. Forgetting the couple tied up inside, they splintered the barn with rifle fire, pockmarking the sides of the building without realizing their target was not even inside. Exhausting their magazines, the two privates stopped to reload. During the lull in the firing, a thin wail could be heard coming from the barn.

"Walks All Day!" someone yelled. Then the cry of alarm was picked up by someone else, and finally Henry Red Shirt called out to the policeman closest to him. "You've gotta hold your fire! You're gonna kill those folks inside." Confused, the two policemen fell back to pick up Jack Wildhorse's body, then retreated to where the spectators had gathered. There they stopped to consider their options.

"We gotta get him off of that barn," one of the policemen said.

"We need more men," the other one replied.

"Some of us can help," Henry Red Shirt volunteered. Both policemen glanced at the disorganized mob of men behind them, before looking back at each other and shaking their heads.

"Maybe," one of them said.

While the Indian police debated their next plan of attack, Boot Stoner reentered the barn and quietly led his horses out the back, pausing only briefly to tell the wailing Indian woman to shut up. It was too dark in the barn to see his penetrating stare, but the gruffness of his voice caused her to cease her crying immediately.

The Creek policemen decided they had no choice

but to rush the barn in an effort to save the lives of the old couple. The flames from the house had died down at that point and the clearing was no longer illuminated brightly, so their plan was to charge into the barn as fast as they could run, and riddle the barn roof with rifle balls. They figured that, even if he was not hit, it would at least make it too hot for him to stay up there.

The plan might have worked if Boot had, in fact, been on the barn roof. The two lawmen were able to make it across the clearing without being shot at. Charging into the barn, one of them almost stumbled over the hostages, but was able to avoid them at the last second. Recovering immediately, he joined his partner in reducing the old roof to lace, firing as rapidly as they could cock and fire up over their heads. All the while, Walks All Day tried frantically to tell them that Boot had left. When they finally understood her frantic screaming, they stood perplexed, the barn floor littered around their feet with spent shells. Soon they were joined by cheering spectators, assuming from the quiet that the fugitive had been killed.

"Gone?" Jonah Feathers exclaimed. "He got away?" He, like his neighbors, found it hard to believe the belligerent savage had survived such a volley of shots. The half-breed had dueled with the entire community and beaten them, leaving many bodies to bury.

"He's lit out from here," one of the Creek police said. "Too dark to track him tonight. We'll have to wait till morning."

"I hope to hell that's the last we'll see of him

around here," Jonah said. Then a thought struck him. "I expect it would be a good idea for somebody to ride over to warn them folks over on Black Rock Creek that trouble might be coming their way." Still feeling a sense of importance for having successfully delivered the Creek Lighthorse, Henry's son volunteered to take on the mission.

"You be careful, Jimmy," Henry cautioned before his son leaped upon his horse and galloped away in the darkness.

Sitting watching from the dark shadows of the cottonwoods that ringed George Longpath's lower field, Boot smiled to himself when the lone rider galloped along the road on the far side of the field. *I wonder where he's going in such a hurry. Might be a good idea to find out.* He waited until Jimmy had rounded the curve at the north end of the field, then started out after him.

Oblivious to the trauma taking place two miles away on the eastern side of the high ridge that bordered Black Rock Creek, Tom Talltree was awakened from a sound sleep by the sound of distant gunfire. "What is it, Tom?" Blue Woman asked when she, too, was awakened and sat up to find her husband standing in the open door.

"Gunfire," Tom answered. "It's coming from Low Hawk—sounds like a war going on."

Blue Woman got up and went to see if Lilly had also heard the noise. In a few seconds, she rushed to the door where Tom was still standing and listening.

"She's gone! Lilly's not there!" Thinking that maybe the girl had gone outside to make water, she walked out on the porch and began calling, "Lilly! Lilly!" When there was no response, Tom went back inside and lit a lantern. Going to Lilly's bed, he gave his wife the news that their niece was not only gone, but so were her things. Tom didn't express his feelings, but there was a slight sense of relief that the troublesome runaway might be out of their lives.

His feelings were not shared by Blue Woman, who immediately began to worry and fret. "Where will she go?" she asked, not expecting an answer. "Maybe she will come back."

Tom, back outside in the yard then, announced, "The shooting has stopped. Maybe I'll ride over in the morning and find out what happened."

"You must find Lilly," Blue Woman said. "She can't be far. Maybe she heard you talking after she went to bed. You should not have said those things," she scolded. "You must go after her."

"I can't look for her till morning," Tom replied, not really enthusiastic about bringing her back. "Maybe it's best for everyone if she finds a better place to stay." When Blue Woman started to berate him, he quickly assured her, "I'll try to find her in the morning when I can see her tracks. She could have gone anywhere. We might as well go back to bed."

Blue Woman was not at all happy with her husband's lack of purpose. She felt a tremendous lack of responsibility on her own part for not taking Lilly in when her parents were killed. Worried now for the girl's safety, she could not go back to bed knowing Lilly was out there somewhere, alone and forsaken. Finally she said, "You go back to bed. I'm going to look for her." Before there was an opportunity to argue about it, they were stopped by the sound of a horse galloping along the narrow path to their house.

Alarmed, Tom ran inside to get his shotgun. Fumbling with the shells, he managed to get it loaded by the time he returned to join Blue Woman on the porch. A moment later, Jimmy Red Shirt rode into the yard, calling out for them. Relieved to recognize Jimmy, but still worried about the cause of his visit in the middle of the night, Tom propped his shotgun by the door and walked out to meet him.

Standing in the middle of the front yard, Tom and Blue Woman listened, horrified by the boy's account of the blatant killings that had taken place in Low Hawk. Jimmy's news confirmed Tom's dread feelings about the potential danger Lilly's arrival had visited upon them. "I knew it. I knew it," he kept muttering to himself as Jimmy related the tragedy of Jack Wildhorse's arrival with the police.

So absorbed were they in the tale of horror, that none of the three noticed the shadowy figure slowly walking his horse up behind them until words suddenly came from the darkness, cold and clammy. "I've come for Lilly. Where is she?"

The words might have come from the evil spirit himself, such was their effect upon Tom Talltree. His blood seemed to turn to jelly in his veins. He at once looked to the door where his shotgun was propped, feeling desperation in knowing he could not possibly reach it in time. Jimmy's reaction was to back away until he bumped into his horse. Of the three, only Blue Woman retained a sense of calm. "She is not here," she said. "She has gone."

"Don't lie to me, bitch. I'll cut your guts out. Where is she?" He glared at the house. "Lilly!" he roared. "Get out here!" When his demands were met with silence, he dismounted and started toward the door. Jimmy, seeing his chance for escape, jumped on his horse. Boot paused for only a moment, just long enough to turn and send a rifle ball to strike squarely between the boy's shoulder blades. As Jimmy's body dropped to the ground, Boot turned back to look at Tom. Then he glanced at the shotgun propped beside the door. Words were unnecessary. His look asked the question *You want to try for it?* Tom backed away.

Boot picked up the shotgun, broke the breech, and extracted the shells. Then he threw it off the porch and went inside. Blue Woman followed right behind him. "I told you she's not here. She's gone where you can't find her, so you might as well go on away from here and forget about her."

Boot cocked his head as he glared into her face. "Old woman, there ain't no place where I can't find her. You're startin' to grind on my nerves. I just might send you to a place where nobody can find you." He continued his search of the cabin. There was no one there, but the corner of the front room caught his eye. It was obviously closed off with quilts to make a bedroom. He turned to form an evil grin for Blue Woman.

"So she ain't here, huh? Then what is this? Did you kick your old man outta the bedroom?" He chuckled at his own joke, then turned brutally serious when he demanded, "Where is she?"

Standing in the doorway, watching the unwelcome guest stalking wantonly through his house, Tom finally spoke up. "She was here, but she left during the night while we was asleep. She can't be too far away."

Blue Woman's head jerked back, recoiling from her husband's betrayal of the girl. Boot grinned, amused by the man's lack of backbone, relishing the fear he knew he generated. "I got a good mind to shoot you for the gutless son of a bitch you are. But I think the old woman is never gonna let you forget it. I'd be lettin' you off too easy. We'll just set back and wait for daylight." He nodded toward Blue Woman. "You can fix me somethin' to eat while we wait."

"I'm not cooking for the likes of you," Blue Woman spat back.

"Then I reckon I'll have to put a bullet hole in that hard head of yours," Boot said, still grinning. When his threat created no visible sign of fear, he said, "Instead of that, I'll shoot this worthless man of yours." He cocked his rifle and aimed it at Tom.

She hesitated for a moment, hating to concede to his demands, but knowing he just might do what he threatened. "All right, but we ain't got much to fix."

Chapter 15

Morning brought a light rain that ended an hour after sunrise. It brought a fresh breeze wafting across the east ridge that bordered the valley of Low Hawk. It brought a parting of the dark clouds that had gathered over the settlement the night before. And it brought John Ward.

Climbing up the east slope of the ridge, he rode easy in the saddle, letting Cousin pick his trail. Behind him, Two Buck followed the buckskin's lead, pulling up beside him when he paused at the top to take a look over the valley beyond. From the ridge, it was possible to see Jonah Feathers' store as well as a couple of the closest houses. There were a few horses tied out front of the store, which struck John as odd for this time of day—for any time of day, for that matter.

"Low Hawk?" Two Buck asked. He had never been in this part of Indian Territory before.

"Low Hawk," John answered him matter-of-factly.

He nudged Cousin forward, and the big gelding started down the west slope.

Two Buck followed obediently behind the deliberate lawman, although he wanted to charge down the slope and across the flat. Sometimes the deputy marshal was a little too patient to suit Two Buck, especially since their destination and maybe the answers to questions burning in the young Indian's mind were so near at hand. Although his recovery from his wounds was not complete, he felt his strength returning gradually as each day passed, and his passion for Boot Stoner's demise was enough to keep him in the saddle all day.

Upon reaching the bottom of the slope, John eased the buckskin to a gentle lope, heading straight for Jonah's store. Flanking him, Two Buck's eyes searched anxiously as if hoping to spot the fugitive. When they pulled up before the store, John had to caution his Cherokee partner when Two Buck started to bound up the steps. "Keep your shirt on. We'll find out what's what."

Entering the building, they walked into the midst of a serious discussion among worried residents of the little community. So intense was the concern that no one noticed the two new arrivals until Jonah glanced up from his position at the counter. "John Ward," he announced respectfully, following it with a small sigh of relief. The group of a dozen or so turned as one to look toward the door.

"Mornin', Jonah, gentlemen," John said, and walked up to the counter to stand beside Jonah Feathers. Before he could say more, the room erupted in a chorus of excited voices, all trying to talk at the same time, all anxious to inform the deputy of the tragedy that had befallen their homes.

Jonah raised his arms and called for calm. Then he took the floor. "He was here, John! Boot Stoner, he was here. He came lookin' for ol' Walking Owl's daughter. She passed through here, went to Black Rock Creek to find her aunt. He's killed four that we know of, and Henry Red Shirt's boy ain't come back from Black Rock Creek. We're afraid Boot mighta done for him, too. One of 'em killed was Captain Jack Wildhorse. He brought two men with him, and Boot shot Jack, drilled him right through the head. We formed a posse last night, and thought we had him cornered at George Longpath's place, but he slipped away."

John listened patiently, glancing at Two Buck when Jonah mentioned Lilly. While Jonah related the events of the previous night, the lawman looked at the faces peering anxiously at him. "Where's the two men Wildhorse brought with him?" he interrupted.

"They said they was gonna try to pick up Boot's trail where he left George's place," Jonah answered. He then told John of the mission to Black Rock Creek that Jimmy Red Shirt undertook.

"And you say the boy never came back?" John asked.

"That's right," Henry Red Shirt answered the question. "He never came home. I'm fixin' to go look for him."

"Black Rock Creek," John said, nodding to Two Buck. "I expect that's where we'll start lookin'."

"We'll go with you," Henry piped up, his words igniting a chorus of willing volunteers.

John remained expressionless as he replied. "I expect it would be best if you don't. I work better when I don't have to look out for anybody else." He glanced at Two Buck again. "I've already got one hot-blooded Cherokee to worry about. I expect that's enough."

"John, I ain't one to question you," Jonah insisted. "But you might be underestimatin' the man you're fixin' to tangle with. He's hell and damnation all by himself. If we had been thinkin' smart, we shoulda sent to Fort Gibson for the soldiers to come get him." He shook his head for emphasis, then added, "Maybe you oughta do that, anyway."

John nodded as if giving serious consideration to what Jonah was telling him. "Much obliged to you gentlemen," he said in ending the discourse, "but I expect we'll just keep the army out of this for the time being. Now I'd appreciate it if you'll just see to the safety of your own homes, and let me do the job I'm paid to do." He turned and walked out of the store, Two Buck on his heels.

Outside, Two Buck could not contain himself any longer. He was at John's elbow before they had time to mount. "You hear that? He's right behind her. We've gotta find her before he does."

"We'll do what we can," John replied, stepping up in the saddle. The attack on the saloon girl in Joplin was still fresh in his mind. Why Lilly was now running from Boot was something to be revealed when they caught up with her or Boot. He wheeled Cousin and headed for Black Rock Creek.

Willy Sharp and Thomas Bluekill, privates in the Creek Lighthorse, were two hours ahead of John Ward. Leading a horse carrying their captain's body, they had picked up Boot Stoner's trail at the point where he had followed Jimmy Red Shirt when the boy rode away from George Longpath's place. The trail had led to Black Rock Creek and Tom Talltree's home, which they now approached with caution. Seeing the two riders approaching, Tom ran out from the house, waving frantically, lest they might decide to ride on.

The two policemen wasted no time talking to Tom and his wife. As soon as they learned that Boot had departed there at sunup, following Lilly's tracks along the creek, they set out after him immediately.

Over halfway between Low Hawk and Black Rock Creek, John and Two Buck met Tom Talltree leading a horse with a body tied across the saddle. Recognizing the deputy marshal, Tom identified himself, and explained that the body on the horse he was leading was young Jimmy Red Shirt. "I'm taking him back to Henry," he explained. Answering John Ward's questions, Tom repeated the details of Boot Stoner's visit to his home, just as he had told the Creek police.

"How long ago did the policemen leave your place?" John wanted to know.

"An hour, maybe an hour and a half," was Tom's answer.

"How much farther is your place from here?" John asked.

"Half hour or so," Tom replied.

"But Lilly left your place sometime last night?" This from Two Buck.

"That's right," Tom answered. "She left while we were asleep. Don't know exactly what time it was."

"And now that devil's on her trail again," Two Buck lamented while looking at John impatiently.

"Much obliged," John said to Tom. "We'll be on our way now."

The stop at Tom's house wasn't an extended one. Lilly's aunt told them much the same story as they had heard from Tom. She did offer a good deal more about Lilly's determination to escape from Boot Stoner, however. This information served to increase the flames of impatience galloping through Two Buck's veins. Watching Two Buck's reactions as the young man questioned Blue Woman in further detail about Lilly, John made no comment. But it caused him to speculate on how he would feel if it was Lucy Summerlin on the run from some renegade like Boot Stoner. He knew that every hour that passed without catching up to Boot was an extension of the hell Two Buck must be living through.

Leaving Blue Woman, they led their horses along the creek bank to study the trail left in the sandy soil.

Their purpose was to identify the different tracks, so as to have some means of telling them apart. The rain that had fallen earlier that morning helped make the job easier, for there was no question the prints standing out the sharpest were left by the two Creek lawmen. Other tracks were fainter, and in some places they had been washed out by the rain. Still, they were frequent enough to indicate the direction of travel. It didn't really require much of a tracker to follow the Creek policemen's three horses, but John wanted to double-check the trail to make sure they were still on track.

About a mile farther on, the trail left the creek bank and veered toward the west. There was no obvious reason for the abrupt change in direction that John could see. To him, it indicated a frightened girl with no idea where she was going. He stood on the creek bank for a long moment, looking in the direction in which the tracks led. If the trail continued along that line, it would lead them to Okmulgee.

Two Buck, bending closely over the tracks along the bank, suddenly exclaimed, "Here!" When John walked over to see what he had found, Two Buck pointed to a single moccasin print in the soft sand near the edge of the water. "It's her footprint!" he said. John nodded in agreement. It was the first real sign they had found that confirmed that Lilly had come this way. The discovery only served to increase the anxiety already at a fever pitch in Two Buck's mind. Wasting no more time, they were in the saddle again, the sense of urgency increased in both men, for the tracks of the horses appeared to be almost as fresh as the moccasin print. As if to emphasize the urgency, they suddenly heard the sound of distant gunfire toward a low line of hills to the west.

"Well, lookie here," Boot Stoner muttered as he looked along his back trail. From his position at the top of a tree-covered hill, he had a view of perhaps a quarter of a mile of the flat he had just crossed. He recognized the riders trailing him as the Creek Nation police who had tried to smoke him out of the barn. A grin slowly crept across his face as he peered back at the three horses, two with riders and one with a body draped across the saddle. "This is Captain Jack Wildhorse of the Creek Lighthorse," Boot recited, mocking the last words of the Indian policeman brief seconds before Boot's rifle ball had split his forehead. The sight now of the two remaining lawmen served to distract him from the growing frustration he had developed because of his failure to run Lilly to ground. He had lost her trail somewhere at the foot of the hills, and had turned back to try to find it again. The fact that he had been forced to turn back turned out to be a stroke of luck, for he might not have discovered the two lawmen following him in time to prepare a reception for them.

Deep down, Boot welcomed the arrival of the two Indian policemen. Crowding his obsession for finding and punishing Lilly was a feeling of invincibility that grew with every life he took. Reaching back into his mother's ancestry, he rejected all traces of his white father's bloodline and was convinced that his *medicine* was strong—too strong to be overcome by any man, white or Indian. There was a special pleasure in the taking of a lawman's life, for it proved his dominance over the authority that would punish him. Looking around him then, he proceeded to choose the best place for an ambush.

At the foot of the first hill, Thomas Bluekill reined his horse to a stop and waited for Willy Sharp to catch up to him. "He stopped here," Bluekill said. "See, his tracks go back and forth across this old game trail."

"He followed the trail up this hill," Sharp added, pointing to a hoofprint farther up the game trail. "We better keep a sharp eye. He might think about doubling back on us."

"Maybe," Bluekill said with a shrug, "but I think his mind is stuck on finding the girl. I don't believe he knows he's being followed."

"Just the same, I think we better be careful," Willy said, and climbed back on his horse. He waited for Bluekill to mount and lead the way up the trail, and then he followed, leading the horse with the body tied across the saddle.

The game trail they followed wound around the first hill, then crossed over a narrow ridge to the next hill. Approaching the top of the hill, Thomas Bluekill rounded a sharp turn to find himself suddenly confronted by Boot Stoner standing boldly in the middle of the trail, his rifle aimed right at him. There was no time for reaction. The Winchester spoke, and Bluekill rolled out of the saddle, dead.

With little more time to react than his partner, Willy released the reins of the captain's horse and wheeled his own mount, plunging down through the brush in an attempt to escape. His emotions on fire, Boot emitted a loud war whoop and ran to the edge of the trail for a better position to take aim. His shot struck Willy in the back, knocking him out of the saddle.

Flushed with the exhilaration of another victorious encounter with representatives of white man authority, Boot hurried down the path to stand over Thomas Bluekill. The policeman was dead. Grunting with satisfaction, he then plunged into the brush after the second lawman. Willy Sharp was still alive when Boot found him, but too badly wounded to defend himself. "You made a big mistake when you came after me," Boot snarled. Willy could only look up at him with eyes that saw the door of darkness opening before him. At first content to let the man die slowly, Boot relieved him of his weapons and cartridges. He stood leering down at the helpless man for a few moments more before a new thought came to him. He drew his knife and took the policeman's scalp, then grinned maliciously while showing it to his screaming victim.

On his way back up the hill, he stopped to take Bluekill's weapons and his scalp. Feeling pleased with himself, he returned to his horses and resumed his search for the woman of his obsession. Having seen no footprints since entering the range of hills, he played a hunch that Lilly would continue to follow the game trail. Since it still led in the general direction of Okmulgee, he felt pretty sure that was where she was going.

A few miles behind Boot Stoner, at the foot of the hills, Two Buck proved to be keener of eye than either the savage half-breed or the Creek policemen. The young Cherokee did not miss the faint toe print that barely disturbed the pine needles beside the game trail. "John Ward," he cried out, when John had also missed the sign and was already starting up the trail. "She don't go that way." He got to his feet and peered through the trees that ringed the base of the hill. "She went that way," he said, pointing toward the south end of the range.

John came back to see for himself. After closely examining the faint marks in the needles beside the trail, he agreed that what they were looking at could possibly be traces of a footprint. "I'd like it better if you could find me another print to back it up," he said. He turned his head to take a glance up the game path where the hoofprints had led, knowing that Boot Stoner was somewhere in that direction, and not too far at that.

Leaving his horse to follow behind him, Two Buck stepped carefully through the pine thicket, stopping every few feet to search the forest floor. Finally he was rewarded when he found a spot with disturbed needles where Lilly's foot had evidently slipped on a root. He looked up at John triumphantly, finding fresh hope in this obvious evidence that Boot had lost Lilly's trail. John nodded in return. There was no decision to be made in his mind; tracking down Boot Stoner held the priority, in spite of Two Buck's anxiety. It was a fortunate circumstance that the trails had separated. The last time they had cornered Boot, Two Buck had managed to get himself shot.

"You stay on Lilly's trail," he told Two Buck. "I'm goin' after Stoner. We still don't know what those shots were about, and I'm afraid those two Creek policemen might be chasin' him all over creation. I had hoped to catch up to Boot when he wasn't on the run."

"You be careful, John Ward," Two Buck said in parting, then hurried off through the pines.

"You be careful yourself," John called after him. "You don't know what that girl might be thinkin' right now. She might just take a shot at you." He knew he should have told Two Buck what he had heard about Lilly's attack on the saloon girl, but now there wasn't time. She was running from Boot, but he didn't know why. He hoped it was for the same reason Two Buck assumed. "If you find her, and she don't give you any trouble, take her on back to her uncle's place in Black Rock Creek. I'll meet you back there. And, dammit, Two Buck, you be damn sure she wants to be rescued before you go stickin' your neck out."

"I will," Two Buck called back over his shoulder, already about to disappear from sight in the thicket.

John shook his head in exasperation. *I hope to hell the boy don't end up with his heart broken,* he thought. Holding his rifle in one hand, he scanned the trail ahead of him, watching for any sign of ambush. It was merely a natural precaution, since he expected to catch up to the Creek policemen before he encountered Boot Stoner. He also had it in his mind, however, that he didn't want to get accidentally shot by the policemen. The trail led upward, to the top of one hill, and crossed over to a second, higher one. There was still no sign or sound that would indicate he was closing the distance between them.

Following the narrow game trail up the second hill, he suddenly stopped to listen. Off to his right, there was something moving in the brush. He quickly slid off his horse and knelt by the side of the path, his rifle ready to fire. Peering through the dense thicket of trees, straining to pick up some movement, there was nothing. And then he spotted it. Moving among the pines was a horse with no rider, but with a body tied across the saddle. *What the hell?* he thought, then immediately remembered that Jack Wildhorse had been killed. "That don't look too good," he muttered. To further concern him, another horse, with an empty saddle, pushed through a bramble of vines to join the first. The fact that they were running loose painted a picture that did not bode well in John's mind.

Even more alert than before, he moved up the path on foot, leading his horse. A few dozen yards more, just past a sharp bend in the trail, he found Thomas Bluekill's body. Kneeling beside the corpse, he first looked all around him to make sure no one was taking a bead on him. "Damn," he swore softly when he saw the crude scalping Boot had done. "Looks like he's turned completely wild." He did not know Thomas Bluekill as well as he had Jack Wildhorse, but he had seen the man before. "Sorry I ain't got time to give you a decent burial," he said, and got to his feet. "Maybe I'll get back this way before too long, and I'll try to do for you then." Having no time to collect the horses left riderless on the hillside below him, nor the inclination to bother with them, he continued up the game trail until he came to the spot where Boot had obviously ambushed the policeman.

Judging by the fresh horse droppings, the horse had stood there while Boot waited for the lawman to round the curve in the path. Looking down at his feet, John saw one spent cartridge. Back on the other side of the hills, he and Two Buck had heard two shots. Where, he wondered, was the other policeman? He decided it was possible there might be another body down the hill, probably near the spot where he saw the horses.

Lilly made her way around the south end of the line of hills, keeping in the trees and trying to disguise her trail wherever possible. She made an effort to cover her tracks out of a general fear of being followed. Had she known that Boot had arrived at her uncle's house, and that he had tracked her from there, she might have been even more frightened. She knew in her heart that Boot was going to show up sooner or later. She feared that she was doomed to live out her life as his chattel. And she knew that she could not go back to the existence she had had with him. The thought of his evil stench upon her drove her to near panic. She would rather die than be taken by him again. The thought of death was not frightening to her at this point in her young life. Even if John Ward eventually caught Boot Stoner, her life was ruined, for who could possibly want her after Boot? The thought almost caused her to laugh at the irony, for she was convinced that Boot would kill her when he caught her this time. It was the pain she knew he would extract before killing her that sickened her. Thinking of it, she rested her hand on the pistol she carried. There were two bullets remaining in the cylinder. One she would use for protection; the other she had resolved to reserve for herself.

Coming out of the trees at last, she found herself facing a seemingly endless prairie of rolling grassland with hills that were almost treeless. She hesitated as she looked out across the exposed expanse. A person walking there could be seen for miles. Feeling suddenly exhausted, she decided to rest there for a while, in the shelter of the trees, before starting out across the prairie.

Startled, she sat up, realizing then that she had fallen asleep. Something had awakened her, some noise, or a stirring in the trees, she thought. But there was no sound now. She listened, but there was nothing but the sound of the wind in the pines. Admonishing herself for falling asleep, she got to her feet and started out across the grassy plain.

Walking as fast as she could, she set a pace that she felt she could maintain for a long period of time. One foot after the other, she walked with determination, for after covering a distance of perhaps a quarter of a mile, she saw the faint outline of distant hills. The sight brought a slim ray of hope. Perhaps she would find some refuge there. The thought was short-lived, however, for she suddenly heard a soft drumming of hooves far behind her. Instantly panicked, she looked around to discover a man on a horse bearing down upon her.

He had found her! Stunned, she could react only in fear, and, in fear, she started to run. Dropping everything but the pistol she clutched in her hand, she ran with frightened abandon, forcing her legs to drive for more speed. Over the low, rolling hills, through grassy ravines, she drove herself until her lungs were bursting from the exertion. The rider was rapidly and steadily gaining on her. Finally, when she feared she was at the end of her endurance, with her legs turning to heavy stones, she stumbled down a narrow ravine and fell.

"Lilly!" the man called out.

Determined to resist him, she raised the pistol and fired. The shot went wide of the mark. When she saw she had missed, she hesitated. The one remaining bullet was intended for herself. She had reached the moment of decision. Still, she hesitated as the horse drew near. It was not an easy decision. She raised the revolver to her head.

"Lilly! It's Two Buck!"

In her state of panic, she heard the words, but she could not be certain that her mind was not playing tricks on her. Her head was swimming from fear and exhaustion, and with the sun at his back, she was not sure of the man's identity. The thought suddenly struck her mind that it was Boot, playing his evil game upon her, and in one final act of defiance, she pulled the trigger.

Leaping from the saddle, Two Buck was horrified by the sight of the young Creek girl holding the pistol to her temple. Knowing he could not get to her in time to stop her, he was stunned moments later by the metallic click of the hammer on an empty cylinder. She had miscounted the number of bullets remaining, forgetting the extra shot she had taken to kill a rabbit on her trek from the Boston Mountains to Low Hawk.

Shattered by the failure of the pistol to fire, Lilly staggered to her feet and tried to run again. Two Buck caught her before she could take half a dozen steps. She fought against him until he pinned her arms in his embrace. "Lilly, it's me, Two Buck," he repeated over and over. "I've come to take you home."

Finally, she was able to hear him and realize that she was not hallucinating. She stopped struggling and gazed into his face. "Two Buck?" she asked. "Two Buck." This time she uttered his name in grateful relief. Suddenly, her eyelids fluttered slightly and her body went limp.

Horrified, Two Buck held the unconscious girl in his arms, afraid at first that she was dead. With no idea what he should do, he held her close to him, rocking her back and forth as if she were a baby. Holding a finger on her neck, he felt a faint heartbeat. Filled with hope again, he gently laid her on the ground, then ran to his horse to fetch a canteen. Cradling her head in his lap, he sprinkled water on her forehead. In a few minutes, she opened her eyes to stare up into his face. The face she saw was the smooth, bronzed face of the young Cherokee boy who worked for her father.

"Two Buck," she uttered. "I thought you were dead. I saw Boot shoot you."

Two Buck smiled, relieved. "He don't kill me. I have to find you."

He picked her up and carried her to his horse. As he lifted her up to sit behind the saddle, she asked, "Where are you taking me?"

"Back to your aunt," he replied. "John Ward say to take you back there, and he'll meet us there."

She was at once alarmed. "I can't go back there. Boot will look for me there. Besides, my uncle doesn't want me there. I heard him tell Blue Woman I bring trouble."

Two Buck stepped up in the saddle. "Boot already been there. Blue Woman don't want you to leave. No matter, anyway. You don't have to stay there if you don't want to. I'll take care of you."

His declaration surprised her. She had no notion of Two Buck's fondness for her. He had never given a clue during the time he worked around Wendell Stoner's place. She had never thought to question the reason Two Buck rode with John Ward to track Boot. Now it occurred to her how unusual it was for John Ward to travel with a partner. Forgetting the specter of Boot Stoner for the moment, she considered the young man whose waist her arms now encircled, and allowed a glimpse of hope to penetrate her troubled mind. She immediately rejected it, telling herself that she had misinterpreted his remarks. She was ruined. No man would want her now, and Two Buck was merely being kind. What did he really know of her? When he had worked for Wendell Stoner, they had often exchanged pleasantries, but little more than that. For her part, she had never given Two Buck serious thought. Why would she even think it now?

Chapter 16

The farther Boot rode on the trail to Okmulgee, the angrier he became. With each mile traveled since killing the two Creek lawmen, his suspicions increased. It was getting along in the afternoon, and since leaving the hills and the end of the game trail he had followed, he had found not one track to indicate Lilly had passed this way. He thought back about Lilly's aunt and uncle. They said she had slipped away in the middle of the night. Now that he pictured it again, Tom Talltree seemed more than a little helpful in pointing out the girl's trail. The whole scene was becoming clear to him now. They figured he was too dumb to see it. They had sent him off toward the hills. Sure, he thought, Lilly had slipped out that way, but wasn't it strange that she had doubled back, and he had found two lawmen on his tail? And now he had ridden half a day away from Low Hawk while she was no doubt back laughing at him with her aunt and uncle. He yanked back hard on the reins, certain at this point that they had figured to pull the wool over his eyes. "By God, they'll all pay for this." He promptly turned around and headed back the way he had come.

Descending the last low slope before the open grass prairie, John Ward followed the single set of hoof-prints along the game trail. Then, unexpectedly, another set of prints appeared, but this second set was headed in the opposite direction, coming toward him before disappearing off to his right. An instant alarm went off in his brain, and he rolled off his horse just as a bullet snapped over his head, followed by the crack of a rifle. He had ridden into an ambush.

He reached up and pulled his Winchester from the saddle sling just as two more shots rang out. Cousin screamed out in pain when the slugs thudded into the horse's flesh. There was no time to lead the horse to cover as Boot continued to crank shot after shot into the dying buckskin gelding. Finally Cousin gave up the fight and collapsed heavily on the path. Still Boot continued his assault upon the fallen horse, hoping to hit the man taking cover behind it.

Even in the midst of the hailstorm of lead flying above his head, John's primary emotion was compassion for the buckskin horse. They had been a team for too many years for him not to feel grief for the loss of a friend and partner. His secondary emotion was anger, though not as much toward the murdering renegade who shot his horse as with himself, for blundering into the ambush. He had never expected Boot to turn around and meet him. He scolded himself for not being alert. It had cost him the best horse a man could have. He now directed his anger at the bushwhacker firing from the cover of a stand of oaks some fifty yards up the slope.

Flat on his belly, he crawled up behind Cousin, and raised his head just enough to watch the stand of oak trees. Detecting a slight movement of branches, he ducked moments before a fresh volley of shots erupted. As soon as it was quiet again, he quickly laid his rifle across his saddle and opened fire on the spot where he had seen movement. Cranking out shots as fast as he could, he peppered the bushes near the base of the trees.

Caught in the process of reloading, Boot had to dive for cover behind a sizable oak tree while the brush and branches around him rattled with a rain of lead. "Damn!" he bellowed, already angry over having missed his opportunity to kill the lawman. There was no way he could be sure, other than instinct, but he felt certain that the man he was shooting at was John Ward. There was no man's scalp he wanted more.

Knowing the deputy marshal had his position pinpointed, Boot finished reloading. He fired two quick shots at the fallen horse, then scrambled away to find cover a dozen yards away. Taking a chance that Boot was retreating to a new position, John did the same, moving away from Cousin to take cover behind a dead tree farther up the hill. There was a brief lull while both men waited to size up the new situation. Boot was the first to break the silence. He rose on one knee and fired three shots before he realized that the lawman was no longer behind the carcass. It was almost a fatal mistake, for he barely got back behind a tree before lead from John's Winchester shredded the leaves around him.

As the afternoon wore on, Boot was forced to realize that killing this particular lawman was not going to be so easy. Twice more he moved to new positions in an effort to get a better angle on John Ward. Each time, John countered to thwart the half-breed's efforts to get a clear shot. Finally Boot had to concede that it was a standoff, and it was getting later and later in the day. His mind returned to the thought of Lilly sitting smugly back with her relatives, thinking that the law was taking care of him. She laughed at him while he was out here in the woods, wasting boxes of cartridges. The image was enough to push him to the boiling point. *To hell with the damn lawman,* he thought. *He's on foot now, and I ain't gonna waste no more time on him.* His mind made up, he did not leave before offering insults and threats. "Hey, John Ward!" he shouted out. "You was mighty damn lucky I didn't kill you this time. Next time you ain't gonna be so damn lucky. It's a long walk back to Low Hawk. By the time you get there, the girl and her whole damn family will be dead."

John didn't bother to answer. He waited, listening until he heard the sound of Boot's horse as it bolted up through the trees. Still keeping a sharp eye in case Boot was trying to trick him into coming out in the open, he moved cautiously back to his fallen horse. What Boot had said was true. It was a long walk back to Low Hawk, but there were other possibilities. If he had any luck going for him at all, the horses ridden by the Creek policemen Boot had killed might still be close to where he had seen them. By his estimate, that was probably three miles through the hills. "Best get started," he said. He then spent a few moments trying to pull his saddle off Cousin, but the stirrup was pinned under the big horse. *Must have caught on a root or something under his belly,* he thought. Under different circumstances, he would have worked at it until he could pull the girth strap and stirrup out, but time was short. The saddle was well worn and needing some repairs, anyway. So, taking cartridge belts and his canteen, he took one last look at his late partner. "I'm sorry, Cousin. I shoulda been on the lookout for some kinda trick from that devil." Then he headed up the game trail, still cautious and alert for another ambush.

He found the horses, all three of them, about a quarter of a mile from the hill where he had first seen them. They had wandered only until finding a stream, and were grazing upon the young grass on the banks. He counted it as a stroke of luck that he happened upon them, because there was not much daylight left in the dense forest by the time he reached them.

Speaking softly, so as not to spook them, he approached slowly. "Easy, easy now," he repeated. All three stood watching him, none threatening to bolt. He walked up to them and collected the reins. Then he took a quick look at the late Jack Wildhorse. "Damn shame," he muttered. "Jack was a good man."

He hesitated for a moment, considering the prospect of taking the body and the three horses back with him. But he knew he didn't have the time to be strapped with the extra burden. Instead, he looked the horses over to decide which one was the stoutest. There was no question. The big gray stallion bearing Jack's body was the best of the lot. With apologies to the late captain of the Creek Lighthorse, he slid the body off the horse and pulled it over next to a dead log. Next, he pulled the saddles off the other two horses and laid them side by side over the body. "That's about the best I can do for the time being, Jack. Maybe that'll keep the buzzards off your face till I get back." He considered hobbling the horses to keep them from wandering too far, but decided not to in case he didn't make it back.

Nightfall found Two Buck and Lilly fording Black Rock Creek some fifty yards north of Tom Talltree's house. During the entire ride back, there had been no more than a word or two between them. Fairly exhausted, Lilly held onto Two Buck, finally succumbing to her fatigue and resting her face against his back. Though unable to express it, the feel of her body close to him, her cheek against his back, created a state of long-sought contentment for him. Since first coming to work for Wendell Stoner, Two Buck had been drawn to the young girl. Knowing she was too young at the time, he had remained silent about his feelings for her, content to wait until she was older. Now, as they approached the house of her uncle, he wondered if he should speak, unsure if it would be proper in light of the trauma she had just experienced.

Breaking the silence then, Lilly gave voice to the concern in her mind. "What will they say when they see me?" she wondered aloud. "My uncle is afraid I will bring Boot Stoner down on him again. He does not want me here."

"Blue Woman wants you to come back," Two Buck insisted. "Besides, John Ward said to bring you back here." In Two Buck's mind, that should have ended all speculation. Just then, their presence was announced by Tom's hound dog. Moments later, the door opened and Tom stepped out on the porch, his shotgun in hand. "It's me and Lilly," Two Buck called out. Then, before advancing any farther, he pulled his horse up and spoke his mind. "Lilly, when I said back there that I'd take care of you, I meant it. I meant that I'd take care of you always."

His words were hurried and stumbling, but the message was clear. Lilly was clearly stunned by his rough proposal, unable to know how to answer. There was really no time at the moment. Her uncle was coming from the porch to meet them. Her aunt, having heard Two Buck call out, came out on the porch. "Two Buck," Lilly hurried to say, "I thank you for what you are saying, but bad things have happened to me. I am not an innocent girl anymore."

"I don't care," Two Buck insisted. "I make you a good husband. I would never treat you bad." Then, with no time left to talk, he said, "Maybe we can talk later."

Properly contrite over his earlier treatment of his late brother's only child, Tom Talltree reached up to help Lilly dismount. As soon as her feet were on the ground, her aunt ran to embrace her. "You had us worried sick, child. You shouldn't have run away like that." She paused then as she remembered. "I guess it's a good thing you did, though, 'cause Boot Stoner was here." She put her arm around Lilly's shoulders and led her toward the house. "Never mind about that. He's gone now, and the main thing is you're safe. We'll be ready if he ever shows up here again."

Tom stood with Two Buck, watching the two women walk to the cabin. "Where's John Ward?" Tom asked. "Did he catch that murderer?"

Two Buck explained that he and John had parted when he picked up Lilly's trail. "He went after Boot, told me he'd meet me back here at your place."

"You can put your horse in with mine," Tom said, "and then we'll see if we can find you something to eat."

Boot Stoner's first visit to the humble abode of Tom Talltree was frightening enough to leave a lasting sense of fearful anticipation in the man. Periodically during the supper reunion with Lilly, Tom would get up and quietly slip out the door, his shotgun in hand, to take a look around the house and barn. He was not afraid to defend his home. His fear was to be taken by surprise, as he had been on the first encounter with the bloodthirsty savage. He could not even count on the dog to warn him of strangers. Half the time the dog would bark, but half the time it would just trot up to be petted. Although his wife seemed to feel the danger from Boot Stoner was now past them, Tom could not release the feeling that the evil half-breed might descend upon them again.

Two Buck sat in a corner of the room, listening to Blue Woman reassure Lilly that her home was with them. His eyes shifted from Blue Woman to Lilly, trying to guess what Lilly's thoughts were. Occasionally Lilly would meet his gaze, and then hold it for a brief instant before looking away. Two Buck hoped with all his heart that Lilly would not think him foolish for his declaration of devotion.

The hastily prepared supper finished, Blue Woman suggested that it was time for bed. She placed her hand on Lilly's arm and teased, "Now I don't expect to wake up in the morning and find you've run off again." When Lilly assured her that she would not, Blue Woman said, "We all need a good night's sleep." She looked at Two Buck, who had expressed his intention to sleep in the barn with his horse. "I don't have any extra blankets, but Tom and I could do without the one on our bed. The nights aren't really chilly anymore."

"No, ma'am," Two Buck replied. "I don't need no blanket. If I get cold, I'll use my saddle blanket." After a lingering glance at Lilly, he bade them all good night and started for the door. He would not admit it, but he was past being ready for bed. Not fully recovered from the bullet wounds in his chest, it had proven to be a long and tiring day for him.

"I'll walk out with you," Tom said and picked up his shotgun again.

Outside, the two men walked to the barn, where Tom helped Two Buck pull some extra hay down to fashion a bed. After Two Buck was settled in, Tom expressed his intention to take a final look around his house, just to ease his mind. "I hope John Ward catches that son of a bitch," he mumbled, mostly to himself after saying good night to Two Buck.

Chapter 17

A full moon, having traced its journey across the Oklahoma sky, was now settling into the distant hills west of Black Rock Creek. Long shadows reached across the yard between the barn and the house, spinning a dark, lacy web across the porch. In the shadow of a large cottonwood near the corner of the barn, a sinister figure knelt, watching the sleeping cabin. With strokes deliberate and unfeeling, Boot Stoner wiped the blood from his knife on the carcass of the dog at his feet. A soft whistle had brought the trusting hound to his hand to be petted.

He paused where he knelt for a few moments while he sized up the situation. He had left his horses back beside the creek so as to silently approach the house. He intended to take no chance on giving the girl an opportunity to escape this time. With one glance at the barn, he considered taking a look inside, but rejected the idea, thinking of the possibility of prompting a horse to neigh and give him away. He remembered the shotgun that had been propped against the door when he was there before. *I should have kept the damn gun, instead of just throwing it in the yard,* he thought. But, at the time, he had no plans of returning.

Moving with the silent grace of his native heritage, he stole across the open space between the barn and the house to a window at the front corner. Peering through the window into the dark interior of the cabin, he could make nothing out at first. Then, as objects slowly took shape in the darkness, he realized that his search was over. There, on a makeshift bed of quilts and blankets, was a slender form that could only be that of the girl who had driven his craving for revenge. A thin, malicious smile slowly formed on his dark face as he anticipated the pleasure he was about to enjoy.

Satisfied that she would not escape him this time, Boot slid along the wall and crossed the porch to the other window on the front of the house. Peering in through the window, he was able to make out the forms of two people sleeping together. *Like lambs ready for slaughter,* he thought and his smile widened.

He moved back to the door and lifted the latch. Pressing slowly against the door, he found that it had been barred. *Damn,* he thought, immediately angry. He carefully lowered the latch and backed away from the door to consider the chances that he could break the timber barring the door. He was mad enough to try, but knowing he was unlikely to break in before waking everyone inside, he paused to consider other options.

Moving around to the back of the house, he found what he was looking for. When he pushed against the back door, it gave just a hair. It was secured, not by a bar, but by a loop of rope. The rope was pulled tight, with no slack to allow the door to open. Not to be denied at this point, Boot strained against the door until he succeeded in stretching the rope enough to create a crack in the door. Then he forced his knife into the crack and sawed away at the rope until it was finally severed.

With nothing to stop him then, he gently pushed the door open and slipped inside. Moving silently, he went from the kitchen into the front room. He stood for a moment watching Tom and Blue Woman sleeping peacefully through the bedroom door. Their totally helpless condition brought him a satisfying sense of pleasure, and a crooked smile came to his face as he imagined their horror upon awakening. He moved then to the corner of the front room, pulled the makeshift quilt partition aside, and leered at the innocent girl lying there. He started to grab her by the ankle and drag her from her bed, but he resisted, preferring to savor his dominance over her for a while longer.

Very carefully, he removed the clothespins that held Lilly's partition in place on the rope stretched across the room for that purpose, and let the quilts fall to the floor. Still, the unsuspecting household slept on, unaware of the monster in their midst. Smug in his satisfaction that they were all helpless to resist him, he proceeded to complete preparations for his evil indulgence. Thoroughly enjoying the invasion of the sanctity of the family's home, he went back to the kitchen and lit a lamp that was on the table. Picking up a chair, he then took the lamp back to the front room and placed it on the floor. He placed the chair by the bedroom door and sat down. Able to see both the bedroom and Lilly in the corner of the front room, he reached down and turned the wick up in the lamp, and waited with his rifle lying across his lap.

The first to awaken was Blue Woman. As the room grew bright from the lamplight, she slowly came out of her slumber. With eyes blinking to adjust to the brightness, she sat up, looking around her, confused by the light. When her gaze finally focused upon the grinning half-breed, sitting watching her from a chair propped against the doorway, she immediately started, then froze. She slowly reached back and prodded her sleeping husband. "Tom, wake up," she gasped.

"Damn if you ain't a helluva sight in the mornin'," Boot sneered, pleased by the blanched look of horror on the woman's face.

Tom stirred then, hastened by the sound of Boot's voice, and the evil chuckle that followed his comment. He sat up, and was about to ask Blue Woman what was wrong when he saw Boot leering at him. Without thinking, he made a sudden move for his shotgun. He was not quick enough. Boot cut him down with one fatal shot through the chest. In the next few seconds, the cabin erupted with terror and confusion. Lilly sprang up with the report of the rifle, followed almost immediately by a loud wail of anguish from Blue Woman. When the frightened girl saw Boot sitting there, she screamed.

"I've come for you, darlin'," Boot snarled, then laughed. "Did you miss me?"

She scrambled out of her bed to crouch in fear on the floor. Boot got up from the chair to go to her, but before he took two steps, he heard Two Buck's boots on the porch and a frantic call for Lilly. Surprised, for he had not suspected there was anyone there but the three of them, Boot nevertheless was quick to react. With Two Buck pounding on the door, Boot walked over and lifted the bar, then stood aside. Seconds later, Two Buck burst into the room, charging past Boot, who was hidden behind the door. The obvious anguish registering on Blue Woman's face told Two Buck that something was terribly wrong. He spun around just in time to catch Boot's rifle barrel squarely across the bridge of his nose. Staggered by the blow, Two Buck dropped immediately, catching himself on one knee, but Boot was ready with a second blow of the rifle barrel against the side of Two Buck's face. The young Cherokee crashed to the floor, out cold. Boot cocked his rifle and aimed directly at Two Buck's head. Lilly screamed in horror, calling out Two Buck's name. Then, forgetting fear for herself, she ran to his side.

"Well, now, ain't that somethin'?" Boot snarled when Lilly took the unconscious boy's head in arms. "So that's the way things are, are they? That makes things a little different." He lowered his rifle. Prepared to execute Two Buck moments before, he decided it would be more satisfying to drag the Cherokee's misery out, in view of Lilly's obvious affection for the boy. Shooting a glance in Blue Woman's direction, he demanded, "Stop that bawling and get me some rope, woman."

Blue Woman, who had left the bed to go to her husband's side, looked up at Boot with eyes filled with tears, the lines in her face etched deeper by the anguish of this horrible moment. She did not reply at once. Instead, her eyes narrowed as she focused on the hateful, smirking face. "You go to hell," she uttered defiantly.

Somewhat surprised, Boot grunted indifferently, then flashed a wide, toothy grin. "I reckon you'll get there before I do, you old bitch." The rifle cracked once more, creating a hole in the middle of Blue Woman's forehead. The old Creek woman collapsed over the body of her husband. Boot turned his attention back to Lilly, who appeared to be in silent shock, unable to scream again. "Well, now, that just leaves the three of us for this little party," he gloated.

A low moan from the injured Cherokee snared Boot's attention once more. "You'd better find me somethin' to tie him up with, else I'll just have to shoot him right now." He pointed the rifle barrel at Two Buck's head. Then he suddenly remembered. "Two Buck," he said. "That's what you called him? I thought he was the one I killed back when that damn lawman jumped us after we left Jackrabbit Creek." He fixed an accusing eye upon her. "He was chasin' me because he's sweet on you. Ain't that right?" He drew back then, pleased with the discovery he had made. Not expecting an answer, he chided her further. "I bet he'd like to know your body like I do—and I mean every inch of it." He threw back his head and laughed as she cowered before him, sick with the thought that her hell would surely start all over again. As suddenly as he had started, he abruptly stopped laughing and roared, "Get me that damn rope, or, by God, I'll gut him like a fish."

"I don't know where any rope is," she whimpered tearfully. "Maybe in the barn."

He smiled knowingly. "Now you don't think I'm gonna let you go out to the barn while I set here watching your boyfriend, do you? I thought he might enjoy watchin' me and you have a little party, but he ain't worth havin' to keep an eye on. It'd be a lot easier to go ahead and kill him." He cocked the rifle.

"Wait!" she cried out, pointing toward the kitchen. There on the back of one of the chairs was a coil of rope that Tom had intended to take back to the barn. She scrambled up to retrieve it.

Still too groggy to put up much resistance, Two Buck was effectively trussed up, then dragged over to sit up against the wall. Gradually, he regained his senses, aided by a splash of water from the bucket near the table. Out of his stupor, he looked with alarm at Lilly crouched trembling in the corner near him. Then he glared at Boot. "You jumped me," he admitted, "but John Ward not so easy to trick."

"Is that so?" Boot replied, delighted that Two Buck was recovered enough to verbally spar with him. "You know where your Mr. John Ward is? Right now, he's on foot way back in the hills. I shot his damn horse out from under him. I expect it'll take him till sometime about noon tomorrow to get back here. By that time, me and your little sweetheart, here, will be long gone." He graced Two Buck with a sinister smile. "And the worms will be makin' a meal off of your carcass."

"Cut me loose, and fight me like a man," Two Buck spat. "Then we see who the worms eat."

Boot just smiled. "Maybe I'll do that," he sneered. "Maybe I'll just untie one arm and one leg. Let you hop around like a rooster while I carve you up with my knife." Eventually tiring of the verbal insults, Boot decided it was time for the final outrage. Propping his rifle against the wall, he walked over and grabbed Lilly by the wrist. She tried to resist, fighting against him as he dragged her over to the bed. Rolling the bodies of Tom and Blue Woman out of his way with the toe of his boot, he threw Lilly on the bed. She tried to scramble out of his grasp, but each time he caught her and she received a vicious blow for her efforts. Soon, she was unable to fight him anymore, and collapsed to submit to his abuse as she had done so many times before.

Dropping his trousers, he forced the sobbing girl's legs apart, all the while grinning at Two Buck and taunting the helpless young Cherokee. Unable to bear the sight, Two Buck closed his eyes tightly and banged his head back against the wall. "You can't stand to watch," Boot goaded, "but you can still hear."

With no physical means to help Lilly, Two Buck

could bear it no longer. In desperation, he tried to undermine Boot's gigantic ego. Forcing himself to look at the savage assault, he commented, "I am surprised to see how small you are. You talk like a big man, but you are very small where you have to make children."

The comment caused Boot to hesitate. "What the hell are you talkin' about?" he demanded.

Seeing that he might have struck the right nerve, Two Buck forced a laugh. "You don't have much to make babies with. You look like small boy."

It had the proper effect. "You talk big for a dead man!" Boot roared. He jerked up his trousers and walked over to deliver a backhand to the side of Two Buck's face in response to the insult to his manhood.

The blow was enough to make Two Buck's already throbbing skull ring, but he forced himself to respond with a wide grin. "A-tsu-tsa," he spat at Boot in his native tongue.

Infuriated, Boot responded with another blow to the defenseless man. "Boy!" he roared. "You are the boy, a dead boy!"

Two Buck's insults had served their purpose of temporarily killing the half-breed's spiteful exhibition, as well as his ability to perform. Lilly was spared for the time being, but Two Buck knew that he was likely to pay a terrible price for her short reprieve. How terrible, he could not have imagined. Expecting to be shot immediately, he was surprised when Boot announced that he was going to spare his life. "Get up from there!" Boot commanded Lilly. "We're leavin'."

Fearful of what might be coming next, Lilly

pleaded, "I'll go with you, but please don't kill him. It's me you want. Leave him in peace."

The malicious grin on Boot's face told her that she was not going to like his response. "Why, that was just what I was plannin' to do. Since you think so much of him, I decided not to shoot him. Is that what you want?"

She did not know how to respond, unable to believe that Boot would actually show compassion just to please her. But he checked to make sure that Two Buck's bonds were secure, then promptly turned away. Grabbing Lilly by the arm, he led her outside. Pulling her back to the horses, he helped her up. Then, as he had done on the day he abducted her from his father's house, he tied her wrists to the saddle horn. As an added precaution, he looped a rope under the horse's belly and tied her ankles to the stirrups. "I wouldn't want you to fall off, darlin'," he teased.

Tying the reins to a porch post, he went to the barn and looked around in the dark interior of the building until he found a pitchfork. With a forkful of dry hay, he returned to the house and deposited it in the middle of the front room floor. He repeated the exercise several times until he had a sizable pile of hay in the small room. When he was satisfied with his efforts, he paused to mock his prisoner. "These mornin's can get pretty chilly, and Lilly wants to make sure you don't get cold."

The brutal half-breed's intentions were obvious, and Two Buck knew there was nothing he could do to save himself. In a defiant gesture, he spat at his

tormenter. The spittle fell short, causing Boot to laugh
at his feeble effort.

"You better start sayin' your prayers, boy," Boot
goaded. He stood there simply grinning at his captive
for a few long moments before going to the kitchen
where he had spied a can of kerosene. After emptying
the can on the floor and furniture, he paused for one
additional moment of gloating. Then he smashed the
lamp on the floor amidst the dried hay. A flame immediately flashed, following the path of the kerosene.
"Damn!" Boot exclaimed, stepping back from the
flame. "I'd like to stay and watch you cook, but this
place is gonna be too hot in a few minutes." He
laughed as Two Buck tried to squeeze back against the
wall. Staying only long enough then to make sure his
fire was strong, he retreated from the burning cabin.

A man was judged by the way he lived his life—or
so Two Buck believed. A man was judged by his bravery in battle, by the way he treated his family and his
neighbors, and the way he faced nature's hardships.
And the Great Spirit, who watched man's trials, also
judged a man by the way he faced death. Two Buck's
time to face death had come, and he was determined
to pass into the spirit world with dignity.

As the flames rose higher around him, reaching up
on the walls within minutes after Boot departed, Two
Buck could already feel the scorching heat closing in
upon him. Through the crackling of the fire as it fed
upon the table, he heard the sound of horses as his ex-
ecutioner departed. He even thought he heard the

sound of Lilly crying, although that could have been the hissing of the turpentine in the log walls.

Like a great beast with an insatiable appetite, the fire crept toward the corner where he struggled in vain to free himself. The heat was now unbearable, closing in to consume the very air he was gasping to breathe. His skin was so hot that it felt blistered. With all hope consumed by the flames, he began to pray that he could be brave, although he now feared that he could not endure the torture. He called upon his native spirits to come to his aid. As the air became too hot to suck into his lungs, he prayed to the Christian God to take him swiftly.

Crying out in painful torment against the unbearable heat, he closed his eyes and prayed for death to take him quickly. With failing breath, he began singing his death chant. When he opened his eyes, there appeared to be a form before him, its outline wavering in the hazy, smoke-filled room. An angel? Hardly. The answer to Two Buck's prayers stood as tall as the door frame, with shoulders that filled the opening. Casting burning chairs and small furniture aside, defying the greedy monster to impede him, John Ward walked through the flaming room. With no time for untying him, he reached down, grabbed Two Buck, and hoisted him on his shoulder. With roof timbers groaning and starting to give way, he retraced his steps to the door and the cool, fresh air outside.

Without pausing, John carried Two Buck down to the creek and laid him in the shallow water while he cut the ropes that bound him. Unable to talk at once,

Two Buck gulped in the cool air. "You gonna make it?" John asked, not sure how close his young friend was to being cooked.

Finally Two Buck spoke. "I think so, but I wouldn't have if you'd been a minute later. I thought I was done for." He pulled himself up to the bank. "How did you know I was in there?"

John shrugged. "I got here too late to catch Boot. The house was burnin' like hell. No one was outside. I didn't figure Boot took everyone with him, and I sure as hell wasn't gonna go in that burning cabin just to make sure. But then I heard you makin' that god-awful noise you call singin'."

Two Buck nodded, remembering that he had cried out when he thought all was lost. Though not overly proud of it, he was glad now that he had not chosen to meet his fate in silence. His appointment with death now effectively postponed, he remembered his main concern. "Lilly!" he gasped. "He's got Lilly again!"

"I figured," John replied calmly. "What about the folks that lived here?" he asked. "Where are they?"

"Dead," Two Buck said. "He shot 'em both."

John shook his head slowly in silent exasperation. The murderous rampage had gone on far too long, and he could not deny a certain frustration over his failure to put a stop to it. Now, however, after arriving on the scene of another slaughter too late, he was not far behind the evil savage. This time, he was certain he had finally caught up with Boot Stoner. "How long has he been gone from here?" he asked.

"I don't know for sure, but it seems like you came

along no more than half an hour after I heard them ride out. I ain't too sure, though. My mind was on other things."

John got to his feet. He glanced back at the burning cabin, and then he looked up at the sky. Already the moon had disappeared behind the hills and the darkness of the sky was softening. Daylight was not far away. "I'm wastin' time standin' here jawin'," he said, even though he knew he would be wasting even more time if he tried to track Boot before there was enough light to see.

Although still a little shaky, and complaining of an ache deep in his chest, Two Buck said that he was ready to ride. John figured the ache was probably due to the overheated air and smoke the young man inhaled. "Most likely you'll get over it in a little while," he said. "Or else you'll just die," he added, teasing.

"I ain't gonna die," Two Buck insisted. "If I was gonna die, I'da done it back there." He gestured toward the house. "I'm startin' to feel cold right now."

"Well, hell, you're soakin' wet. Maybe you oughta go stand close to the fire."

"I ain't goin' close to that fire no more. My clothes will dry out before long." He was impatient to get under way, imagining any number of atrocities that might be happening to Lilly.

"Suit yourself," John said. "Let's get ready to ride."

With Two Buck on his feet again, they went to the barn, where they discovered Two Buck's horse missing. He took a long, cynical look at Tom Talltree's old mare, but there was no other choice, so he looked around until he found a bridle and saddle. John watched him patiently while he saddled the mare. When he was done, John unbuckled his gun belt and tossed it over to him. "Here," he said. "You don't wanna go after Boot Stoner naked."

At first light, they picked up Boot's trail. It led in the general direction of Low Hawk. With Two Buck certain that Boot had not had breakfast before leaving Black Rock Creek, John was hoping that the outlaw might stop to eat soon after daybreak.

That was not the case, however. Boot planned to head south to the Canadian River and beyond to the Chickasaw Nation, and eventually into Texas. His plan included a stop first at Jonah Feathers' store in Low Hawk, where he intended to pick up supplies for the journey.

It was still early when Boot rode into the little community of Low Hawk. With no concern at all for the risk of encountering vengeful residents of the town, he rode up to the store leading Lilly's horse, with Two Buck's behind hers. He tied his horse up at the hitching rail, pulled his rifle out of the saddle sling, and took a long look around before entering the store. Due to the early hour, there was no one about. Satisfied that he would not be disturbed during his dealings with the store's owner, he went inside.

Jonah Feathers almost tipped his chair over backward when he saw who his first customer was. The coffee cup in his trembling hand sloshed hot coffee over the sides and down upon his fingers. The sensation of the hot liquid over his hand went unnoticed by Jonah as his whole body went numb with fright.

"Don't shit your britches," Boot snarled. "I ain't gonna kill you if you do like I tell you." He glanced quickly around the store. "Where's your woman?"

"In the house," Jonah managed to squeak, swallowing hard to keep his Adam's apple from coming up to choke him.

"Call her in here," Boot ordered.

Jonah did as he was told, and in a few minutes, Ruth Feathers came through the doorway from the attached living quarters. "What is it, Jonah? I'm trying to roll out some biscuits . . ." She stopped in midsentence when she saw Boot standing there with his rifle cradled across his arms. "What are you doing here, you murderer?" she demanded, unconcerned with his reaction to the contempt in her tone.

"You better tell her to shut up," Boot immediately snarled.

"Ruth, for the love of God, hold your tongue!" Jonah implored. He could not believe his wife's disregard for the trouble she might invoke.

Realizing Jonah's fear then, she said nothing more, but she fixed the half-breed outlaw with a scorching gaze. Boot answered her gaze with a sneering look of scorn. Then he informed Jonah that he was there to get supplies. He walked around the little store, pointing out items he saw on the shelves and calling out the quantities he needed of each. Jonah hustled back and forth to fetch the items indicated, and placed them in a stack on the counter. Ruth backed away behind the end of the counter, where she stood silently watching. When she was sure Boot's attention was on something on one of the shelves, she reached under the counter to retrieve the butcher knife used to cut side meat. She slipped it into the deep pocket of her skirt. She was not certain what she would do with it, but she was determined to have some form of protection.

When he could see nothing else he fancied, Boot said, "All right, load that stuff up on them horses outside." When Jonah jumped to comply, Boot motioned him back with his rifle. "Not you. Let her load it up." He stood then, gazing insolently at the frowning woman, waiting for her response.

Ruth's eyes narrowed again, her lips pressed tightly together, about to reply, but Jonah spoke first. "Do as he says, Ruth. It ain't worth gettin' shot over."

"Yeah, *Ruth*," Boot repeated, emphasizing her name, "it ain't worth gettin' shot over."

Still Ruth hesitated, giving her husband a scalding look before she relented and picked up two sacks of supplies. Walking out the front door, she was startled to see Lilly sitting on one of the horses, her hands and feet tied to the saddle. "Oh, dear Lord, child," she gasped. "That savage found you."

With soulful eyes, Lilly replied, "I'm so sorry, ma'am. I'm sorry I brought all this trouble down on you."

"It's not your fault, child," Ruth insisted. She looked behind her to see if she was being watched as she hurriedly tied the cloth sacks behind the saddle. "I'll try to cut you loose, and then you run."

"Don't make him mad, ma'am. He'll hurt you," Lilly implored, afraid for her.

"Never you mind that," Ruth replied, and began sawing the rope that held Lilly's foot to the stirrup.

Before she made any progress on the rope, she heard Boot's voice behind her. "Hey, I didn't tell you to do no talkin'. Get back in here and get the rest of my goods." Shielding her knife with her back turned to him, she quickly hid it in her skirt again. Turning around, she marched back inside to get the other sacks. "Put them two behind my saddle," Boot instructed when she came back.

Lilly saw the look of dismay in Ruth's eyes when she realized she was not going to get an opportunity to finish working on the ropes. The captive girl showed Ruth a grateful smile and nodded in way of thanking her for trying. Heartbroken, Ruth returned a smile of apology. She stepped over to stand by Lilly's horse when Boot stepped off the porch and prepared to mount.

Standing helplessly by, watching four full sacks of his merchandise about to be carried away, Jonah could not resist saying, "I don't suppose you'd consider payin' for those goods."

Boot laughed at the notion. "Hell, I am payin' you for them goods," he said. "I'm lettin' you and that old crow you're married to live. I might could even do you a bigger favor, and shoot your old lady. How'd that be?" He leveled the rifle in Ruth's direction.

"No! No!" Jonah quickly blurted. "You take the merchandise."

Boot threw his head back and laughed, only to stop cold when he heard an authoritative voice call out from the edge of the trees by the creek. "Boot Stoner! You're under arrest for murder. I'm givin' you a chance to surrender peacefully."

Boot's reaction was immediate, and it was not to surrender. Swinging his leg over, he kicked his horse hard, and the animal bolted away with Boot lying low on its neck. Thinking quickly, Ruth severed the lead rope when Boot's sudden departure pulled the line taut, causing Lilly's horse to bolt after Boot's before veering to the side and galloping off in another direction with Two Buck's horse following. The crack of John Ward's Winchester split the air as the deputy tried for a lucky shot.

He knew there was little chance of hitting the fugitive, but he took the shot anyway. If he could have waited until he was within closer range, he would have had a better chance. His instructions from Judge Parker were to always give the fugitive the opportunity to surrender, no matter how heinous the outlaw. He had done that, so he now felt that his obligations to uphold the law were satisfied. From this point on, he considered his job to be that of eliminating a mad dog. As the two galloped up to the store, John yelled to Two Buck, "Go after her!" Two Buck was already riding after Lilly as fast as Tom's old horse would run. John asked the gray stallion for all the speed the big horse could deliver, and the horse responded, chewing up the grassy plain in huge chunks. At long last, the duel was on. Weeks of frustrating search had finally boiled down to a deadly dash across a grass-covered sea of prairie. This time, John felt certain, win or lose, the issue would be settled.

The two horses were a match. The lawman could realize no gain, and the outlaw could not increase his lead. Urging his horse desperately, Boot swung back toward the creek that ran through Low Hawk, through a stand of cottonwoods on the bank, and splashed through the creek to the other side. Still, the lawman was relentless, matching stride for stride. Striking a narrow wagon road, Boot turned his horse to follow it. Its hooves thundered along the hard-packed clay as Boot looked back to see John Ward still bearing down on him.

"Damn him!" Boot complained. There was something in him that feared the relentless lawman. He had boasted of a desire to face John Ward, even convinced himself of his strong medicine. Yet, at the fateful moment, he was not sure of himself. Now his horse began to show signs of fatigue, and he looked back again at his pursuer, hoping to see signs of the deputy's horse foundering. Then, rounding a curve in the road, he came upon a burned-out cabin with a barn still standing. In the panic of the moment, he failed to realize it was George Longpath's house, a house he had burned down. Aware that his horse had not much left to give, he swung into the path and urged the weary animal toward the barn.

John rounded the bend in the road in time to see Boot ride into the barn, coming out of the saddle before the horse came to a full stop. He pulled up hard on the gray's reins, and the thankful horse skidded to a stop. John quickly looked around him for some position of cover. Not a moment too soon he dived behind a large oak about thirty yards from the front of the barn, and cocked his rifle just as shots rang out from the building. He rolled over to the other side of the tree when bullets kicked up dirt around the roots, and fired three quick shots at the barn, then rolled back to the other side of the tree. He didn't have to wait more than a few seconds before his shots were answered. While Boot fired a barrage of shots at the opposite side of the tree, John watched carefully to pinpoint their point of origin. *He's in the hayloft,* he thought as the dull smack of shot after shot struck the oak.

This could take all day, John thought, realizing they were at a standoff at this point. Determined to bring the altercation to a close, he decided it was time to take a risk. Rolling back to the other side again, he waited for another barrage from the barn. When he figured Boot was reloading, he rose up on one knee and pumped six rounds into the door of the loft. As soon as the last shot rang out, he sprinted for the open barn door. Boot only managed to partially reload his magazine before he realized what was happening. By the time he moved to the door to spot the lawman, John had reached the cover of the barn below him. Frustrated, Boot shot blindly through the loft floor, as John rolled under Boot's horse. It was only for a moment, however, for the horse reared wildly as the shots kicked up dirt around it; then it bolted through the open end of the barn with John just barely out of the way of its hooves.

John hustled to the side wall and the ladder to the loft. Boot, distracted by the sudden flight of his horse, ran to the door again. Climbing quickly up the steps with his rifle in one hand, John reached the loft floor just as Boot turned to discover him. Finding himself dead in the lawman's sights, Boot jumped from the loft door to the ground below. John scrambled up onto the floor of the loft and moved to the door, expecting to see Boot running for cover. Instead, Boot was trying to drag himself back inside the barn, his leg having been broken in his jump from the hayloft.

Not willing to risk the same fate, John moved quickly back to the ladder and descended the plank steps two at a time, landing on the floor of the barn at nearly the same time Boot struggled inside the door. Boot reached back to pull his rifle to him, only to scream in pain as a bullet from the lawman's rifle shattered his arm. He looked back at John Ward, the deputy standing with his rifle aimed right at him, and realized he was done for. "Don't shoot!" he screamed. "I give up!" Seeing John hesitate, he begged the lawman, "You got me. My leg's broke. I think you broke my arm, too. I give up. You're a federal marshal—you can't shoot me in cold blood!"

Still standing with his rifle aimed at the vile outlaw's head, John Ward had to think about that for a moment. What the wounded half-breed said was true in principal, but this mad dog needed killing badly. The people he had murdered demanded it. His sense of honor won out in the end, and he slowly lowered the rifle and approached the crippled outlaw.

"You're gonna have to help me up," Boot said. "My leg's broke, and I can't put no weight on this arm." He held his bleeding hand up for John to see.

John hesitated for a moment, studying the man who had terrified such a large part of the Nations for weeks. After a long pause, he spoke. "All right," he said softly, and bent down to give him a hand. The two adversaries looked each other in the eye at that moment. Boot's eyelids narrowed and his eyes quivered slightly as he suddenly lunged up with his long skinning knife, thrusting up at John's belly. Just as suddenly, Boot's wrist was met and locked in the steel grip of John Ward's hand. At the same time, he jammed his rifle barrel up under Boot's chin. He smiled and said, "I was hoping you'd try that." Boot's eyes opened wide with fright a split second before the bullet tore through the top of his head.

Chapter 18

It was a long ride back to Fort Smith—a long way to carry a worthless corpse. It gave a man a lot of time to think. It had taken some time to finally track down Boot Stoner, but once again John Ward had gotten the job done. Thankfully there weren't many as bad as Boot Stoner. *But, damn,* John thought, *one's bad enough.* He thought of the evil that the savage half-breed had wrought, the lives he had taken, and those he had altered. There was some good that had come of it. Lilly had gone back to the Cherokee Nation with Two Buck. She hadn't agreed to marry the young man who worshipped her, but John supposed she eventually would.

Thoughts of the young couple, finding happiness in a world of misery, triggered other thoughts. And for the first time he could remember, John Ward was lonely. As he made his way across the Canadian River, north of the San Bois Mountains, he wondered if it had been him lying across the saddle of a horse, instead of Boot, would there have been anyone to grieve? "What the hell would it matter?" he uttered. But he knew what was really bothering him: Lucy Summerlin. Thoughts of the doctor's daughter had penetrated his concentration on too many occasions during the past few weeks, far too many to ignore. In his line of work, thoughts of a woman could influence a man's decisions. "Maybe I'm in the wrong business," he declared.

"I'm glad to see you back safely, John," Judge Parker said after Boot Stoner's body had been turned over to the undertaker. "I know this was a tough one."

John nodded. "I'm sorry it took so long. A lot of people got killed."

"Couldn't have been helped, I guess. The main thing is that he's no longer a threat." Thinking that he noticed a troubled look in his deputy's eye, the judge affected a casual note. "I guess you'll be wanting to get back to that time off I interrupted before. Maybe do some hunting and fishing."

"Maybe," John replied. "I'm takin' the time off. There's some other things I need to take care of."

When the big lawman failed to offer details, Judge Parker decided not to pry. "Well, you've certainly earned it. Enjoy yourself."

"Thank you, sir," John replied respectfully. There was some urgent business he had in mind, and he had not definitely made up his mind until that moment.

*   *   *

Feeling a slight pressure from John's heels, the big gray stallion picked up the pace as horse and rider approached the little settlement of Red Bow. Dr. Summerlin was sitting on the front porch of his clinic, holding a coffee cup in his hand. As the big deputy pulled up at the hitching post, the doctor got up and stepped down from the porch to greet him.

"Well, John Ward, did you ever catch that outlaw you were chasing?"

"Yes, sir, I caught him," John replied.

"How about my gunshot patient? What was his name?"

"Two Buck."

"Right, Two Buck. How's he doing?"

"He's gettin' along fine. I think he's gonna get himself married," John replied.

"Well, come on in and sit down. There's still some coffee left in the pot."

"Uh, no, thanks," John responded. "I ain't forgot the last time I tried some of your coffee." Summerlin threw back his head and laughed. Anxious to get to the point of his visit, John said, "I was hopin' to talk to Lucy."

A slight frown crossed the doctor's face. "Why, John, Lucy's not here. She's gone back to St. Louis to stay with my sister. A place like Red Bow is kinda hard on a young woman. I think she stayed with me a lot longer than she wanted to."

John was devastated. It had taken so long to bring himself to the point where he knew what he wanted. And to find out now that he had missed his opportunity was almost too much to bear. She had waited for him to commit to her. He was sure of that now, and because of his lack of confidence, he had lost her.

Seeing the obvious disappointment in the honest lawman's eyes, Summerlin said, "Damn, I'm sorry, John. She just left yesterday. One of my patients took her over to Deer Creek, and she's going to catch the train there tomorrow morning."

"Deer Creek," John repeated. "She's catchin' the train in the mornin'?" Summerlin nodded. "Deer Creek's a day and a half ride from here," John calculated. "Or half a day and a night." With no further decision to be made, he bade the doctor good-bye and jumped into the saddle.

Riding straight through the night, stopping only periodically to rest his horse, John sighted the small gathering of homes and stores that made up the settlement of Deer Creek close to midmorning. Already worried that he was not going to make it before the train arrived, he was at once dismayed to see the train not only there, but already pulling out. "No! Dammit, no!" he shouted, once again devastated. "By God," he vowed, and dug his heels into the gray's flanks. The horse responded as before, galloping past the water tank and the telegraph shack, out beside the track, racing the gradually accelerating locomotive.

Pulling even with the engineer's cab, he grabbed the hand rail and swung himself aboard. "Stop the train," he commanded to a startled engineer. When the engineer did not respond at once, John pulled his badge out of his pocket and shoved it in the poor man's face. "Stop this damn train. I'm a deputy federal marshal, and I'm arresting a criminal on this train." Left with no choice other than to comply, the engineer brought the train to a stop.

Wasting no time, John ran back along the track to the passenger cars. There were only two, and she was not on the first one. Charging into the second car, he saw her at once. Stunned, her eyes wide as saucers, Lucy Summerlin could scarcely believe what she saw. "John," was all she could say as the big man strode straight up the aisle toward her, amid the puzzled stares of the other passengers.

Just finding her had dominated his thoughts up to that moment. He had not given thought to what he would say if and when he found her. Stopping abruptly at her seat, and gazing down into her still-mystified face, he spoke his peace. "Lucy, your pa told me you were goin' to St. Louis. And I reckon that's what you oughta do if that's what you want. But I couldn't let you go without tellin' you I wanna marry you. If you think you could tolerate me, I'd be obliged if you'd be my wife."

Lucy's mouth dropped open in amazement, and she thought that surely she was not hearing what she thought she had just heard. She was unable to answer for a long moment, as she gazed up into his now-tormented face. Then she laughed, unable to help herself. "John Ward, that is about the worst proposal of marriage I've ever heard."

Becoming more and more nervous as the other

passengers began to crowd in to better hear the proposition of marriage, John asked, "Well, whaddaya say?"

"Well, I don't know," she replied, her smile growing by the second. "Do you love me?"

"What? . . . I don't know . . . I mean, I reckon."

"Which is it? You don't know, or you reckon?"

"Hell, I love you. I love you bad."

"Then I'll marry you."

There was a spontaneous round of applause from the spectators. The cheers accompanied the red-faced lawman as he carried Lucy's suitcase along the aisle and down the steps. Following in his wake, Lucy smiled as she acknowledged the good wishes. There was nothing she desired in St. Louis. Everything she needed was right there in the Nations.

Ready to find
your next great read?

Let us help.

Visit prh.com/nextread